PENGUIN  CLASSICS

MOZART'S JOURNEY TO PRAGUE
AND A SELECTION OF POEMS

EDUARD MÖRIKE (1804–75) was the seventh child of a large family in Ludwigsburg (Württemberg). His father was a doctor who died when Mörike was thirteen. He studied theology in Tübingen and became a Protestant pastor in 1834, a profession in which he was seldom happy and from which he retired after nine years. His novel *Maler Noten* was published in 1832 and a first volume of poetry in 1838. Between 1851 and 1866 he taught literature at a seminary in Stuttgart, and continued to write, including his masterpiece *Mozart's Journey to Prague* (1855). Mörike never travelled beyond his native Württemberg and led a quiet and increasingly reclusive life with his Catholic wife and two daughters. He spent the last decade of his life in virtual solitude, anxious to avoid the fame his writing had brought him.

DAVID LUKE is an Emeritus Fellow of Christ Church, Oxford. Among the German authors he has written about and translated are Goethe, Kleist, the brothers Grimm and Thomas Mann. His translation of Goethe's *Faust* won the European Poetry Translation Prize. His previous work for Penguin includes Goethe's *Selected Verse* and *Selected Tales* of the brothers Grimm.

EDUARD MÖRIKE

Mozart's Journey to Prague
and a Selection of Poems

Translated and with an Introduction and Notes by
DAVID LUKE
Scots translations by GILBERT MCKAY

PENGUIN BOOKS

PENGUIN BOOKS

Published by the Penguin Group
Penguin Books Ltd, 80 Strand, London WC2R ORL, England
Penguin Putnam Inc., 375 Hudson Street, New York, New York 10014, USA
Penguin Books Australia Ltd, 250 Camberwell Road, Camberwell, Victoria 3124, Australia
Penguin Books Canada Ltd, 10 Alcorn Avenue, Toronto, Ontario, Canada M4V 3B2
Penguin Books India (P) Ltd, 11, Community Centre, Panchsheel Park, New Delhi – 110 017, India
Penguin Books (NZ) Ltd, Cnr Rosedale and Airborne Roads, Albany, Auckland, New Zealand
Penguin Books (South Africa) (Pty) Ltd, 24 Sturdee Avenue, Rosebank 2196, South Africa

Penguin Books Ltd, Registered Offices: 80 Strand, London WC2R ORL, England

www.penguin.com

First published by Libris 1997
Revised edition published by Penguin Books 2003
1

Translation, Introduction and Notes copyright © David Luke and Gilbert McKay, 1997, 2003
All rights reserved

The moral rights of the translators has been asserted

Set in 10.25/12.25 pt PostScript Adobe Sabon
Typeset by Rowland Phototypesetting Ltd, Bury St Edmunds, Suffolk
Printed in England by Clays Ltd, St Ives plc

Contents

1837–1863

Introduction

As the half-forgotten author of poems which are among the most remarkable in the German language but became famous chiefly as the texts of songs, and of a minor masterpiece of imaginative musical biography, an inspired narrative prose poem about Mozart which lives chiefly in the borrowed glory of the greater masterpiece it celebrates, Eduard Mörike suffers the paradox of owing his exalted but inconspicuous place in German literary history largely to the genius of others. How many readers, even in Germany, listening to the most exquisite of Hugo Wolf's Mörike settings, remember who wrote the words, and how many will understand the modest and mysterious title of *Mozart auf der Reise nach Prag* (literally *Mozart en route to Prague*) if they do not already know the story as a Mozartian fantasy, a brilliant literary footnote to *Don Giovanni*? And yet it seriously distorts Mörike's achievement to overlook either the story itself or the poetry to which it is closely related. Both are Mörike's essential legacy: *Mozart's Journey to Prague*, a work created at the height of his maturity but charmed into existence by memories that went back thirty years to the beginning of his adult life, and the lyrical development to which it essentially belongs.

Mörike lived all his life hidden away in south-west Germany, in the cultural region of Swabia, corresponding approximately to the political territory of Württemberg, in which he was born in 1804 and whose borders he almost never crossed. 1804, as it happened, was the year in which Napoleon became Emperor of the French and began rearranging Germany. The old medieval Holy Roman Empire of the German Nation still nominally

existed during the first two years of Mörike's life, and Württem-
berg, also the native land of Schiller and Hölderlin, was a
medium-sized state within it, half Catholic and half Protestant.
Napoleon, to reward the reigning Duke who had earned his
favour, made the duchy a kingdom in 1805, before abolishing
the Empire in 1806; and Württemberg was still a medium-sized
kingdom when another German Empire, this time courtesy of
Bismarck, came into being four years before Mörike's death in
1875. The poet had been virtually untouched by these events
or by any of the intervening political perturbations of the
nineteenth century. He remained an introverted and neglected
provincial dreamer, though in his later life he did gain some
recognition in Germany, even outside the Swabian heartlands.
Even in Germany, after his death, he was again forgotten for
about another thirty years, but from the turn of the century
until now German literary scholars have taken an increasing
interest in him, and a historical-critical complete edition of
his works and letters, begun in 1967, is still being slowly put
together. In England and elsewhere outside his linguistic sphere
he remains almost entirely unknown.

Mörike's native Ludwigsburg had been built near Stuttgart at
the beginning of the eighteenth century, in the formal Italianate
style, as a garrison town and the summer residence of the
Württemberg court. His mother was a Protestant clergyman's
daughter and his father at first considered adopting the same
career, but became a doctor instead and died from a stroke in
1817. There were thirteen children, of whom seven survived
infancy; Eduard's brothers Karl and August and his sisters Luise
and Klara were especially close to him. His education seems to
have been based from the outset on the assumption that he
would become a pastor like his grandfather, though personal
suitability or conviction commonly played a lesser part in such
decisions than the fact that the Church offered long years of
elaborate vocational training at public expense, leading eventu-
ally to modest but secure life-long employment. When Eduard
was thirteen, the traumatic loss of his father threatened to
interrupt this programme; fortunately, his rich and cultivated
uncle Friedrich Eberhard von Georgii, a high legal official,

offered him hospitality for a year to enable him to complete the
first stage of his schooling. Living in his uncle's large rococo
mansion in Stuttgart, the boy encountered the *ancien régime*
elegance he was later to celebrate in *Mozart's Journey to Prague*,
as well as being encouraged to further study of the Latin and
Greek classics to which his poetry is substantially indebted.

Mörike failed his all-important *Landexamen* at the age of
fourteen, but his uncle's influence nevertheless secured his
admission to the Lower Theological Seminary in Urach, an
enchanting small fortified town surrounded by wooded hills,
one of the medieval Swabian duchies. His commitment to theo-
logical studies was less than total, but he was later to remember
his years in Urach with great nostalgia. It was here, and later at
the Theological Seminary in Tübingen, that he formed close
youthful friendships, some of them lifelong, as with Wilhelm
Hartlaub, who, like Mörike himself, ended up as a simple village
pastor, and Johannes Mährlen, who became a Professor of
Economics at the Stuttgart Polytechnic. With Ludwig Bauer, a
fellow poet whom he met at Tübingen and who was to remain
one of his chief intimates, Mörike found, Tolkien-like, that he
could construct elaborate private mythologies: the imaginary
remote island kingdom of Orplid, with its tutelary goddess
Weyla, its lineage of kings and disappearing civilization, was
their joint invention, and was to play a significant part in
Mörike's rambling, never-finished novel *Maler Nolten* (*Nolten
the Painter*) as well as in some of his poems. Other friends
included the future critic and scholar Friedrich Theodor Vischer
and the future philosopher David Friedrich Strauss, both of
whom he had known since their early schooldays together.
Vischer and Strauss had little patience with Mörike's interest in
Märchen and myth, but were to retain a stimulating influence
on him. Strauss later made himself notorious by suggesting in
his *Das Leben Jesu* (*Life of Jesus*, 1835–6), a book which
cost him his university career, that the Gospel narratives were
themselves mythical.

On record from Mörike's years as a theological student,
more especially after his move to Tübingen in 1822, are some
emotional experiences that found their way into his verse: his

childhood association with his cousin Klara Neuffer, for
instance, had developed into an adolescent romance, but in
1823 she gave him up in favour of another candidate for the
ministry. Much more traumatic and of lasting effect, as it seems,
was his infatuation with the mysterious Maria Meyer (1802–
65), a beautiful and unstable girl of questionable reputation.
Her unmarried mother Helena Meyer had been the weak sister
in a large and otherwise respectable Swiss family, and had ended
in the local workhouse, the paternity of her several children
remaining obscure. The adolescent Maria, who probably suf-
fered from epilepsy as well as religious hysteria, had for a time
been a protégée of Juliane von Krüdener, a mad Baltic baroness
who travelled around Switzerland in 1817 as the leader of a
peripatetic evangelical sect, before retiring to her Livonian
estates and never again emerging. Maria was now also, like her
mother, locked up in Schaffhausen and put to work knitting
and spinning, but released in 1819. Her movements during the
next four years are uncertain, but in 1823 she was found by a
Ludwigsburg innkeeper lying unconscious beside the road from
Stuttgart, and entered his employ as a 'bartender'. One of her
many male visitors at the inn was the painter Rudolf Lohbauer,
an intimate friend of Mörike's, and it was thus that the latter,
visiting Ludwigsburg during the Easter vacation of 1823, met
'Peregrina', as he was to call her in his poems. Maria, apart
from her remarkable beauty, was not without some degree of
cultivation, and her personality fascinated a number of those
who met her. She liked to make a mystery of herself and would
tell fanciful stories about her origins and her family. Whether
or not Mörike, like Lohbauer in all probability, became her
lover for a time (and everything that might be evidence of this
has been carefully destroyed) there is no doubt that she stirred
his emotions more deeply than any other woman in his life.
After returning to Tübingen he and Lohbauer kept up a corre-
spondence with her, until suddenly and without explanation
she vanished from Ludwigsburg and resumed her wandering
lifestyle. The following year she reappeared in Tübingen and
sought out Mörike, who refused to see her. Torn by conflicting
feelings, he characteristically took refuge at home in Stuttgart

with his mother and his sister Luise, in whom he had confided. In 1826 Maria again tried to visit him in Tübingen, but again he would not see her; evidently this was in self-defence, a shrinking retreat from a passion that had disturbed him too painfully. Maria returned to Switzerland, where she eventually married a carpenter's apprentice in her native Schaffhausen and tried to make an honest living with him; Mörike never learnt of this change of heart, having long ago lost touch with her. The five poems he eventually published as a cycle under the title 'Peregrina' are partly more direct, partly more stylized and fictionalized treatments of the Maria Meyer experience. The first and fourth in particular, set to music by Wolf with incomparable pathos, momentarily reveal the tragic depths of feeling of which the poet was capable. His novel *Maler Nolten* incorporates four of them, and develops 'Peregrina' as one of the central figures of the story: the wandering, mentally deranged gipsy Elisabeth, who evidently symbolizes the darker side of the hero's nature. The mysterious power she exercises over him frustrates all his attempts to integrate himself by marriage into normal society, and in the end destroys him as well as Elisabeth herself, though their fatal bond seems to continue on a mystic plane after their death.

In 1824, the year of Mörike's renunciation of Maria, two other significant events occurred in his life within a few days of each other. One was his visit to the Hoftheater in Stuttgart with his favourite brother August, his sister Luise and two friends, to see a performance of *Don Giovanni*. This was his first, never-to-be-forgotten introduction to Mozart's greatest and most disturbing opera. Five days after they had seen it together the seventeen-year-old August died suddenly in mysterious cir-cumstances. The family had on financial grounds dissuaded him from his chosen career of medicine, and as a compromise he had taken a job as an apothecary's assistant in Ludwigsburg. On the morning in question he was found dead in the cellar at his place of work, having apparently poisoned himself. The town's medical officer, to spare the family of his deceased col-league, officially certified a 'nervous stroke' as the cause of death. The shock to Eduard, as one of the few who probably knew the truth, was profound, and left its trace in a poem not written, or at least not published, until thirteen years later, the ode 'To an Aeolian Harp' ('An eine Äolsharfe', 1837), in which the motif of lamentation for the death of a beloved boy is muted in the text of the poem itself, but reinforced in the Latin epigraph. Mörike appears to have felt that the two events of 1824, so close to each other in time – the encounter with *Don Giovanni* and the death of August – were a significant coincidence, and it seems likely that this was the early emotional and imaginative root of *Mozart's Journey to Prague*, which is in fact not only a celebration of the composer's genius but also a meditation on his tragically early death and on mortality in general. The story ends with a poem, 'Denk es, o Seele' ('O soul, remember'), a lyrical *memento mori* now relatively well known as an anthology piece, which Mörike actually wrote in 1851 and which may at first not have specifically referred to Mozart. In 1855, passing it off as a Bohemian folk-song, he incorporated it into *Mozart's Journey* as the story's concluding comment.

After four years as a seminarist at Urach and four at Tübingen, Mörike passed his final examination in 1826, though without great distinction. He was now required to practise for some years as a curate or supply-preacher (*Vikar*) before being given a parish of his own. This interim period was in his case unusually prolonged and peripatetic; he was plagued by scruples about his suitability for the ministry (he had, for instance, considerable sympathy for the views of his friend David Strauss) and kept applying for release from his duties on the grounds or pretext of ill health. He considered seriously whether he might be able to earn his living as a freelance writer, and even resigned his curacy for more than a year to try this out, but soon realized that despite the burdens of his vocation, the stability and security it could offer made it, if he was to be a poet, the least unacceptable option. Fortunately the Church authorities treated him with considerable tolerance. Mörike's *Vikariat* lasted eight years and involved ten transfers from parish to parish. One of them was the parish of Plattenhardt, to which he was assigned in May 1829, shortly after his year of absence. Here the incumbent had recently died, and his widow and daughter, the twenty-two-

year-old Luise Rau, were still living in the parish house; Mörike
fell in love with Luise and they quickly became engaged. Over
the next four years he wrote passionate and exalted letters to
her, overwhelmed her with poems, urged her to read Goethe and
Lichtenberg. What the unsophisticated Luise understandably
wanted, however, was above all a husband who would be settled
in his own parish, as her late father had been, and she and her
mother became less and less confident that the eccentric and
frequently ailing Mörike would ever be fit for this role. The
engagement was broken off in 1833. Less than a year later,
however, in May 1834, the consistory did at last appoint the
wayward *Vikar* to a living of his own, in the tiny village of
Cleversulzbach near Heilbronn. Mörike took his mother and
sister to live with him there instead of a wife.

On the face of it, settling down at Cleversulzbach should have
been entirely favourable to his genius: a peaceful sedentary
existence, freedom from interference, time enough to wait for
the moment of inspiration – this was exactly what he himself
said it needed. And in fact, at Cleversulzbach, he published the
first collection of his poems in 1838, and in 1840 a 'Classical
Anthology' of Latin and Greek poetry, in his own translations
or in edited versions of others. But the rural idyll of the contented
country parson, the role in which Mörike was long to be stereo-
typed, was not what it seemed. Everything was to his liking –
except his actual job of preaching, which remained a torment
to him. He himself now required supply-preachers, he continued
to ask for frequent sick leave, he borrowed sermons from his
old friend and more dedicated colleague Wilhelm Hartlaub,
who had his own parish not far away at Wermutshausen. Again
the consistory was patient; but in the end Mörike had no option
but to write formally (this being the *démarche* required in such
cases) to the *Landesvater*, King William I of Württemberg,
asking to be released from his office. His request was granted
immediately: at thirty-nine, Mörike became a country parson
in early retirement and on half pay. His mother had died at
Cleversulzbach, and he and his sister Klara now stayed with
Hartlaub and his family for six months, before moving to the
health resort of Bad Mergentheim. Here again he was free to

spend his days as he pleased, writing, reading, drawing, collecting stones, but marriage seemed financially impossible. In Mergentheim, however, Klara formed a bosom friendship with the twenty-seven-year-old Margarethe Speeth, the daughter of their landlord Valentin von Speeth, a retired army officer who had served in Napoleon's Russian campaign. Mörike felt drawn into the relationship between the 'two dear sisters', partly because Margarethe, like Luise Rau, had recently become fatherless: the veteran of Borodino, commending his daughter to Eduard's care, had died a few months after the Mörikes moved into his house. Apparently on the basis of a proposal of marriage which must in effect have been from the brother and sister jointly, the three continued to live together for six years, an arrangement which no doubt attracted some local comment, if only because Margarethe was a Catholic like everyone else in Mergentheim. The marriage was officially formalized in 1851, the parties having decided to move back to Stuttgart and settle there.

Stuttgart, the capital of Württemberg, now became Mörike's permanent place of residence, and it was here, in middle life, that he began to enjoy increased reputation, even something like fame. He found himself under royal patronage, received in audience by the King, appointed to give weekly lectures on literature at Stuttgart's Katharinenstift, a finishing-school for young ladies founded by William's previous wife Catherine. It was an aristocratic but relatively liberal institution, with an international clientele; its director was a friend and admirer of Mörike's who had been active on his behalf. The Queen now even attended one of the poet's lectures, accompanied by her ladies-in-waiting, her small dog and her knitting. His salary began very modestly but was rapidly and generously increased, and he was kept on full pay after his retirement in 1866. In 1852 he was awarded an honorary doctorate at Tübingen, and became a titular professor by royal decree four years later. His reputation was now spreading to other parts of Germany and beyond. In 1856 he received, but declined, an offer of patronage from King Maximilian II of Bavaria, who invited him to settle in Munich. In 1855 and 1857 respectively two eminent literary

figures from the remotest north, the *Novelle*-writer Theodor
Storm and the dramatist Friedrich Hebbel, entered into corre-
spondence with him and came to visit him in Stuttgart; another
visitor, in 1865, was Ivan Turgenev, who came to demonstrate
to the poet that he could recite 'The Auld Steeplecock' ('Der alte
Turmhahn', 1840, 1852) by heart. Mörike's two daughters were
born at this time, Fanny in 1855 and Marie in 1857. The
marriage itself, however, was gradually and predictably being
destroyed by the jealous tensions between Klara and Mar-
garethe; a long overdue separation was agreed in 1873, Mar-
garethe going to live with Fanny and Mörike with Klara and
Marie. The last years of his life were increasingly barren and
isolated. He found the growing number of admiring visitors
irksome, and kept changing his lodgings to avoid them. After
his separation from Margarethe he withdrew into seclusion with
his sister and younger daughter, increasingly frail and refusing
to see anyone except his oldest friends. He died, almost in
penury, on 6 June 1875, after a show of reconciliation with
Margarethe only a few days earlier.

Mörike belongs to the elite of European poets who lack massive-
ness of output, and whom some would for this reason exclude
from the category of greatness. By the same token, Goethe owes
his commanding position in literature generally, his quasi-
Shakespearian status, not least to the sheer volume and diversity
of his writings. But we should remember that Coleridge, author
of two of the greatest poems ever written in English ('The Rime
of the Ancient Mariner' and 'Kubla Khan'), wrote virtually
nothing else; and that much the same might be said of, for
example, Hölderlin, Keats, Baudelaire and T. S. Eliot. As a
compromise, Mörike has been called a great minor poet.
Alternatively, certain features of his relatively exiguous work –
his variety of forms, his development from a lush romantic
manner in his youth to his own kind of classical maturity –
perhaps qualify him to be described as a minor provincial
Goethe. But Mörike, here again resembling Goethe, both invites
and resists definition, as does the nineteenth century generally,
which we must probably call the age of realism, or of the

transition from romanticism to realism, or of realism in its
various subclassifications such as poetic realism and bourgeois
realism. If Mörike has a terminological home, it is somewhere
here. For the early-to-middle part of the century there is also, as
German literary historians tell us, the term 'Biedermeier' (the
Biedermeier epoch, the Biedermeier style). Having originally
done duty in literary and social satire, then in application to a
modest and elegant style of furniture, interior decoration and
painting, 'Biedermeier' was extended to serious literature by
later critics but has never become very serviceable or fashionable
for English readers. It does not designate a 'school' or project,
but a trend, detectable in a certain number of writers in different
genres and independently of each other, of whom Mörike was
certainly one. It was appropriate to an epoch of extreme political
conservatism, the Metternich police state, in which the intellec-
tual middle classes could do little but retire, so to speak, to their
respective provinces. If there is a 'Biedermeier' attitude, it is one
of disillusioned withdrawal from political engagement of any
kind, as well as from passionate love and anything else that
might disturb the resigned tranquillity, the *aurea mediocritas* of
life. This quietistic ideal is perfectly expressed by Mörike in at
least two of his most characteristic poems, 'Seclusion' ('Ver-
borgenheit', 1832) and 'A Prayer' ('Gebet', 1832, 1845–6). The
term 'Biedermeier' is also often applied to the Austrian novelist
and *Novelle*-writer Adalbert Stifter, the Austrian dramatist
Grillparzer and some other less-well-known figures. But there
is much to be said for preferring, in the case of Mörike, the
label 'poetic realist', given the widely recognized special affinity
between what is called poetic realism and the *Novelle* form as
such, and given in particular the central importance, in his work
as a whole, of his *Novelle* about Mozart.

The term *Novelle* was borrowed by Goethe from the Italian
word *novella*, a story or item of news. He saw it exemplified in
Boccaccio's *Decameron*, which he attempted to imitate, adopt-
ing in particular Boccaccio's device of a cycle of stories within
a narrative frame. Goethe thought of the *Novelle* as a story
reporting some novel or interesting event, and as one that made
some use of the framing technique. Since his time, these and

certain other features (such as careful construction, conden-
sation, flashback narratives, dramatic elements, a central sym-
bolic object or moment) have more or less attached themselves to
the *Novelle* tradition, though whether they are in fact formally
essential to it is not certain. Some critics indeed have been
content to define the *Novelle* simply as 'eine Erzählung mittlerer
Länge', a tale of middling length, what we would call a long-
short story. The matter remains controversial, and there is not
even a generally agreed distinction of form or content between
the *Novelle* and the *Erzählung*. The first and, some would
say, still unsurpassed master story-teller in German literature,
Heinrich von Kleist, published his tales (1810) simply as *Erzäh-
lungen*, and this was also, in the twentieth century, the term
preferred by Thomas Mann and Kafka. On the other hand,
we should probably try to distinguish the *Novelle* from the
Märchen. Mörike wrote a small number of stories, none of them
important except *Mozart's Journey to Prague*; some of them
(including *Mozart's Journey*) he called *Novellen* and others
Märchen, but he does not seem to have had in mind any clear
criterion for the distinction. It seems probable, however, that a
Novelle is intended as a more 'realistic' story, and that a realistic
story is thought of as one excluding all fantastic or supernatural
material, one that operates entirely within the world of social
and historical reality. The word *Märchen*, on the other hand, is
usually mistranslated into English as 'fairy-tale', which as Tol-
kien has pointed out would be all right if by 'fairy' we under-
stood not a small white creature with wings, but the world of
féerie (faery), the folk-tale world of wish-fulfilments, the world
(as the brothers Grimm called it in their famous collection) of
'once upon a time, *when wishing still helped*' (*wo das Wünschen
noch geholfen hat*), the world of magic spells, of be-wishments
(*Verwünschungen*) which are bewitchments. 'Realism' only
exists here in an indirect sense, as the communication of inner,
psychological realities. Stories of this kind, which for clarity's
sake should really be called folk-tales (*Volksmärchen*) or tales
of magic (*Zaubermärchen*), are anonymous or of obscure
origin, like the traditional folk-songs (*Volkslieder*) which were
seen as a parallel manifestation of the folk psyche. To German

romanticism in its high phase, coinciding roughly with the period of the Napoleonic wars between 1805 and 1815, both were objects of the most intense interest, as attested by the collection by Arnim and Brentano of more than 700 German folk-songs under the title *Des Knaben Wunderhorn* (*The Boy's Magic Horn*, 1805–8) and of the even more monumental *Kinder- und Hausmärchen* (*Household Tales for Children*, 1812–) by the brothers Jakob and Wilhelm Grimm, which laid the foundation of European folklore studies. These were two of the most important documents of the German romantic movement.

A further development was the artificial or literary *Märchen* (*Kunstmärchen*) which the author wrote under his own name, blending folk-tale material with his own narrative and themes and comments, usually to more or less ironic effect. These hybrid creations were denominated by coinages such as *Märchen-Novellen* or even *Novellen-Märchen*. The Danish tales (1835–) of Hans Christian Andersen, well known in England, belong to this mixed genre, and a brilliant example from the German romantic period is Adalbert von Chamisso's *Peter Schlemihls wundersame Geschichte* (*The Strange History of Peter Schlemihl*, 1813), which uses several traditional folk-motifs: the devil's bargain, the man without a shadow, the magic purse, the magic bird's-nest, the cap of invisibility and the seven-league boots. It has been widely described as a pure romantic *Märchen*, though Thomas Mann called it '*eine phantastische Novelle*'. Three years earlier, and in some ways standing apart from romanticism in general, the eight stories of Kleist appeared, a year before his suicide. None of them could be called a *Märchen*; some are chronicles as strictly realistic or naturalistic as present-day detective stories (*Das Erdbeben in Chili* [*The Earthquake in Chile*], *Die Verlobung in Sankt Domingo* [*The Betrothal in Santo Domingo*], *Der Zweikampf* [*The Duel*]); in others the supernatural intrudes to some extent (the ghost in *Das Bettelweib von Locarno* [*The Beggarwoman of Locarno*], the mysterious *Doppelgänger*-figures in *Michael Kohlhaas*, *Der Findling* [*The Foundling*] and *Die heilige Cäcilie* [*St Cecilia*]). Kleist calls this last story 'a legend', as if to disclaim responsibility for its historical truth. Another Christian legend, also involving a devil's bargain, is the Swiss novelist Jeremias Gotthelf's *Die schwarze Spinne* (*The Black Spider*, 1842), written at the height of the '*Novelle*' period and transformed by compelling realistic detail and consummate art into one of the greatest examples of the genre.

It is evident that in subtitling his story about Mozart 'a *Novelle*', Mörike was boldly attaching himself to a flourishing literary tradition of some fifty years' standing, rich in its variety of conventions, and which still provokes critical controversy today. At the time of writing *Mozart's Journey* he was at the height of his powers and had already produced most of his finest poetry. To give some rough indication of his development as a poet over nearly forty years, the poems in the present selection are arranged more or less chronologically and divided into two periods, the first nominally ending in 1838, the year of the publication of his first volume of collected verse. Successive editions, gradually enlarged over the years, followed in 1848 and 1856, with a final collection (the definitive 'Ausgabe letzter Hand') appearing in 1867, some years after he had stopped writing. There could be said to be a perceptible difference between the work of Mörike's first, youthful period, the 1820s and 1830s, and that of his mature period after 1838. In the former, he normally wrote in rhymed forms of considerable diversity, often echoing romanticism in his adoption of the *Volkslied* style. In his maturity, with some important exceptions, rhymeless 'classical' forms predominated. Many of the earlier poems, being shorter and lending themselves more readily to musical setting than hexameters and pentameters, are partly for this reason relatively well known. A perfect synthesis of Mörike's words and Hugo Wolf's music, for instance, is achieved in 'At Midnight' ('Um Mitternacht', 1827), which rivals the status of Goethe's 'Über allen Gipfeln' ('Wanderer's Night Song') as the profoundest evocation of the stillness of night in German literature. The solitary observer watches the darkness slowly rise out of the sea and cover the mountains; in its silence he can hear the mountain streams murmur, representing the movement of time within its stasis, the diurnal cycle to which midnight also belongs. This is a detailed magic, the casting of an entirely realistic spell. Equally extraordinary, without the addition of music, is the longer ode 'On a Winter Morning before Sunrise' ('An einem Wintermorgen, vor Sonnenaufgang', 1825) which Mörike always placed at the beginning of his collections. Once again the solitary lyric self is totally absorbed, exploring the nuances of his emotions as they respond to the nuances of the natural world; the special quality of the light of a winter dawn mirrors the ambiguous state of the soul, its luminous darkness, its stillness still in motion, its state between waking and dreaming. In 'Urach Revisited' ('Besuch in Urach', 1827) he wanders nostalgically through the landscape of his youth, vainly trying to recapture the lost absorption, to understand the speech of the waterfall which is the earth's perpetual self-colloquy. These are solitary lyrical utterances, as is the sonnet 'To My Beloved' ('An die Geliebte', 1830), one of several addressed to Luise Rau during the years of their engagement. Here the beloved is ethereal but evanescent. The tragic 'Peregrina' cycle, though written a few years earlier, betokens a maturer suffering: its note of authentic anguish is one which Mörike's love poetry would never strike again.

  The romantic 'folk' style, on the other hand, a poetry of *Märchen* in the widest sense, could seem less personal in that the poet often disappeared behind a conventional role-figure: the speaker or 'singer' is the young huntsman, the humble groom or gardener winning the favour of the princess, the abandoned lover, the lover telling his story to the stream or the green leaves. The background is the landscape of forests and rolling hills, castles and medieval towns, rivers and mill-wheels murmuring in valleys – the abiding elements of a certain sort of German, and especially south German, romanticism, which those who have never fallen under its spell will call its paraphernalia and its clichés. This whole lost world is glimpsed in some of Mörike's poetry of the 1820s and 1830s; most perfectly in the ballad 'Sweet-Rohtraut' ('Schön-Rohtraut', 1838), inspired, as he recalled, by the mere sound of the old Germanic name 'Rohtraut' which he found by chance in a dictionary. Other examples are 'The Forsaken Girl' ('Das verlassene Mägdlein', 1829), 'A

Huntsman's Song' ('Jägerlied', 1837) and in the comic manner
'News from the Storks' ('Storchenbotschaft', 1837). After 1838
the ballad and the *Volkston* largely disappear from Mörike's
poetry, with the notable exception of 'The Auld Steeplecock'
('Der alte Turmhahn', 1840, 1852). The brief visionary utter-
ance of the Orplidian 'Song of Weyla' ('Gesang Weylas', ?1831),
an isolated and mysterious curiosity in the earlier work, remains
without later parallel, while the free verse ode 'To an Aeolian
Harp' anticipates in more ways than one the great classical
valediction 'Erinna to Sappho' ('Erinna an Sappho', 1863) writ-
ten twenty-six years later.

Mörike's renewed interest in classical poetry dates from the
mid-1830s when, bored with his parish work at Cleversulzbach,
he turned again to the Greek and Latin poets he had read at
school and in his uncle's house. Three of his own translations
from Catullus (including the famous epigram 'Odi et amo' ['I
love and I hate']) were included in his first collection, a strophe
from Horace became the epigraph for 'To an Aeolian Harp',
and the first *Klassische Blumenlese* (*Classical Anthology*)
appeared in 1840, featuring Homer, Theocritus, Catullus,
Horace, Tibullus and others. Mörike used existing translations,
which he revised and annotated, in all cases preserving the
original metres or, more strictly speaking, the usual modern
German accentual adaptations of the ancient quantitative
metres. The rhythmical and syntactical affinities between Ger-
man and Latin or Greek have always meant that it could be used
more readily than other modern European languages as an
acceptable medium for translating and imitating the ancient
classics, and since the mid-eighteenth century the German
equivalents of hexameters and other ancient verse-forms con-
tinued to flourish. Their extensive use by Goethe, above all,
must have influenced Mörike at least as much as his study of
the Greek and Latin texts themselves. No doubt for a variety of
reasons, this exploration of classical poetry marked a turning-
point in Mörike's own creative work, and from now on most
(though not all) of his important poems are written in the
classical rhymeless forms: dactylic hexameters as in the mock-
Homeric 'Tale of the Safe and Sound Man' ('Märchen vom

sichern Mann', 1837–8) and the *Lake Constance Idyll* (*Idylle vom Bodensee*, a short sentimental 'epic' of country life in seven cantos, inspired by a visit to Lake Constance [the Bodensee] in 1840 and indebted to Goethe's *Hermann und Dorothea* [1795]); elegiac distichs as in 'The Beautiful Beech-Tree' ('Die schöne Buche', 1842) or 'A Domestic Scene' ('Häusliche Szene', 1852); the iambic trimeter or senarius (the metre of ancient tragedy and comedy) as in 'On a Lamp' ('Auf eine Lampe', 1846), 'Divine Remembrance' ('Göttliche Reminiszenz', 1845), 'An Edifying Meditation' ('Erbauliche Betrachtung', 1846), 'The Woodland Pest' ('Waldplage', 1841), 'A Visit to the Carthusians' ('Besuch in der Kartause', 1861) and others. Like Goethe he also made good use of the traditional short form, the ever-flexible comic or serious classical epigram, originally a tombstone inscription and restricted in length for that reason but prized since later antiquity for its laconic antithetical wit and pointed ending. Typically it was in elegiac distichs and only one or two distichs long: Catullus's 'Odi et amo' is an example; others in Mörike are 'To Sleep' ('An den Schlaf', 1838) (another translation), and 'At Daybreak' ('Bei Tagesanbruch', 1837, 1867). 'Inscription on a Clock with the Three Hour-Goddesses' ('Inschrift auf eine Uhr mit den drei Horen', 1846) and 'On a Lamp' (both in trimeters) are probably both short enough to be classified as epigrams, as are 'Johann Kepler' (1837) and 'The Falls of the Rhine' ('Am Rheinfall', 1846). Deservedly the best-known poem from the later Mörike's whole 'classical' repertoire has always been the elegiac idyll 'The Beautiful Beech-Tree', but it is almost the only one to have been received into the canon, while others of comparable beauty and elegance have been largely neglected.

The 'Tale of the Safe and Sound Man', for instance, a remarkable early exercise in Homeric hexameters standing more or less at the point of Mörike's transition to his later manner and looking ironically both forward and back, is a *Kunstmärchen* of enormous comic verve. The opening line seems to indicate that it is addressed to an audience of children, though a personal allegory may also be intended. The grotesque giant Suckelborst ('safe' because he was hidden inside a womb-like mountain to survive the Flood) is a figure from the imaginary Orplid world which Mörike and Ludwig Bauer invented in their student days. A letter from Bauer to Hartlaub (9 October 1829) and the later reminiscences of the poem 'An Edifying Meditation' both suggest that Suckelborst had been a persona sometimes adopted by the poet himself in exuberant mimic improvisations. Mörike seems to have been gifted with a special kind of creative verbal sensuality, and the 'safe and sound man' perhaps came into being in his drunken, inarticulate bass-voice gurglings in the same way as the princess Rohtraut was born out of the sound of her name. In any case, it is easy enough to detect an ironic self-caricature of the poet in this clumsy, childlike dreamer, supposedly endowed with the special insights of genius into cosmic truths and called upon to commit them to writing, but usually too lazy to do so. To the rural community (comically and affectionately evoked as a Swabian village called Igelsloch, literally 'hedgehog-hole') he is an outsider, a mischievous hur-lothrumbo, but not wholly isolated or rejected (the village barber secretly trims his beard for him with hedging-shears). Obeying, with a bad grace, the orders brought to him by a messenger of the gods, he writes his mysterious work on barn doors lashed together to form an exercise book, and sets off to the underworld, carrying a walking-stick and wearing a hat like a nineteenth-century professor, to read it to his proper audience, the timeless dead. Mörike whimsically mixes three different mythologies: the Orplid world of Weyla and Lolegrin, the Homeric gods whose unquenchable laughter ends the poem, and the Christian Devil who interrupts Suckelborst's lecture in Hades. The giant punishes the Devil's schoolboy antics by tear-ing out his tail, which he then uses as a bookmark, after proph-esying that the Devil will at the end of days be finally put to scorn and the improbable hero received into the company of the gods; a Goethean note, for good measure. The story of Suckelborst is a substantial comic masterpiece by the later Mörike which has lacked due recognition.

Another is 'The Auld Steeplecock', though like Goethe's *Her-mann und Dorothea* it was published to popular acclaim. Excep-tionally, Mörike reverted here to rhyming verse, the doggerel

and archaizing style (*Knittelvers*) revived by the young Goethe
in the 1770s. As a publisher's note explained when the 'Steeple-
cock' first appeared in a periodical in 1852, the 'cock' is 113
years old and can therefore only talk in archaic German. The
poem was conceived and the first twenty-two lines written in
1840, when Mörike was still at Cleversulzbach; by his own
account the incident of the replacement of the church steeple-
cock took place in reality, and Mörike kept the retired cock in
his study. He then dropped the poem and did not finish it for
another twelve years. Sending it to Storm in 1854, he explained
that he had somewhat idealized his country parson, providing
him for example with a wife and children (though in the text
they appear only fleetingly). The cock, which by a bizarre deflec-
tion of roles does all the talking itself, describes in vivid lan-
guage, and with a mixture of humour and resignation, its own
situation and that of its 'maister dear' the minister. It has been
rescued from the scrap-heap but moved from its proud position
at the top of the church steeple to perch on the more modest
'tower' of the minister's ornamental stove. The sublime panor-
ama has been reduced to a limited and snug enclosure, well
locked up and itself enclosed within a small village community.
The minister's study, a true Biedermeier nest of the kind seen
in the paintings of Carl Spitzweg (1808–1885), is full of old
leather-bound books, the smell of good tobacco, a walnut desk
and other treasured objects. The minister evidently has a
Biedermeier tendency to collect things, of which indeed the
steeplecock itself is one and the Dutch stove with its elaborate
picture-tiles another. Collecting is characteristic of this careful
middle-class lifestyle. The Prior in 'A Visit to the Carthusians'
has a 'box of curiosities'; the schoolmaster Preceptor Ziborius
in 'A Domestic Scene' collects varieties of home-brewed vinegar;
Mörike himself (like the elderly Goethe) collected mineralogical
specimens. Like the 'Tale of the Safe and Sound Man', 'The Auld
Steeplecock' includes a detectable element of self-caricature:
the slightly absurd snugness of the priest tucked away in the
remote countryside with his pensioned-off cock, and the 'safe
and sound' outsider with his neglected duty of preaching to
the dead. Unlike it, however, it is also coloured by elegiac sad-

ness, the resigned sadness of the solitary eccentric and of the discarded cock itself. In common with other important works of Mörike's later period, including *Mozart's Journey to Prague* and 'A Visit to the Carthusians', it is both an idyll and a meditation on death.

This is not paradoxical if we consider the rather complex sense of the concept 'idyll' as it developed in the literary theory and practice of the German classic-romantic era. Traditionally, the 'idyll' had since ancient times been simply the more or less sentimental evocation of pastoral life, but by the late eighteenth century, notably in Schiller's classic theoretical account *Über naive und sentimentalische Dichtung* (*On Naive and Reflective Poetry*, 1797), it came to mean the portrayal, in poetry or prose, of an ideal human condition, a past golden age or future utopia. Certain motifs remained characteristic: natural simplicity and innocence, harmony and contentment within accepted limitations, a state of things scarcely troubled by history and time. Schiller defined *Idylle* radically and widely as a mode of presentation (theoretically possible in any genre) depicting reality as the harmonious perfection it should be but empirically is not. Its opposite, defined even more widely, was 'satire', the representation of reality as the disharmonious imperfection it is but should not be. The poet writes from a vision of harmony and wholeness or from a vision of disharmony and conflict. The idyllic presentation can be humorous or serious or both, it can be tinged with irony, with a sense that the harmony is fragile, that the happiness is under threat, subject to mortality and change. Schiller argued that this should indeed always be so in idyll at its best: idyll and satire are in principle inseparable, since true satire should be a protest in the name of implied positive values, and true idyll should be coloured by awareness that potential tragedy is still there, next-door to the idyllic world because pushed back to just beyond its boundaries. Goethe's *Hermann und Dorothea* was essentially humorous, but nuanced with dramatic and tragic elements: it was an idealized portrayal of German middle-class society in a small country town, but this symbolically stable way of life was set against the threatening chaotic background of the French Revolution, war and refugees.

The threatened idyllic condition is a social one. Most of the poems by Mörike that can reasonably be classified as idylls or near-idylls are humorous (though subtly expressing serious themes) and portray idyllic social states: the idyllic condition is one of social harmony, dependent not on mysterious higher powers but on civilized human behaviour and the recognition of human limitations.

'The Auld Steeplecock', expressly described as 'an idyll' in Mörike's subtitle, presents a limited order of human life in which things are as they should be. It does not document Mörike's existence as a simple country pastor in Cleversulzbach or anywhere else, but abstracts from this reality and transforms it into a model, a should-be, a place where 'lichtsome sweet contentment dwalls'. In a sense it is the cock himself who transforms it, who so to speak creates the idyll. The cock sees it all as a peaceable and secure place, his contentment is heightened by the warm stove on winter nights, the good locks and bolts that keep out thieves, the stout wood of the henhouse that keeps out the fox, and even by his own final positive recognition that at the age of 113 it is time to accept mortality: to acknowledge, as in 'A Visit to the Carthusians', that 'all things have their time'. This story of the Carthusian monastery, told in a late poem in trimeters (1861), is another variant of the social-domestic idyllic genre. The poet remembers his previous visit fourteen years ago, when things were as they should be: the idyllic state now in the past and half forgotten, the peaceful life of the monastic community in the old Prior's day, the tables loaded with baked eel and succulent fresh artichokes and the 1834 house vintage. The house has become a brewery now, and little is left of its former happier state. The poet recognizes only the house doctor, who happens to be there on his return visit and now shares a glass with him, and an ornamental clock still standing on its shelf, its dial bearing the ominous motto *Una ex illis ultima*, to remind anyone who cares to look at it that one of these hours will be his last. Jocularly, the doctor tells him how the Prior bequeathed the clock to the Steward, who was so alarmed by its motto that he parcelled it up tight, sealed it ten times and hid it away behind the chimney in an out-of-the-way room. The clock had seemed to threaten the old order, or rather it had relativized it by spelling out its impermanence, but it was still an integrated part of that order. The Steward broke the convention required by the idyllic harmony, and became comically eccentric by hiding the clock; but the clock has come to light again, it has outlived the Steward and the Prior and the whole brotherhood, and to the poet it still ticks out its warning message.

'A Visit to the Carthusians' is a serious-comic social idyll. Idylls of solitude, of solitary encounter, on the other hand, are purely serious. One is 'To a Christmas Rose' ('Auf eine Christblume', 1841), in which Mörike reverts again to rhymed verse. The flower (a kind of winter-flowering hellebore) was a real one which Mörike found, suddenly and by chance, when walking in a churchyard, and which he describes in a letter to Hartlaub (29 October 1841) with botanical precision. Mörike, the poetic realist, was a dreamer with a strong sense of physical realities. This poem is the celebration of a harmonious and perfect physical phenomenon for its own sake. The flower is a thing, an object, a living entity, studied, described, contemplated, praised, held aloft as it were, but still a distinct *Gegenstand*, literally something standing 'over against' the poet. It is fully itself, though made fully 'symbolic' by a nexus of associations: the death of Christ, and at the other end of the cycle the annunciation of his birth, but also the world of innocent nature – the snow and the moonlight, the grazing deer, the inquisitive elf, the insect whose winter ghost circles the mysterious flower in eternal salutation. Very similar, and one of the most compelling of all Mörike's poems, is another *Dinggedicht* ('thing poem'), 'The Beautiful Beech-Tree' (written in elegiac distichs). This famous 'thing poem', or, as we might say, 'object poem' (or, as Brian Rowley prefers, 'entity poem'), is another wholly serious idyll of solitude and numinous timelessness, an absolute synthesis between mature classical form and the romantic experience of 'forest solitude' (*Waldeinsamkeit*), the visionary and ecstatic contemplation of a mysterious yet wholly real Object within nature. Again, the poet has found the beech-tree – which later attempts have failed to identify – by chance, and yet, as it seems to him, not quite by chance. He feels that something has led him to the place, that it is being shown to him by 'a sprite friendly to man', one of the pagan tutelary spirits of the forest. As Romano Guardini pointed out, an accumulation of details gives the impression that the tree and its surroundings are more than beautiful or idyllic: they are sacred, numinous, almost uncanny. The forest is explicitly called a 'grove', and the space in which the tree stands, though no human hands have cleared it, is circular: the sun is at its zenith, and the tree's foliage casts a circle of shade which almost fills the clearing but is bounded by a bright ring of sunlight. All this suggests the precinct, the τέμενος, of an ancient temple. The visitor is stricken with awe, the soft grass round the tree is like a precious carpet with magical powers, on which he 'scarcely dares' to walk; it receives him ceremoniously, and when he reaches the great tree in the centre it does not occur to him to sit down under it or loll against its trunk. Instead, with instinctive reverence, he stands upright. In this 'high hour of noon', the dangerous hour at which Pan sleeps, there is an air of nameless expectancy. Even the birds are silent, and the visitor remains motionless, he feels drawn into something that is not simply the absence of sound or motion but their other side, their positive countersphere. He listens to what Giacomo Leopardi, some twenty years earlier, in his famous poem 'L'Infinito' ('Infinitude', 1819) had called *'sovrumani silenzi e profondissima quiete'*. It is what Mörike calls 'daemonic silence, fathomless stillness'. The phrase carries no suggestion (as the modern spelling 'demonic' might) of evil or malignity, only of a strong, indwelling, non-human power and a profound harmony. Its representative, another listener, has been alert (*'auflauschend'*) to the poet's approach, and has drawn him to a place to which no path leads: it is 'off the path', there is no signpost, one finds it only when one is not looking for it. And again the moment, the encounter, as so often in Mörike, comes 'suddenly'.

Another symbolic Object is the Schaffhausen waterfall in 'The Falls of the Rhine'. In this classical elegiac epigram a phenomenon, which Goethe had also found awe-inspiring, is perceived and imaginatively mythologized into an eternal gigantomachy, the gods with their silver-maned steeds eternally subduing the monstrous primal rage. The watching 'wanderer' feels a joy that almost shakes his heart out of his body. Similarly in 'A Walk in the Country' ('Auf einer Wanderung', 1845), which it is instructive to compare with the much earlier 'A Journey on Foot' ('Fußreise', 1828). Both are in free rhymed forms. 'A Journey on Foot' refers to the poet's walking-stick, his mood of religious euphoria, and the woods, hills and birds in general terms. In 'A Walk in the Country', as a variant of Mörike's characteristic theme, there is not so much an Object as a Moment, a momentary, personal, magical disclosure: the 'little town' entered just as the sun is setting, and from a window the clear voice suddenly singing (Auden's phrase will do as well as any) just as he arrives, a specific moment in which he seems suffocated (*lustbeklommen*) with sudden, uncovenanted joy.

These are poems that have a certain festive solemnity, they are at the serious end of the spectrum, the opposite end to the broad farce (somehow heightened by classical metres) of the 'Tale of the Safe and Sound Man'. 'The Woodland Pest' on the other hand (in trimeters), written a year before 'The Beautiful Beech-Tree', could be read as a comic pendant to it. The daemonic presences here take the form of a plague of gnats, which drive him out of his poetic solitude and so enrage him that prudish dryads request him to moderate his language or quit their peaceful maidenly domain. The poet must recognize that the minor pains and disturbances of life are 'almost unavoidable'. In 'A Domestic Scene' (in elegiac dialogue) the potential idyllic condition of contentment between the schoolmaster and his wife, with the husband pursuing his quaint but harmless hobbies of silkworm-breeding or brewing experimental varieties of vinegar, is disturbed and threatened when his activities grow into eccentric obsessions: the vinegar jars have spread all over the neat middle-class household, and the wife protests that he is a laughing-stock with the neighbours. Like the Carthusian Steward, Preceptor Ziborius becomes comical by his excess, his lack of irony. The balance must be restored, the pentameter must be spoken to close the distich, the measure must be respected: an ancient Horatian message, not far from the '*Friede*' ('sweet contentment') of Mörike's 'Auld Steeplecock' or the '*holdes*

Bescheiden' ('contentment sweet and wise') which 'A Prayer'
('Gebet') places neither at one extremity nor the other, but '*in
der Mitte*'.

The most extraordinary and elaborately encapsulated of the
Encounter or Object poems is 'Divine Remembrance', in which
the poet again adopts the persona of a 'wanderer' (this could be
a convention borrowed from the young Goethe). He is making
his way through a wild, rocky landscape, when he suddenly
recalls a painting seen years ago in his much-visited Carthusian
monastery: a painting of the Child Jesus as a beautiful five-year-
old boy sitting on a rock in wild countryside, where his com-
panion, an old shepherd, has picked up a curiously shaped
petrifact and shown it to him. The Object captured by the
painter, then perceived and now recalled by the poet, could
hardly be more momentous and sacred: it not only goes back
through the centuries to the earthly life of Jesus, but seems to
return to the beginning of time. An almost imperceptible nuance
of wonderment appears on the Child's face as he stares at it,
and in a flash of 'divine remembrance' recalls for a fleeting
moment the creation of the world by his own act. The piece of
stone, found by chance and appearing both in the painting and
in the poet's description of the painting, a memory within a
memory, thus becomes a symbol of the world itself.

It is not clear whether this poem is to be construed as an
expression of religious belief on the narrator's part, of assent to
the traditional Christian doctrine of the incarnate Logos 'by
whom all things were made', as the Johannine epigraph states.
Mörike has made this a rather more complex point than it
seems. For instance, there is also the prior question of whether
the painter (whoever he was, and if indeed the painting ever
existed) himself held the traditional belief. It might be thought
prima facie that this must have been so, because if it were not,
half the point of the painting would disappear. It would have
lost the profundity, the paradox that this five-year-old child is
simultaneously the Creator, who in undergoing human incar-
nation has (as the classic formulation puts it) 'emptied himself'
of divine knowledge and therefore of any consciousness of his
divine actions, unless by some exceptional momentary anam-

nesis. In the absence of this theological dimension it would still be a religious painting, but in a quite commonplace sense: an attractive scene, marginal to the biblical story, of the Christ Child playing with a piece of rock. On the other hand, this may indeed be what the real or imaginary painting was: the christological hint may be no more than an interpretative contribution by the poet, whose thoughts about the Child and his plaything are more complicated than the artist's were. This is perhaps the more likely reading both of the painting and of Mörike's reception of it. But even on this view the poet can be said to be at one or two removes from an expression of faith: he may be merely touched by the faith of the unidentified painter, or he may have invented the painting altogether, perhaps thus implying that the divine Child as such may also never have existed. In any case the poem is not telling us of the poet's encounter with the painting itself, or his thoughts about it when (as he claims) he first saw it, but of his memory of it which he suddenly now recovers in rocky archaic surroundings; and this memory of the painted scene is now enriched, becomes more moving, by his added reflections (with or without doctrinal assent) on the identity of the divine Child. Moreover, an exact parallel is here suggested between this psychological process of recollection (which may have prompted the writing of the poem) and the mysterious return, at the sight of the archaic stone, of the Child's lost memory of his act of creation. The stone (a petrified growth 'from the sea's depths'), the Child, the painting and the mountain landscape, all take on their significance from the nexus of their encounters and associations. Both the natural Object and the art-Object are transformed and exalted, the two psychological events combine to disclose a pattern: the link between creativity and buried but recovered memories. Somehow we are again taken back here to the story of the child-giant Suckelborst: he has ancient knowledge of the beginning of things, he lived before the Flood, he himself is like something in a creation-myth, in his naive uncouthness he represents the creative force. Similarly, it is a returning childhood memory that prompts Mozart's creativity when he first sits down by the orange-tree.

In *Mozart's Journey to Prague*, the idyllic and tragic elements coexist, and each heightens the effect of the other. The half-historical, half-fictional tale is both a celebration of supreme art and a valedictory acknowledgement of the creative artist's tragic destiny. Its central significant event is Mozart's idyllic-fictional, unintended, serendipitous visit to the Schinzberg household on his way to Prague to produce the première of *Don Giovanni*, and the centre of this centre is the significant Object, the orange-tree. His encounter with it, and consequently with the Count and his family, involves more than one quite fortuitous but highly meaningful coincidence. He happens to arrive on the day of the betrothal festivities for the Count's young niece Eugenie, happens to wander into the Count's garden, and happens to sit down beside the particular tree that has acquired and will now further acquire such especial importance. It is now standing near a fountain, flourishing and fertile, bearing fruit as if to greet Mozart's arrival. It is at this point that the 'idyll' begins, only to be rudely threatened almost at once. Mörike's astonishing account of the onset of the mysterious creative process in the composer's mind is the poetic high point of the *Novelle*, becoming dramatic as Mozart's musical trance is interrupted. As in 'Divine Remembrance', creativity is triggered by a memory – in this case, as he looks at the oranges and listens to the fountain, a childhood memory of the golden balls thrown by dancing jugglers in Naples, and of the melody, or one like it, of Zerlina's wedding dance. He becomes oblivious of his surroundings and is unconscious of the strange, instinctive, geometrical gesture with which he cuts the fruit into two hemispheres, parting and rejoining them as his musical idea develops. This is an internal idyll of creative harmony. The ensuing comic confrontation with the indignant head gardener marks the moment of maximum distance between genius and society; he is seen as 'some kind of tramp wandering about', who is 'not right in the head' and 'says his name is Moser'. The satisfying anagnorisis that follows is the turning-point, the dénouement by which Mozart is reintegrated into the social idyll. The family joyfully invite him and his wife to break their journey to Prague for at least one night, to stay with them and join in the festivities.

In the course of these he plays them one of his piano concertos, Eugenie sings an aria from *Figaro*, and she and Mozart together perform the new duet for *Don Giovanni* which he has written by the orange-tree and now dedicates to her. In the morning they continue their journey in a new carriage, which the Count has given them as a present. The artist's relationship with society is shown to be as it should be.

Mozart's Journey to Prague is somehow both prose and poetry, both an eloquent conversation-piece and a subtly constructed *Novelle* complete with flashbacks, criss-crossing narrations and a central symbolic Object. It is both an ornamental fountain of words and music, and at the same time the detailed record of a unique and idyllic social event, by a writer who has left behind him the youthful rhetoric of romantic isolation and adopted the voice of a narrator communicating with a real public, with a like-minded readership of cultivated friends: a narrator who has something to tell them, a story about something he has seen or found or experienced, a place he has visited ('I know a place . . .', 'long ago I saw a picture . . .'). His narrative poems are sometimes (reviving here another ancient convention) 'epistles' to real or fictitious recipients, and their stories are as often as not told quite casually, in a low-key, understated, conversational style (*Plauderton*). This applies pre-eminently to *Mozart's Journey to Prague*, in which Mörike's predilection for narrative is very evident. His authorial story is interspersed with secondary, internal stories, by Mozart himself and by his wife Constanze. One of these is Mozart's eloquent account of the Neapolitan water-pageant he saw seventeen years ago and of which he has been reminded by the orange-tree's golden fruit; another is his account of the circumstances in which he was moved to write the sinister music of Don Giovanni's meeting with the Statue. Later we hear Constanze's reminiscences, her confession of her anxieties about her husband's poor health and human weaknesses, and her eager hopes that the expected success of *Don Giovanni* in Prague may give a new turn to his fortunes. She describes at length the future she imagines for him, his happy and prosperous life in Berlin under the King of Prussia's patronage. But Mörike's authorial comments make it clear that none of this will ever happen, they refer to Mozart's inability to thrive in this world, the self-consumption of his burning genius, his presentiments of death and terrible fits of paralysing depression. The narratives interweave, and the theme of his death interweaves with them. Through the high-spirited chatter of the story, it appears and disappears, hinted at, half mentioned, left unmentioned, finally confronted at the end in the *memento mori* of 'O soul, remember'.

'A Visit to the Carthusians', written six years after *Mozart's Journey to Prague*, resembles it in several ways: firstly in being a sophisticated complex of low-key, conversational narratives, secondly in combining a social idyll of 'lichtsome sweet content- ment' with presages of death, thirdly in making elaborate use of a symbolic Object (the clock). In both the story and the poem, the primary or external narrative (Mozart travelling to Prague to produce *Don Giovanni*; the poet revisiting the abandoned monastery) contains a subtext, the underlying inner theme (the transitoriness and fragility of great cultures and of the creative artist himself; the certainty of death for every man). In both cases there is a historical dimension, and the Object relates the present to the past. In *Mozart's Journey* we are given two stories about the orange-tree, two episodes of its history: one reaching back about a century to the great age of Louis XIV, when Madame de Sévigné gave the cutting to Count Schinzberg's grandmother, and the other in which the tree (having now been carefully preserved as a symbolic heirloom of the family and thus a symbol of the *ancien régime* at its best) is intended as a betrothal gift for Eugenie – only to have its value for her and for everyone else unexpectedly and miraculously enhanced when Mozart himself sits down by it and picks one of its oranges as he composes part of *Don Giovanni*. From this moment, the fruit becomes something scarcely less consequential than the apple in the garden of Eden ('your paradise', as Mozart himself calls it in his letter to the Countess). Similarly, in 'A Visit to the Carthusians', the clock plays its role twice: in the past, fourteen years ago, when the poet-narrator first visited the monastery and found it prosperous and hospitable, and now again on his return visit when the doctor tells him the story of the clock and how the Steward hid it, while the clock itself still stands there with its menacing admonition. Both the clock and the doctor connect the past with the present, and bring with them the poem's essential theme: the theme of death, of readiness or unreadiness for death, of the fear of 'the last hour'.

In the story about Mozart, the idylls are also threatened: the idyll of perfect order represented by his art, and the social idyll represented by his fictional, transient visit to a place invented for him by Mörike as the artist's ideal social setting. Here all is festivity and conviviality, badinage and *Lebenslust*, memories of an earlier golden age of culture. But hidden beneath everything are Mozart's melancholy, his forebodings, his vulnerability to 'daemonic' forces. They rise darkly to the surface as he sits at the piano and plays extracts from his new opera which the world has not yet heard, ending with the Cemetery scene and the erotic hero's terrifying descent into hell. Two years later, European culture will be shaken by the French Revolution, and four years from now Mozart himself will be dead. Eight years after finishing *Mozart's Journey to Prague*, Mörike wrote another 'letter' poem, a last work before the twelve years of his final silence. In 'Erinna to Sappho', the young poetess Erinna writes to her beloved mentor of her happiness with 'all our friends, and the graceful art of the Muses' – and of how, that morning, she had suddenly found herself alone, confronted by strange omens of her imminent death and descent into 'night's dreadful abyss': the sinister *Doppelgängerin* in the mirror, the rush of Apollo's black-feathered arrow grazing her temple. Death isolates: and Mozart too, even in his present privileged company, seems isolated by the darker side of his own music. His hearers were delighted by *Figaro* and by Zerlina's 'Giovinette che fate all'amore', but the music of the Stone Guest is the voice of the unspeakable. No one can find an adequate comment. Mörike seems to suggest that there are two kinds of art: on the one hand the 'graceful art of the Muses' which adorns and enhances social intercourse, and on the other the art of isolation, of the abyss, of compulsive self-destroying genius. Only Eugenie, the most gifted and sensitive of the Schinzberg circle, perceives something of the latter in her admired master: she too cannot put it into words, but then she finds the words in the 'Bohemian folk-song' with which Mörike ends the story, and weeps as she re-reads it. She nevertheless seems to accept the truth of its message, and her tears are tears of sadness rather than of despair. She is thus the essential link between Mozart and her friends, between the divine-daemonic genius and the civilized society to which he gives delight. The at least partial bridging of this gap corresponds to Mörike's known intention that in his story about Mozart the idyllic feeling, though inseparable from elegiac sadness, should nevertheless predominate.

Further Reading

Among biographical and critical sources here used I should
mention above all the massive and authoritative systematic
study of Mörike's poetry by Renate von Heydebrand (*Eduard
Mörikes Gedichtwerk*, Metzler-Verlag, Stuttgart, 1972). Others
to which I am indebted to a lesser extent include Romano
Guardini's lectures on five poems (*Gegenwart und Geheimnis*,
Werkbund-Verlag, Würzburg, 1957), Benno von Wiese's analy-
sis of *Mozart's Journey to Prague* in his book *Die deutsche
Novelle von Goethe bis Kafka* (Bagel-Verlag, Düsseldorf, 1959),
Siegbert Prawer's fascinating documentation of the reception of
the poetry (*Mörike und seine Leser*, Ernst Klett, Stuttgart, 1960),
Gerhard Storz's *Eduard Mörike* (Klett, 1967), Hans Egon Hol-
thusen's short illustrated biography (Rowohlt, Reinbek, 1971),
Peter Lahnstein's mainly biographical *Eduard Mörike* (List-
Verlag, Munich, 1986), and Birgit Mayer's indispensable factual
résumé in the Metzler *Realien* series (*Eduard Mörike*, Stuttgart,
1987). Material on Mörike in English is unfortunately scanty,
but readers not fluent in German may wish to consult Margaret
Mare's biography (*Eduard Mörike: the Man and the Poet*,
Methuen, London, 1957), Lionel Thomas's selection of the
poems (with introduction and notes, Blackwell's German Texts,
Oxford, 1960), R. B. Farrell's article 'Mörike's Classical Verse'
(*Publications of the English Goethe Society*, London, 1955/6)
and his short monograph on *Mozart's Journey to Prague*
(Studies in German Literature no. 3, London, 1960), the article
by W. D. Williams 'Day and Night Symbolism in Some Poems
of Mörike' (in *The Era of Goethe: Essays Presented to James
Boyd*, Oxford University Press, Oxford, 1959), J. P. Stern's

essay on Mörike ('Recollection and Inwardness') in his collection *Idylls and Realities* (Methuen, 1971), and the studies by B. A. Rowley, 'A Long Day's Night. Ambivalent Imagery in Mörike's Lyric Poetry' (*German Life and Letters*, 1975/6), 'The Nature of Mörike's Poetic Evolution' (in the collection of commemorative essays for Lionel Thomas, Hull University Press, Hull, 1980), and 'Brimstone, Beech and Lamp Bowl: Eduard Mörike's Things' (*Publications of the English Goethe Society*, 1993/4). See also J. Rolleston, 'The Legacy of Idealism: Schiller, Mörike and Biedermeier Culture' (*Modern Language Quarterly*, December 1990), and J. Adams (ed.), *Mörike's Muses: Critical Essays on Eduard Mörike* (Camden House, Columbia, SC, 1990).

Note on the Text

Twelve years after *Mozart's Journey to Prague*, Mörike published the fourth and last edition (*Ausgabe letzter Hand,* 1867) of his collected poems, that is to say his final selection of those he thought worth publishing. The two best modern editions currently available, that by H. G. Göpfert (1954, revised 1981) and that by Helga Unger (1967–70), are both based on this text, while taking account of earlier printings and manuscripts in which interesting variants are occasionally to be found. The Reclam selection by Bernhard Zeller (1987) is based on Göpfert, and thus indirectly on the 1867 edition. For purposes of the present anthology I have used the Reclam texts simply because of their modernized punctuation; a few poems not in Reclam are taken from Unger. The question of the order in which the poems should be arranged is slightly more problematic. It is thought (though there has been some controversy on this point) that Mörike himself was responsible for the traditional sequence, which remained essentially the same in all four of his own editions, and which most subsequent editors have in practice adopted. It is not, however, chronological or dictated by any other discernible principle; for instance Mörike did not group the poems under subheadings according to form or theme, as Goethe in his own collected editions had tried to do. Suitably enough, he placed the great early meditation on the winter sunrise, 'On a Winter Morning before Sunrise' ('An einem Wintermorgen, vor Sonnenaufgang', 1825), at the beginning of the collection, and ended it with a still relatively early piece, the comical 'Good Riddance' ('Abschied', 1837), in which the poet very satisfyingly kicks his critic downstairs. In the bilingual selection here offered, the actual choice of poems is inevitably influenced by personal preferences and considerations of translatability, but I have also tried to illustrate the already discussed broad dissimilarity between Mörike's earlier and later work, and have therefore abandoned his own order for one that is almost consistently chronological. This is then divided into two slightly overlapping sections (the first, as a concession to tradition, beginning with 'On a Winter Morning' and ending with 'Good Riddance'). The greater length of the second section reflects an obvious bias in favour of poems in the later and 'classical' style, but this may serve as a corrective to the opposite bias of most previous Mörike anthologies. In the most important and influential anthology of all, Hugo Wolf's volume (published in 1889) of musical settings of fifty-three of the poems, the emphasis also falls on the 'romantic' or 'lyrical' poems of the earlier period, though this of course is not a case of bias but a necessary requirement of the *Lied* form. Wolf's *Mörike-Lieder* are discussed in a separate excursus (pp. 195–204). About half the poems chosen in the present edition are among those composed by Wolf, but I have made no attempt to relate the translations to the music or devise singable versions, if only because this would have required excessively close imitation of Mörike's metrical patterns, with consequent excessive semantic distortion.

Mozart's Journey to Prague

In the autumn of 1787 Mozart, accompanied by his wife, travelled to Prague, where he was to stage the first production of *Don Giovanni*.

On the third day of their journey, at about eleven o'clock in the morning of 14 September[1] and not more than thirty hours distant from Vienna, the couple were driving in the best of spirits in a north-westerly direction, beyond the Mannhardsberg and the German Thaya, not far from Schrems and the highest point of the beautiful Moravian mountains.

'Their carriage,' writes Baroness von T— to her friend, 'a handsome orange-yellow vehicle drawn by three post-horses, was the property of a certain old lady, the wife of General Volkstett,[2] who always seems to have rather prided herself on her acquaintance with the Mozart family and the favours she has shown to them.' This imprecise description of the conveyance in question is one to which a connoisseur of the taste of the 1780s may well be able to add a few details. The doors on both sides of the yellow coach were decorated with floral bouquets painted in their natural colours, and it was edged with narrow gold trimming, but the paintwork in general was still quite without that glossy lacquered finish favoured by modern Viennese carriage-builders. The body moreover was not fully rounded out, though lower down it curved inwards with coquettish boldness; the roof was high and the windows had rigid leather curtains, though at present these were drawn back.

Here we might also make some mention of the costumes of the two travellers. Frau Constanze, carefully saving her husband's new clothes for special occasions, had packed these in the trunk and chosen a modest outfit for him to wear: over an embroidered waistcoat of rather faded blue his usual brown topcoat with its row of large buttons, each fashioned in a starlike pattern with a layer of red-gold pinchbeck glinting through the outer material; black silk breeches and stockings, and shoes with gilt buckles. The weather being quite unusually hot for the time of year, he had removed his coat and for the last half hour had been sitting bareheaded and in shirt sleeves, chattering contentedly. Madame Mozart was wearing a comfortable travelling dress, light green with white stripes. Loosely bound, her beautiful auburn hair fell in abundant curls over her neck and shoulders; all her life she had never disfigured it with powder, but her husband's vigorous growth of hair, tied in a pigtail, was today merely powdered more casually than usual.

The road rose gently between the fertile fields which here and there intersected the wooded landscape; at a leisurely pace they had reached the top and were now at the forest's edge.

'I wonder,' said Mozart, 'how many woods we've passed through, today and yesterday and the day before yesterday! I've never given them a thought, still less did it occur to me to get out and set foot in them. But now, my darling, let's do just that, and pick some of those bluebells growing so prettily in the shade. Coachman! Give your horses a bit of a rest!'

As they both stood up, a minor disaster came to light for which the maestro was soundly scolded. By his carelessness, a phial of very expensive eau-de-Cologne had lost its stopper and spilled its contents, unnoticed, over his clothes and the upholstery. 'I could have told you so!' lamented his wife. 'I've been noticing a sweet smell for some time now. Oh my goodness, a whole flask of *Rosée d'Aurore* completely emptied! I'd been saving it like gold!'

'Why, my dear little silly!' he consoled her, 'don't you see that this was the only way your divine elixir could do us some good? First we were sitting in an oven, and all your fanning was useless. But then suddenly the whole carriage felt cooler. You thought it was because of the few drops I put on my ruffles; we were both revived, and our conversation flowed happily on, when otherwise we should have been hanging our heads like sheep being carted to the slaughter. And we shall be reaping the benefit of this little mishap for the rest of our journey. But come on now, let's stick our two Viennese snouts straight into this green wilderness!'

Arm in arm, they stepped over the ditch at the side of the road, plunging at once into the shade of the pine-trees, which very soon thickened to darkness, sharply broken only here and there by shafts of sunlight that lay across the velvet mossy ground. The refreshing chill, suddenly contrasting with the heat outside, might have proved dangerous to the carefree traveller had his prudent companion not induced him, with some difficulty, to put on the coat which she was holding in readiness.

'My goodness me, what a splendid sight!' he exclaimed, gazing up at the tall tree-trunks. 'You'd think you were in church! I don't believe I've ever been in a forest before, and it never entered my head till now what sort of a thing it is, this whole tribe of trees standing together! No human hand planted them, they all arrived here by themselves, and there they stand, just because they enjoy living and keeping house together. You know, when I was young I used to travel around all over Europe, I've seen the Alps and the sea and all the great and beautiful things of creation: and now by chance here I am, poor simpleton, standing in a pine-wood on the Bohemian border, amazed and enraptured to find that such a thing actually exists and is not merely *una finzione di poeti*, like nymphs and fauns and other things they invent, and not just a stage wood either, but one that has really grown out of the ground, growing tall on moisture and the warmth and light of the sun! This is where the stag lives, with his extraordinary antlers zig-zagging out of his head, and so does the funny little squirrel and the wood-grouse and the jay.'

He stooped down and picked a toadstool, praising its splendid scarlet colour and the delicate white gills on the underside of its cap; he also pocketed an assortment of pine-cones.

'One might think,' remarked his wife, 'that you had never yet taken twenty steps into the Prater, which after all also boasts these rare treasures.'

'Prater forsooth! God bless my soul, what a place to mention here! Nothing but carriages, gentlemen with swords, ladies in all their finery with fans, music, the whole spectacle of high society – how can one ever notice anything else there? And even those trees that give themselves such airs, I don't know – all the beechnuts and acorns that cover the ground, they're scarcely distinguishable from all the corks that have fallen among them, discarded corks from a thousand bottles. Two hours' walk away from the Prater woods and you can still smell waiters and sauces.'

'Oh, hark at him!' she exclaimed, 'that's how he talks now, the man whose chief pleasure's to dine in the Prater on roast chicken!'

When they were both back in the carriage and the road, after running level for a short way, began dipping downwards into a smiling landscape which merged with the hills in the further distance, our maestro was silent for a while and then resumed his theme. 'This earth of ours, you know, is really beautiful, and we can't hold it against any man if he wants to stay on it as long as possible. Thank God I feel as fresh and well as ever, and there are a thousand things I could fancy doing; and sure enough, their turn will come to be done just as soon as my new work has been finished and produced. How much there is out there in the world and how much here at home, how many remarkable and beautiful things of which I still know nothing: wonders of nature, sciences, arts and crafts! That black-faced lad by his charcoal kiln, he knows exactly as much as I do about a whole lot of things, even though I too have a wish and a fancy to take a look at many matters that just don't happen to be in my line of business.'

'The other day,' she replied, 'I found your old pocket diary for the year '85; you'd made three or four jottings at the back, things to remember. The first was "Mid-October: casting of the great bronze lions at the Imperial foundry"; the second, heavily marked: "Visit Professor Gattner!" Who is he?'

'Oh yes, I know – that's the dear old man at the Observatory who invites me there from time to time. I've been wanting to take you along some day to see the moon with me, and the man in the moon. They've got a vast great telescope up there now;

they say you can look at the huge disc and see mountains and valleys and ravines, as clear as if you could touch them, and the shadows cast by the mountains from the side the sun doesn't shine on. For two years now I've been meaning to go, and I can't get round to it, to my eternal shame and disgrace!'

'Well,' she replied, 'the moon won't run away. There'll be time to catch up on what we've missed.'

After a pause he went on: 'And isn't that how it always is? Ugh! I can't bear to think how much one misses and puts off and leaves hanging in the air – to say nothing of duties to God and man – I just mean how many of the small innocent pleasures that offer themselves every day of one's life.'

Madame Mozart could see that her husband's lively mood was now increasingly taking a direction from which she was neither able nor willing to divert him, and sadly she could do no more than wholeheartedly agree as with mounting emotion he continued: 'Have I ever even had the pleasure of being with my children for as much as an hour? How half-hearted it always is with me, how fleeting! Lifting the boys up to ride on my knees, chasing about the room with them for a couple of minutes, and *basta!* that's it, down they go again! I can't recall that we've ever made a day of it out in the country together, at Easter or Whitsun, in a garden or a wood or in the fields, just us together, romping around with the little ones and playing with the flowers, just to be back in one's own childhood again. And meanwhile life goes by, it runs and rushes past – Oh, God, once you start on such thoughts, what a sweat of fear you break into!'

With the utterance of these self-reproaches, the intimate and affectionate conversation now developing between the couple had unexpectedly taken a more serious turn. We prefer not to acquaint our reader with its further details, but offer instead a more general survey of the situation which in part, expressly and directly, supplied the theme of their discussion, and in part merely constituted its familiar background.

We must at the outset sadly acknowledge that Mozart, despite his passionate nature, his susceptibility to all the delights of this life and to all that is within the highest reach of the human imagination, and notwithstanding all that he had experienced, enjoyed and created in the short span allotted to him, had nevertheless all his life lacked a stable and untroubled feeling of inner contentment.

Without probing deeper than we need into the causes of this phenomenon, we may in the first instance perhaps find them simply in those habitual and apparently insuperable weaknesses which we so readily, and not without some reason, perceive as somehow necessarily associated with everything in him that we most admire.

His needs were very various, above all his passion for the pleasures of society was extraordinarily strong. Honoured and sought out as an incomparable talent by Vienna's noblest families, he seldom or never declined invitations to dinners, parties and soirées. In addition he would entertain his own circle of friends with befitting hospitality. The Sunday musical evening, a long-established tradition in his house, or the informal luncheon at his well-furnished table with a few friends and acquaintances two or three times a week, were pleasures he refused to forgo. Sometimes, to his wife's dismay, he would bring unannounced guests straight in off the street, a very varied assortment of people, dilettanti, artistic colleagues, singers and poets. The idle parasite whose sole merit lay in an untiring vivacity, ready wit and the coarser sort of humour was made as welcome as the learned connoisseur and the virtuoso musician. For the most part, however, Mozart sought relaxation outside his own home. As often as not he was to be seen playing billiards in a coffee-house after lunch, or passing the evening in a tavern. He was very fond of driving or riding in the country with a party of friends; being an accomplished dancer, he liked going to balls and masquerades, and he particularly enjoyed taking part in popular festivals several times a year, especially the open-air fête on St Bridget's Day, at which he would appear in pierrot costume.

These pleasures, sometimes wild and boisterous and sometimes attuned to a more peaceful mood, served the purpose of giving his creative intellect much-needed rest after its enormous tensions and exertions; and they had the additional and incidental effect, following the mysterious unconscious play of genius, of communicating to it those subtle and fleeting impressions which sometimes quicken it to fruitful activity. But unfortunately it also happened at those times, when it was so important to drain the auspicious moment to its last drop, that no other consideration whether of prudence or of duty, of self-preservation or of good housekeeping, was able to make itself felt. In his creative work as in his pleasures, Mozart exceeded any limit he could set himself. All his nights were partly devoted to composition, which he would revise and finish early next morning, often while still in bed. Then, from ten o'clock onwards, called for on foot or by carriage, he would go the rounds of his lessons, which as a rule would take up some hours of the afternoon as well. 'We're working ourselves to the bone to make an honest living,' he himself once wrote to a patron, 'and often it's hard not to lose patience. One happens to be a well-accredited cembalo player and music teacher, and lo and behold one has a dozen pupils on one's back, and then another and another, no questions asked whether they're any good or not provided they pay cash on the nail. Any old mustachioed Hungarian from the Corps of Engineers is welcome, if Satan has put an itch in him to study ground-bass and counterpoint for no reason whatever; or any conceited little countess who receives me red as a turkeycock if I don't turn up on her doorstep dead on time, as if I were Master Coquerel the coiffeur! . . .' And then, when these and other professional labours, classes, rehearsals and so forth had tired him out and he needed some fresh air to breathe, he would often find that his exhausted nervous system could only be restored to a semblance of life by fresh excitement. All this imperceptibly undermined his health, at least nourishing if not actually causing his recurrent fits of melancholy, and so inevitably fulfilling that premonition of early death which dogged his footsteps to the last. Every kind of anguish, including remorse, was familiar to him like a bitter flavour on all his joys. And yet we know that these sorrows too, purified and serene, all met and mingled in that deep fountain from which they leapt again in a hundred golden streams, as his changing melodies inexhaustibly poured forth all the torment and rapture of the human heart.

The ill-effects of Mozart's way of life were most plainly to be seen in his domestic arrangements. The reproach of foolish, irresponsible extravagance was well merited, and even went hand in hand with one of his most lovable traits of character. A caller who turned up in dire need to ask him for a loan, to beg him to stand surety, had usually calculated in advance that Mozart would not bother to negotiate any terms or guarantee of repayment; and indeed it was no more in his nature than in a child's to do so. He liked best to make an immediate outright gift, and always with laughing generosity, especially when he felt that for the time being he had money to spare.

The expense involved in such lavishness, in addition to ordinary household needs, naturally far exceeded his income. His earnings from theatres and concerts, publishers and pupils, together with his pension from the Emperor, were quite insufficient, if only because his music was still far from commending itself decisively to public taste. The pure beauty, complexity and profundity of Mozart's work were commonly found less palatable than the more easily digestible fare to which his hearers were accustomed. It is true that *Il Seraglio*, thanks to the popular elements in this piece, had in its time so delighted the Viennese that they could scarcely have enough of it. *Figaro*, on the other hand, competing a few years later with the charming but far slighter *Cosa rara*, had been an unexpected and lamentable failure, which was certainly not only due to the Director's intrigues.[3] Yet this very same *Figaro* had then almost at once been received with such enthusiasm by the better educated or less prejudiced audiences of Prague, that the master, touched and grateful, had decided to write his next great opera specially for them.

Notwithstanding the unpropitious times and the influence of his enemies, Mozart might still, if he had exercised a little more circumspection and prudence, have earned a very respectable income by his art. As things were, however, he fell short of success even in those ventures which won him acclamation from the great mass of the public. It seemed, in fact, that fate, his own character and his own weaknesses all conspired to prevent this unique man of genius from prospering and surviving.

We may readily understand with what difficulties a housewife who knew her duty must have been faced in such circumstances. Although herself young and lively, the daughter of a musician and no stranger to artistic temperament, as well as having been brought up to live frugally, Constanze willingly did her utmost to stop the waste at its source, to cut short some of her husband's excesses and make good the large-scale loss by small economies. But it was perhaps in this last respect that she lacked the right skill and experience. It was she who kept the money and the household accounts; every bill, every demand for repayment and all the unpleasantness fell only to her to deal with. Thus there were times when she almost lost heart, especially when these household worries, the privations, the painful embarrassments and the fear of public disgrace, were compounded by her husband's moods of depression, which would overwhelm him for days on end. Idle and inconsolable, he would sit sighing and lamenting beside his wife, or brooding by himself in a corner, and as a screw follows its endless thread, so he would dwell endlessly on the single gloomy theme of his wish to die. Nevertheless her good humour seldom deserted her, and her clear common sense usually stood them in good stead, even if only for a short time. In the essentials there was little or no improvement. Even when she did, with a mixture of seriousness and cajolery, of flattery and pleading, succeed in persuading him, just this once, to take tea with her or to enjoy dinner with his family and then spend the evening at home, what good did it do? Occasionally, indeed, noticing with dismay and emotion that his wife had been shedding tears, he would sincerely abjure this or that bad habit, promise complete reform and more than she had asked – it was all in vain, for he would soon slip back into his old ways. It was tempting to believe that to do otherwise was simply not in his power, and that somehow to have forcibly imposed on him a completely different way of life, conforming to our ideas of what is proper and beneficial for mankind generally, would in his case have been the very way to destroy this unique and miraculous individual.

Constanze nevertheless kept on hoping that a favourable turn of events might be brought about by external causes, that is to say by a radical improvement in their financial position, which in view of her husband's growing reputation she fully expected. If only, she thought, the constant pressure could be relieved, the economic pressure which he himself directly or indirectly felt; if only he might follow his true calling undividedly, without having to sacrifice half his strength and his time merely to earn money; and if only he no longer had to chase after his pleasures, but could enjoy them with a far better conscience and with twice the profit for his body and soul! Then indeed his whole state of mind would become easier, more natural, more peaceful. She even planned that they would one day move and live elsewhere, convinced as she was that despite his absolute preference for Vienna there was no real future for him there, and that she might in the end be able to persuade him of this.

But there was now a next, decisive step to be taken towards the realization of Madame Mozart's thoughts and wishes: and this, she hoped, would be the success of the new opera which was the purpose of their present journey.

Its composition was well over halfway completed. Close friends well qualified to judge, who had followed the progress of this extraordinary work and were well placed to form some idea of its character and probable reception, spoke everywhere of it in a tone of such wonderment that even among Mozart's enemies many were prepared to see *Don Giovanni*, before it was six months old, stirring and taking by storm and changing the face of the entire musical world from one end of Germany to the other. Other well-wishers, speaking with greater caution and reserve, based their forecasts on the present state of musical fashion, and were less hopeful of a general and rapid success. The maestro himself privately shared their only too well-founded scepticism.

Constanze for her part, like any woman of lively temperament and especially when her feelings are dominated by an entirely understandable wish, was much less susceptible than men to such misgivings and second thoughts of one kind or another, and held fast to her hopeful view, which indeed, now in the carriage, she yet again had occasion to defend. She did so in her most charming and high-spirited manner and with redoubled energy, for Mozart had become noticeably more depressed in the course of their foregoing talk, which of course had been quite inconclusive and had broken off in deep dissatisfaction. Still full of good humour, she explained in detail to her husband how, when they got home, she proposed to spend the hundred ducats for which they had agreed to sell the score of the opera to the Prague impresario: it would cover the most urgent items of debt as well as some other expenses, and she had good hopes of managing on her household budget through the winter and into the spring.

'Your Signor Bondini,'[4] she declared, 'will be feathering his nest on your opera, you may be sure of that; and if he is even half the man of honour you keep saying he is, he'll be paying you back a tidy percentage from the royalties he'll get for copies of the score from one theatre after another. And if not, well then, thank God, we have other possibilities in prospect, and much sounder ones too. I can foresee quite a few things.'

'Let's hear about them.'

'The other day a little bird told me that the King of Prussia[5] needs a new Kapellmeister.'

'Oho!'

'Director-General of Music, I should say. Let me have my little daydream! It's a weakness I inherited from my mother.'

'Dream away; the crazier the better!'

'No no, it's all quite sane. First, let's assume – in a year's time, let us say –'

'On the Pope's wedding-day –'

'Oh do be quiet! I predict that in a year come St Giles there will no longer be any Imperial court composer answering to the name of Wolf Mozart.'

'Well now, devil take you, my dear.'

'I can already hear our old friends gossiping about us, telling each other all sorts of stories.'

'For instance?'

'One morning, for instance, our old admirer General Volk-stett's wife comes sailing straight across the Kohlmarkt soon after nine o'clock on a visiting expedition, all on fire after three months' absence: she has finally made that great journey to her

brother-in-law in Saxony that she's chattered about daily ever
since we first met her. She got back last night, and now her heart
is full to bursting – fairly brimming over with happy travel
memories and impatience to see her friends and delightful titbits
of news to tell them – and off she rushes to the Colonel's wife
with it all! Up the stairs she storms and knocks on the door and
doesn't wait for a "Come in". Just picture the jubilation and the
huggings and kisses! "Well, my dearest Madame Colonel," she
begins, when she's caught her breath again after the prelimi-
naries, "I've brought you a multitude of greetings, just guess
from whom! I didn't come straight back from Stendal, we made
a little detour, we took a left turn to Brandenburg." "What!
Is it possible? You went to Berlin? You've been visiting the
Mozarts?" "For ten lovely days!" "Oh my sweet, my dear, my
darling Madame General, tell me about it, describe them! How
are our dear young friends? Are they still as happy there as they
were at first? I find it so extraordinary, unthinkable, even now,
and all the more now that you've just been to see him – Mozart
a Berliner! How is he behaving? How does he look?" "Oh, him!
You should just see him. This summer the King sent him to
Carlsbad. Can you imagine his best-beloved Emperor Joseph
thinking of that, eh? The two of them had only just got back
when I arrived. He's aglow with health and energy, he's round
and plump and lively as quicksilver, with happiness and content-
ment just written all over his face."'

And now Constanze, speaking in her assumed role, began to
paint her husband's new situation in glowing colours. From his
apartment in Unter den Linden, his country house and garden,
to the brilliant scenes of his public activity and the intimate
Court circles where he would be invited to accompany the
Queen on the piano: all this seemed to become real and vividly
present in her descriptions. Whole conversations and delightful
anecdotes came tumbling out of her as if by magic. She truly
seemed more familiar with the Prussian capital, with Potsdam
and Sanssouci, than with the Imperial palaces of Vienna and
Schönbrunn. She was also roguish enough to endow the person
of our hero with a good number of quite new domestic virtues
which had supposedly grown and prospered on the solid Prus-

sian soil, and among which our friend Madame Volkstett had
noticed above all, as a phenomenon proving how often *les
extrêmes se touchent*, a most wholesome parsimonious tendency
which suited him wonderfully well. '"Yes, just think, he gets
his three thousand thalers cash down, and all for what? For
conducting a chamber concert once a week and the grand opera
twice – oh, dearest Madame Colonel, I saw him, saw our dear
little treasure of a man, with his superb orchestra all round him,
the orchestra he trained and that worships him! I was sitting
with his wife in their box, almost opposite the royal family! And
what, I ask you, what was on the programme? – I brought one
for you, I've wrapped up a little present in it from the Mozarts
and myself – here it is, look, read it, it's printed in letters a yard
long!" "What? Heaven help us! *Tarare!*"[6] "Yes, you see, my
dear; who would have thought it! Two years ago, when Mozart
wrote *Don Giovanni*, that accursed, poisonous Salieri, all black
and yellow with envy, was already plotting in secret to repeat
the triumph he had in Paris with his own opera, to repeat it
without delay on home ground. There was our dear Viennese
public, dining on wood-snipe and listening to nothing but *Cosa
rara*; well, now he would show them another kind of bird
too. So now he and his accomplices were whispering together,
planning subtle ways of producing *Don Giovanni* with its
feathers well plucked, bald and bare as *Figaro* had been and
neither dead nor alive – well, do you know, I made a vow that
if that man's infamous opera reached the stage, nothing would
induce me to go to it, nothing! And I kept my word. When
everyone was running along to see it – you too, my dear Madame
Colonel! – I sat on by my stove with my cat on my lap, eating
my pastry-cake; and I did the same thing the next few times it
was given. But now, just think: *Tarare* at the Berlin Opera, the
work of his arch-enemy, conducted by Mozart! 'You must go
to it!' he exclaimed before we'd been talking a quarter of an
hour, 'even if it's only so that you can tell them in Vienna that I
didn't harm his precious brain-child. I wish he were here himself,
the envious pig, and he'd see that I don't need to ruin another
man's work in order to prove that I still am what I am!'"'

'*Brava, bravissima*!' shouted Mozart, and took his little wife by the ears, and kissed and cuddled and tickled her, until her fanciful game, the many-coloured dreams that floated from her imagination of a future that would, alas, never even begin to be realized, came to an end in high-spirited, mischievous caresses and laughter.

Meanwhile they had been continuing their descent into the valley and were approaching a village which they had already seen from the top of the hill; just beyond it, in the charming plain, was a small country mansion of modern appearance, the residence of a certain Count von Schinzberg.[7] They were planning to feed the horses, rest and have lunch in this village. The inn where they pulled up stood at the end of it by itself on the main road, from one side of which a poplar avenue not six hundred paces long led to the castle grounds.

When they had alighted from the coach, Mozart as usual left it to his wife to order lunch. In the meantime he ordered a glass of wine for himself in the parlour downstairs, while she asked only for a drink of cold water and some quiet corner where she might sleep for an hour. She was shown upstairs, and her husband followed, merrily singing and whistling to himself. The room was whitewashed and had been quickly aired. In it, among other old furnishings of finer origin which had no doubt found their way here at one time or another from the castle, stood a clean and elegant four-poster bed with a painted canopy resting on slender green-lacquered columns. Its silk curtains had long ago been replaced with a commoner material. Constanze made herself comfortable, he promised to wake her in good time, she bolted the door behind him, and he now went to seek his own entertainment in the public parlour. There was however no one there except the landlord, and his guest, finding that neither the man's conversation nor his wine was much to his taste, indicated that he would like to take a short walk towards the castle until lunch was ready. The park, he was told, was open to respectable visitors, and in any case the family was not at home today.

He set off and soon covered the short distance to the open park gates, then strolled along an avenue of tall old lime-trees, at the end of which, a little way to the left, the front of the house suddenly came into view. It was built in the Italian style, its walls washed in a light colour and with a double flight of steps grandly projecting from the entrance; the slate roof was decorated with some statues of gods and goddesses in the usual manner and with a balustrade. Our maestro, passing between two large and still profusely blossoming flower beds, walked towards the shadier parts of the garden; he made his way past some groups of beautiful dark pines, along a tangle of winding paths and into the more sunlit areas again, where he followed the lively sound of leaping water and at once found himself standing by a fountain.

The pool was imposingly wide, oval in shape and surrounded by a carefully tended display of orange-trees[8] growing in tubs, which alternated with laurels and oleanders; round them ran a soft sanded pathway, and opening on to this was a little trellised summerhouse which offered a most inviting resting place. A small table stood in front of the bench, and here, near the entrance, Mozart sat down.

As he listened contentedly to the plashing of the fountain and rested his eyes on an orange-tree of medium height, hung with splendid fruit, which stood by itself outside the circle and quite close to him, this glimpse of the warm south at once led our friend's thoughts to a delightful recollection of his own boyhood. With a pensive smile he reached out to the nearest orange, as if to feel its magnificent rounded shape and succulent coolness in the hollow of his hand. But closely interwoven with that scene from his youth as it reappeared before his mind's eye was a long-forgotten musical memory, and for a while his reverie followed its uncertain trace. By now his eyes were alight and straying to and fro: he was seized by an idea, which he immediately and eagerly pursued. Unthinkingly he again grasped the orange, which came away from its branch and dropped into his hand. He saw this happen and yet did not see it; indeed so far did the distraction of his creative mood take him as he sat there twirling the scented fruit from side to side under his nose, while his lips silently toyed with a melody, beginning and continuing and beginning it again, that he finally, instinctively, brought out an enamelled sheath from his side pocket, took from it a small silver-handled knife, and slowly cut through the yellow globe of the orange from top to bottom. He had perhaps been moved by an obscure impulse of thirst, yet his excited senses were content merely to breathe in the fruit's exquisite fragrance. For some moments he gazed at its two inner surfaces, then joined them gently, very gently together, parted them and reunited them again.

At this point he heard footsteps approaching and was startled into sudden awareness of where he was and what he had done. He was about to try to hide the orange, but stopped at once, either from pride or because it was too late anyway. Before him stood a tall broad-shouldered man in livery, the head gardener of the estate. This fellow had no doubt observed the suspicious movement Mozart had just made, and was momentarily lost for words. The composer, also speechless and evidently riveted to his seat, stared half laughingly, visibly blushing yet with a certain impudence, straight up into the man's face with his great blue eyes; and then – an onlooker would have found this very comical – he set the seemingly undamaged orange with a bold, defiant and emphatic gesture down in the centre of the table.

'Excuse me,' began the gardener with barely concealed annoyance, after taking a look at the inauspicious dress of the stranger, 'I do not know whom I have the –'

'Kapellmeister Mozart from Vienna.'

'No doubt, sir, you are known to the family?'

'I am a stranger here and on my way through. Is his lordship at home?'

'No.'

'Her ladyship?'

'Her ladyship is busy and not receiving visitors.'

Mozart rose to his feet and turned to go.

'By your leave, sir – may I ask by what right you simply come in here and help yourself like this?'

'What?' exclaimed Mozart, 'help myself? Devil take it, man, do you think I meant to steal this thing here and eat it?'

'Sir, I think what my eyes tell me. These oranges have been counted and I am responsible for them. His lordship selected this tree specially for use at an entertainment, it is just about to be taken to the house. I cannot let you go until I have reported the matter and you have given your explanation of how this happened.'

'Very well. I shall wait here until you do that. You can depend on it, my good fellow!'

The gardener looked about him with some hesitation, and Mozart, thinking that perhaps a tip might settle the matter, put his hand in his pocket, only to find that he had not a penny in his possession.

They were in fact now joined by two under-gardeners, who loaded the tree on to a hurdle and carried it away. In the meantime the maestro had taken out his pocketbook, extracted a sheet of paper, and with the gardener still standing over him had begun to pencil the following lines:

Most gracious Lady,

Here I sit, poor wretch, in your paradise, like our fore-father Adam after he had tasted the apple. The damage is already done, and I cannot even shift the blame for it to my dear Eve, who at this very moment, with the graces and amoretti of her canopied bed fluttering round her, lies at the inn enjoying the sweet sleep of innocence. Command me, and I will personally answer to your Ladyship for a misdeed which I myself find incomprehensible. In sincere mortification

Your Ladyship's most humble servant
   W. A. Mozart,
      en route to Prague.

Folding up the note rather clumsily, he handed it to the servant, who was still waiting uneasily, and told him to deliver it as directed.

No sooner had the enemy withdrawn than a carriage was heard entering the courtyard at the back of the castle. It was the Count bringing home his niece and her fiancé, a rich young baron, from the neighbouring estate. Since the Baron's mother had for years been confined to her house, today's betrothal ceremony had taken place there, and now an additional happy celebration, with a number of relatives invited, was to be held

at the castle, for it was here that Eugenie, whom the Count and
Countess treated like a daughter, had found a second home
since her childhood. The Countess and her son, Lieutenant Max,
had returned a little earlier to make various arrangements,
and the whole house was now a hive of activity upstairs and
downstairs, so that it was only with difficulty that the gardener
at last managed to hand the note to the Countess in the ante-
room; she however, paying little attention to what the messenger
said, did not open it at once but went hastily about her affairs.
He waited and waited, but she did not return. One after another
of the servants, valets and lady's maids and footmen, hurried
past him. He asked for the Count and was told that his lordship
was busy changing his clothes. Then he looked for Count Max,
but he was deep in conversation with the Baron, and fearing that
the gardener was about to make some inquiry or announcement
which would prematurely reveal something about the evening's
plans, cut him short as he spoke: 'Yes, yes, I'm coming, off you
go now.' Some time passed before the father and son eventually
appeared together and received the painful news.

'Why, damnation take it!' exclaimed the good-natured, stout
but somewhat irascible Count, 'that's absolutely intolerable! A
musician from Vienna, you say? Some sort of tramp, I suppose,
wandering about begging for alms and grabbing whatever he
can find?'

'By your leave, my lord, that is not quite what he seems to be.
I think he's not right in the head. And he's very arrogant. He
says his name is Moser. He's down there waiting to hear from
us. I told Franz to stay near by and keep an eye on him.'

'What's the point of that now, damn it! Even if I have the fool
locked up, the damage can't be repaired. I've told you over and
over again that the main gate must always be kept shut. But the
mischief would have been prevented anyway if you'd taken
proper precautions sooner.'

At this point the Countess, with Mozart's note open in her
hand and in a great state of joyful excitement, hurried in from
the adjoining room. 'Who do you think is in our garden?' she
cried. 'For God's sake, read this letter – it's Mozart from Vienna,
the composer! We must go down at once and invite him in – if

only he hasn't left already! What will he think of me! I hope you treated him politely, Velten? Whatever happened?'

'Happened?' retorted her husband, whose annoyance could not be immediately and completely assuaged even by the prospect of a visit from such a celebrity. 'Why, the crazy fellow has picked one of the nine oranges off that tree I was keeping for Eugenie! It's monstrous! This means that the whole point of our little pleasantry has been spoilt, and Max may as well scrap his poem straight away!'

'Oh, nonsense!' insisted his wife. 'The gap can be filled easily, just leave it to me. Go to him now, the two of you, release the dear man and make him welcome, as kindly and flatteringly as you can! He shall not travel any further today if we can possibly keep him here. If you don't find him still in the garden, look for him at the inn and bring him back with his wife. What a splendid present, what a wonderful surprise for Eugenie, on this day of all days! There couldn't have been a happier chance.'

'Certainly!' replied Max. 'That was my first thought too. Quick, Papa, come along!' And as they hurried out and down the steps, he added: 'You can set your mind at rest about the lines. The ninth Muse shall not be the loser; on the contrary, I shall turn this mishap to particular advantage.'

'Impossible!'

'Most certainly!'

'Well, if that is so – but I'll have to take your word for it – let us find this strange fellow and do him all the honour we can.'

While this was happening at the castle, our quasi-prisoner, not greatly concerned about the outcome of the incident, had sat on for some time writing busily. But since no one appeared, he began to pace uneasily to and fro; and now, too, an urgent message came for him from the inn to say that lunch was ready and waiting, that he must please come at once, that the postilion was anxious to continue the journey. And so he gathered his things together and was just about to leave without further ado, when the two gentlemen appeared outside the summerhouse.

The Count greeted him heartily in his loud booming voice, almost as if he were an old friend, cutting short all his attempts to offer an apology, and at once expressing his wish to have both Mozart and his wife spend at least this afternoon and this evening with him and his family. 'My dearest Maestro,' he declared, 'you are so far from being a stranger to us that I may say I know of no other place in which the name of Mozart is mentioned more often or with more fervent admiration than here. My niece sings and plays, she spends almost her entire day at the piano, knows your works by heart, and it has been her dearest wish that one day she might see you at closer quarters than was possible last winter at that concert of yours she went to. We are going to Vienna for a few weeks before long, and her relations have promised her an invitation to Prince Galitzin's[9] where you are often to be found. But now you are going to Prague, you'll be staying there for some time and God knows whether your return journey will bring you our way again. Give yourself a holiday today and tomorrow! We can send your carriage back at once, and if you will permit me I shall take care of the rest of your journey.'

The composer, well used to making much greater sacrifices to friendship or pleasure than the Count's invitation involved, very gladly accepted his hospitality for the rest of the day, on the understanding that he must resume his journey early the following morning. Count Max requested the pleasure of fetching Madame Mozart from the inn himself and of making all the necessary arrangements there. He set off on foot, giving instructions for a carriage to follow him immediately.

We should remark in passing that this young man combined the happy temperament he had inherited from his father and mother with a talent and enthusiasm for intellectual pursuits, and although military life was not really to his taste, he had also distinguished himself as an officer by his wide knowledge and good education. He was well read in French literature, and at a time when German poetry was not very highly regarded in fashionable circles, he had won praise and favour by writing in his native tongue, using the poetic forms with considerable facility and deriving them from good models such as Hagedorn, Götz[10] and others. Today, as we have already heard, he had been presented with a particularly agreeable opportunity to make use of his gift.

Madame Mozart, when he arrived, was sitting at the laid table chattering to the innkeeper's daughter, and had already helped herself in advance to a bowl of soup. She was too well accustomed to unusual incidents and bold impromptu behaviour by her husband to be unduly surprised by the young officer's arrival or the message he brought. With undisguised pleasure, and using all her good sense and competence, she at once discussed and took charge of the needful arrangements. The luggage was repacked, the bill paid, the postilion dismissed; and making herself ready without too much anxious attention to her toilet, she drove in high spirits with her escort to the castle, little suspecting how strange her husband's introduction to it had been.

He in the meantime was already very contentedly installed there and enjoying the best of entertainment. It was not long before he met Eugenie and her fiancé. She was a most graceful, sensitive girl in the flower of youth: blonde, slender, festively dressed in lustrous crimson silk trimmed with costly lace, and wearing round her brow a white fillet set with splendid pearls. The Baron, only a little older than his bride, was of a gentle and open disposition and seemed worthy of her in every way.

The first and almost too generous contributor to the conversation was the genial and temperamental master of the house himself, whose rather boisterous manner of speaking was plentifully larded with jests and anecdotes. Refreshments were served, and our traveller did them full justice.

Someone had opened the piano, the score of *The Marriage of Figaro* was lying there ready, and the young lady, accompanied by the Baron, was about to sing Susanna's aria[11] in the garden scene – that aria in which the very essence of sweet passion seems to pour into us with the fragrant air of the summer night. The delicate flush on Eugenie's cheeks gave way for a moment to extreme pallor; but with the first melodious note her lips uttered, all the bonds of diffidence dropped from her heart. She moved smilingly and effortlessly along the high wave of the music, inspired by this moment which was surely one that she would treasure as unique for the rest of her life.

Mozart was clearly taken by surprise. When she had finished

he approached her and spoke in his artlessly sincere manner: 'My dear child, what can I say? You are like the sun in the sky, which sings its own praises best by shining and warming us all! When one's soul hears singing like that, it feels like a baby in its bath: it laughs, it is amazed, it has not another wish in the world. And believe me: hearing one's own music rendered with such purity, such simplicity and warmth, indeed with such complete-ness – that's not a thing that happens to one every day in Vienna!' And so saying he took her hand and kissed it affection-ately. Eugenie was so overwhelmed by his great charm and kindness, to say nothing of the honour he did to her talent with such a compliment, that she came near to fainting, and her eyes filled suddenly with tears.

At this point Mozart's wife arrived, and soon after her came new and expected guests: a baronial family, neighbours and close relations, whose daughter Francesca had been Eugenie's bosom friend since childhood and knew the castle as her second home. Greetings, embraces and congratulations were ex-changed all round, the two visitors from Vienna were intro-duced, and Mozart sat down at the piano. He played part of one of his own concertos, one which Eugenie happened to be studying at the time.

The effect of such a recital in a small circle of this kind is naturally distinguished from any given in a public place by the infinite satisfaction of immediate personal contact with the artist and his genius in a familiar domestic setting. The concerto was one of those brilliant pieces in which pure beauty, as if by gratuitous choice, freely submits to the service of elegance, but in such a way as to seem merely disguised by the exuberant play of forms, merely hidden behind a myriad dazzling points of light: for in its every movement it discloses its own essential nobility and pours forth its own passionate splendour in rich profusion.

The Countess privately observed that most of the small audi-ence and perhaps even Eugenie herself, despite the rapt concen-tration and reverent silence with which they listened to so enchanting a performance, were nevertheless very much in two minds between listening and watching. With one's eyes involuntarily drawn to the composer, to his simple, almost rigid posture, his kindly face, the rounded movement of those small hands, it must have been scarcely possible to dispel from one's mind a whole complex of conflicting thoughts about this miraculous prodigy.

When the master had risen to his feet again, the Count turned to Madame Mozart and said: 'How lucky the kings and emperors are! It's no easy matter, you know, to meet a famous artist and praise him as a wit and a connoisseur should. But in a royal mouth, anything at all sounds pointed and remarkable. What liberties they can take! How easy it would be, for example, to come right up behind your good husband's chair, and at the final chord of some brilliant fantasy to give the modest classical master a clap on the shoulder and say "My dear Mozart, you are a hell of a fellow!" The word would no sooner be spoken than it would go round the room like wildfire: "What did he say to him?" "He said he was a hell of a fellow!" And all the fiddlers and pipers and music-makers would be beside themselves at this one phrase. In short, that's the grand style, the inimitable homely imperial style I've always envied in the Josephs and Fredericks of this world, and never more than at this moment. For may the devil take me if I can find in all my pockets even the smallest coin of any other compliment to pay him!'

The roguish manner of the Count's speech was well enough received, and the company could not help laughing. Now, however, at their hostess's invitation, they proceeded to the richly decorated circular dining-room, where a festive scent of flowers greeted them and a cooler air sharpened their appetite as they entered.

Places at table were suitably allocated and the company sat down, the guest of honour finding himself opposite the bridal pair. As neighbours he had on one side an elderly little lady, an unmarried aunt of Francesca, and on the other the charming young Francesca herself, who quickly captivated him by her intelligence and gaiety. Madame Constanze sat between their host and her obliging escort the Lieutenant, and the rest disposed themselves appropriately, making a party of eleven, with the

sexes alternating as nearly as possible, and the lower end of the
table left empty. In the middle were two enormous porcelain
centrepieces with painted figures holding up large bowls heaped
with natural fruit and flowers. Magnificent festoons hung on
the walls. The remaining provisions already served or following
in due course were appropriate to a prolonged banquet. Noble
wines stood ready between the dishes and plates or gleamed
from the sideboard, a whole variety ranging from the deepest
red to the pale gold with its merry foam that is traditionally
kept back to crown the latter half of a feast.

Until about this time the conversation, in which a number a
lively participants joined, had been flowing in all directions.
From the outset, however, the Count had several times alluded,
at first obliquely but then ever more directly and boldly, to
Mozart's adventure in the garden; and since some of those
present reacted to this only with a discreet smile, while others
were vainly racking their brains to guess what he might be
talking about, our friend felt it was incumbent upon him to
address the company.

'Since I needs must,' he began, 'I will confess how it was that
I had the honour of becoming acquainted with this noble house.
It is a story that does me little credit, and but for the grace of
God I should now be sitting, not at this very happy table, but
on an empty stomach in some remote dungeon of his lordship's
castle, counting the cobwebs on the walls.'

'Goodness me!' exclaimed Constanze, 'now I shall hear some
fine story!'

Whereupon Mozart described in detail first how he had left
his wife behind in the White Horse, his walk in the park, then
the calamity in the arbour, his confrontation with the garden
constabulary, in short the facts more or less as we already know
them, narrating them all with the greatest candour and to the
extreme delight of his audience. Their hilarity was almost
unstoppable, and even the quiet Eugenie could not refrain, but
simply shook with laughter.

'Well,' he continued, 'as they say, bad luck like this never
comes amiss! The affair has stood me in good stead, as you shall
see. But first of all let me tell you how it came about that a silly

fellow like me could so forget himself. It came about partly because of a memory from my childhood.

'In the spring of 1770, as a little boy of thirteen, I travelled to Italy with my father. From Rome we went to Naples. I had played twice at the Conservatoire there and at several other places as well. The nobility and clergy showed us great kindness; in particular a certain Abbé attached himself to us, who took pride in being something of a connoisseur and was also well connected at Court. The day before we left, he took us with some other gentlemen to a royal garden, the Villa Reale, which runs along the fine boulevard by the seashore. A troupe of Sicilian actors was performing – *figli di Nettuno* they called themselves, as well as various other fancy names. There we were, with many distinguished onlookers, among them the charming young Queen Carolina herself with two princesses. We were sitting on a long row of benches, shaded by the tent-like canopy of a low loggia with the waves lapping against the terrace below it. The sea was ribboned with many different colours, reflecting the splendid blue sky. Straight ahead was Vesuvius, with the gentle curve of the lovely shimmering coastline to our left.

'The first part of the performance was over; it was given on the dry wooden boards of a kind of raft moored offshore, and there was nothing specially remarkable about it. But the second and most beautiful part consisted entirely of boating and swimming and diving displays, and it has remained in my memory ever since, fresh in every detail.

'Two vessels, elegant and very lightly built, were approaching each other from opposite directions, each of them seemingly on a pleasure trip. One of them was slightly larger, it had a half deck and rowing benches, but also a slender mast and a sail; it was splendidly painted, with a gilded prow. On board, five conventionally handsome and scantily clad youths, their arms, legs and chests apparently naked, were either rowing or disporting themselves with an equal number of attractive girls who were their sweethearts. One of these, sitting in the middle of the deck weaving garlands of flowers, was taller and more beautiful as well as more richly adorned than the rest of them. The latter were willingly serving her, spreading an awning to shelter her from the sun and handing her flowers from the basket. Another girl sat at her feet playing a flute, accompanying the singing of the others with its bright tones. This exceptional beauty also had her own particular protector; but the two of them behaved to each other with a certain indifference, and her lover almost seemed to me to be treating her rather roughly.

'In the meantime the other, plainer vessel had drawn nearer. The young people in it were all male. The colour worn by the boys in the first ship was scarlet, and these were in sea-green. Their attention was caught by the sight of the pretty girls; they waved greetings to them and signalled that they desired their closer acquaintance. The liveliest of the girls now took a rose from her breast and held it up coquettishly, as if asking whether such gifts would be acceptable, to which the others replied with unambiguous gestures. The red youths looked on scornfully and angrily, but there was nothing they could do when some of the girls decided at least to throw the poor devils something to satisfy their hunger and thirst. There was a basket of oranges standing on the deck; probably they were only yellow balls made to look like the fruit. And now an enchanting spectacle started, accompanied by music from the players on the quayside.

'One of the maidens began by lightly tossing a few oranges across, which were caught with equal dexterity and at once thrown back; and thus it continued to and fro, with gradually more and more of the girls taking part, until oranges by the dozen were flying hither and thither at ever-increasing speed. The beautiful girl in the middle took neither side in this contest, merely watching eagerly from her seat. We were lost in admiration for the skill shown by both parties. The two boats circled each other slowly, about thirty paces apart, sometimes lying broadside on, sometimes aslant with bows converging. About twenty-four balls were constantly in the air, but in the confusion there seemed to be many more of them. At times a regular crossfire developed, and often they rose and fell in a high curving trajectory. Only a very few missed their mark, for as if by some power of attraction they fell of their own accord straight into the grasping fingers.

'But delightful though all this was as a spectacle for the

eye, our hearing was equally charmed by the accompanying melodies: Sicilian airs, dances, *saltarelli*, *canzoni a ballo*, a whole medley of pieces lightly interwoven with each other like garlands. The younger princess, a sweet innocent creature of about my age, was nodding her head very nicely in time to the music; to this day I can still see her smile and her long eyelashes.

'Now let me briefly tell you how this comedy continued, although it is not relevant to my theme! It really was the prettiest thing you could imagine. While the skirmishing was gradually coming to an end and only a few more missiles were being exchanged, as the girls collected their golden apples and returned them to the basket, a boy in the other boat, as if in play, had seized a large net of green cords and held it for a short time under water; then he lifted it out, and to everyone's astonishment it had caught a great fish of shimmering colours, blue and green and gold. The others eagerly leapt up to him to pull the fish out, but it slipped out of their hands as if it were really alive, and dropped back into the sea. Now this was an agreed stratagem to fool the red youths and entice them out of their ship. They, as if bewitched by this miracle, had no sooner noticed that the animal did not attempt to dive but continued to play on the surface, than without a moment's hesitation they all hurled themselves into the sea; the green youths did the same, and thus we saw twelve fine-looking expert swimmers, all intent on catching the fleeing fish, which danced about on the waves, disappeared beneath them for minutes on end, and then surfaced again, now here and now there, now between the legs of one of the youths and now between the breast and chin of another. Suddenly, just as the red swimmers were most passionately absorbed in their chase, the other party spied its advantage, and quick as lightning climbed aboard their opponents' vessel, on which the only persons left were the girls, who now set up a great shrieking. The noblest-looking of the boys, who was like the god Mercury in stature, sped straight up to the chief beauty and embraced and kissed her, his face aglow with joy; and she, far from joining in the cries of the others, likewise passionately flung her arms round the neck of this youth, whom she evidently knew well. The other group, thus outwitted, at once came swimming alongside, but were driven off with oars and weapons. Their futile rage, the maidens' startled shrieks, the strenuous resistance of some of them, their pleas and entreaties – all this noise, almost drowned by that of the waves and the music, which had suddenly changed its character – it was all beautiful beyond description, and the audience burst into a storm of enthusiastic applause.

'Now at this moment the sail, hitherto loosely furled, opened out and released from its midst a rosy-cheeked boy with silver wings, with a bow and arrows and quiver, who hovered freely above the mast in a graceful posture. Already all the oars were being plied and the sail was swelling, but the presence of the god and his energetic forward gesture seemed to drive the vessel on more powerfully than either, so much so that the swimmers, in almost breathless pursuit, and with one of them holding the golden fish with his left hand high above his head, soon gave up in exhaustion and were forced to take refuge on the abandoned ship. In the meantime their green opponents had reached a little wooded peninsula, from behind which a handsome vessel full of armed comrades suddenly appeared. With such a threat confronting them, the first group ran up a white flag to signal that they were prepared to negotiate amicably. Encouraged by a similar signal from the other side, they put in at the same landing-place, and soon we saw the good-natured girls, all except the leading one who voluntarily stayed behind, happily going aboard their own ship with their lovers. And that was the end of this comedy.'

There was a short pause in which everyone greeted the narrative with acclamation, and Eugenie, her eyes shining with excitement, whispered to the Baron: 'Surely what we have just been given is a whole symphony in colour from beginning to end, as well as a perfect allegory of the Mozartian genius itself in all its joy and serenity! Am I not right? Does it not embody all the grace of *Figaro*?'

Her fiancé was just about to repeat her remark to the composer when the latter began speaking again.

'It's seventeen years now since I saw Italy. What man who has seen it, and seen Naples above all, does not remember it for the rest of his life, even if, like myself, he was still half a child at the time! But scarcely ever have I experienced so vivid a recollection of that beautiful evening by the Gulf as today, in your garden. Every time I closed my eyes, there it was – quite plain and clear and bright, its last veil lifting and drifting away, that heavenly panorama spread out before me! The sea and the sea-shore, the mountain and the city, the motley crowd of people on the embankment, and then that wonderful complicated game with the balls! My ears seemed to hear that same music again, a whole rosary of happy melodies, some my own and some by others, all and sundry, all following on from each other! Suddenly a little dancing song jumped out, a motif in six-eight time, quite new to me. "Hang on!" I thought, "what's this? Now that's a devilish neat little thing!" I took a closer look, and – good God above, it's Masetto and it's Zerlina!' And he looked laughingly across at Madame Mozart, who at once understood him.

'The fact is simply this,' he continued. 'In the first act of my opera there's an easy little number which I hadn't yet written: a duet and chorus for a country wedding. Two months ago, you see, when it was the turn of this piece to be composed, I couldn't get it right first time round. A simple, childlike melody, bubbling over with happiness, like a fresh posy of flowers and a fluttering ribbon fastened to the girl's dress: that was what I needed. But because one must never try to force anything, and because trifles of this kind often simply write themselves, I just passed it by, and scarcely gave it another thought as I carried on with the main work. Quite fleetingly, as I sat in the carriage today, just before we drove into the village, I remembered the text of that song; but no musical idea developed from it, at least not so far as I know. In fact, only an hour later, in that arbour by the fountain, I picked up a happier and better tune than I could ever have invented at any other time and in any other way. In art one sometimes has strange experiences, but I had never known a trick like that before. For lo and behold, a melody, fitting the line of words like a glove – but let me not anticipate, we're not quite there yet. The little bird had only just stuck its head out of the egg, and at once I began to scoop it out clean and complete.

As I did so, I clearly saw Zerlina dancing there before my eyes, and in a strange way that laughing landscape of the Gulf of Naples was there as well. I could hear the voices of the bride and the groom turn about, and the lasses and lads singing in chorus.'

And at this point Mozart began merrily trilling the opening lines of the song:

> 'Giovinette, che fate all' amore, che fate all' amore,
> Non lasciate che passi l'età, che passi l'età, che passi l'età!
> Se nel seno vi bulica il core, vi bulica il core,
> Il remedio vedetelo quà! La la la! La la la!
> Che piacer, che piacer che sarà!
>   Ah la la! Ah la la!' etc.[12]

'Meanwhile, my hands had done the great mischief. Nemesis was already lying in wait for me just round the hedge, and now it stepped forth in the guise of that terrible man in braided blue livery. An eruption of Vesuvius, if it had really occurred on that divine evening by the sea, and had suddenly smothered and buried the spectators and actors and the whole Parthenopean[13] splendour in a black rain of ashes: by God, it would not have been a more unexpected and dreadful catastrophe than this. Devil take him! I can't recall when any man has ever put me in such a pother. A face that might have been cast in bronze – rather like the cruel Roman emperor Tiberius! If that's what the servant's like, I thought after he had left, how am I to look his lordship himself in the eye! And yet, to tell the truth, I was even now rather relying on the protection of the ladies, and not without some reason. For my little wife Connie here, who's a trifle nosy by nature, had already in my presence made the fat woman at the inn tell us most of what we needed to know about this noble family and all its members; I was standing there and heard –'

Here Madame Mozart could not refrain from interrupting, and assured the company most emphatically that on the contrary, it was he who had asked all the questions: this gave rise to a good-natured disputation between husband and wife, which caused much amusement. 'Be that as it may,' he declared, 'the fact is that I heard some story somehow about a dear adopted daughter who was engaged to be married, and not only beautiful but kindness itself, and with a voice like an angel. And the thought came to me now: *Per Dio*! that will help me out of my pickle! I'll sit down straight away and write that little song as far as it goes, then I'll give a truthful account of my foolish prank, and the whole thing will be a great joke. No sooner said than done! I had time enough, and even a clean sheet of green-lined paper on me. And here is the result! I lay it in this lady's fair hands – an impromptu bridal song, if you will allow it to count as such.'

So saying, he handed his meticulously written manuscript across the table to Eugenie, but her uncle's hand anticipated hers: he snatched it up, exclaiming: 'Have patience just a moment, my dear!'

At a sign from him the double doors of the dining-room opened wide, and a procession of servants appeared, quietly and ceremoniously carrying in the fateful orange-tree and setting it down on a bench at the end of the table; at the same time two slender myrtles were placed to the left and right of it. An inscription fastened to the trunk of the orange-tree declared it to be the property of the bride; but in front of it, on the surrounding moss, stood a porcelain plate covered with a napkin. When this was removed, an orange cut into two halves was revealed, and beside it on the plate, with a meaningful look, Eugenie's uncle laid the master's autograph. All this was greeted by the company with prolonged and tumultuous applause.

'I really think,' said the Countess, 'that Eugenie still does not even know what is standing there before her. I'll wager she doesn't recognize her beloved old tree in its new glory and all covered with fruit!'

Startled and unable to believe her eyes, the young lady looked from the tree to her uncle and back again. 'It's not possible!' she said. 'I know it was so far gone that it couldn't be saved.'

'So you think, do you,' he replied, 'that we just picked up some kind of substitute to present to you? That would have been a fine compliment! No, just take a look at this – now I have to do what they do in comedies, when long-lost sons or brothers have to prove their identity by birthmarks and scars. Look at this lump! and this crack where the branches divide – you must have noticed it a hundred times. Well now: is it, or isn't it?' And she could doubt it no longer; her amazement, her emotion and her joy were indescribable.

For the family, this tree was associated with a memory that went back more than a hundred years, the memory of a great lady, who well deserves that we should give a brief account of her here.

The grandfather of Eugenie's uncle, whose diplomatic accomplishments had won him honour in the Imperial ministry and who had enjoyed the equal trust of two successive rulers, was no less fortunate in his domestic affairs as the husband of an excellent wife, Renate Leonore. Her repeated visits to France brought her into frequent contact with the brilliant court of Louis XIV and with the leading men and women of that remarkable period. And although she shared the spontaneous *joie de vivre* of that society, its constant flow of highly cultivated pleasures, she nevertheless always retained in word and deed her innate German firmness of character and moral seriousness – qualities that were unmistakably impressed on the strong features of the portrait of this Countess still hanging on the wall. It was this very disposition that enabled her to play in court circles a distinctive role of naive opposition, and in the letters she left behind her there are many instances of her candour and ready wit, displayed equally in matters of religion, literature, politics or anything else. With great originality she would defend her sound principles and views, or criticize the weaknesses of society without giving the least offence. Accordingly her lively interest in such guests as might be met, for instance, at Ninon de Lenclos's house,[14] that true centre of refined intellectual culture, was of such a character as to be wholly compatible with the exalted friendship that bound her to one of the noblest women of the age, the Marquise de Sévigné.[15] In addition to many whimsical pleasantries addressed to her by the poet Chapelle[16] and scribbled in his own hand on sheets of paper with a silver floral border, the deeply affectionate letters of the Marquise and her daughter to their good Austrian friend were discovered in an ebony casket by the Count after his grand-mother's death.

And it was also from the hands of Madame de Sévigné that one day, on a terrace in the garden during a fête at the Trianon, she had received the flowering orange branch, which she at once casually planted in a pot: here it happily struck root, and she took it back with her to Germany.

Gradually, for some twenty-five years, the little tree grew before her eyes, and later her children and grandchildren tended it with the utmost care. In addition to its personal value, it could stand for them as a living symbol of the subtle intellectual charm of an almost idealized bygone age: an age, to be sure, in which we can today find little that is truly admirable, and which was already pregnant with a disastrous future, a world-shaking calamity already not too far removed in time from the events of this innocent tale.

It was Eugenie who most devotedly loved this heirloom from her excellent ancestress, and that was why her uncle often remarked that one day it would become her special property. It had therefore been a great sorrow for the young lady when, during her absence in the previous spring, the tree had begun to wilt, its leaves to turn yellow and many of its branches to wither. Since there was absolutely no discernible cause for its deterioration, and no remedy seemed to be effective, the gardener soon gave up hope of its recovery, although in the ordinary course of nature it should easily have lived to twice or three times its age. But the Count, advised by an expert in the neigh-bourhood, had it secretly treated in a separate enclosure, apply-ing a strange and indeed mysterious recipe of a kind often known to country people; and his hope of one day being able to surprise his beloved niece by giving her back her old friend with its vigour and fertility restored was fulfilled beyond all expectation. Overcoming his own impatience and his anxious concern that the oranges, some of which had by now reached full maturity, might drop off their branches too soon, he had postponed this pleasure for several weeks until the day of the present feast; and we need hardly describe what the good gentle-man must have felt on finding that at the very last moment he was to be deprived of this happiness after all by the action of a stranger.

The Lieutenant had found time and opportunity, before sitting down at table, to revise his in any case perhaps rather too solemn poetic contribution to the presentation ceremony and, by altering his closing lines, to fit them reasonably well to the new circumstances. He now drew out his manuscript, rose from his chair, turned to his cousin, and recited his poem, the contents of which may be briefly summarized as follows:

Long ago, on an island in the far west, the famous Tree of the Hesperides had sprung up in the garden of Juno as the Earth Mother's wedding gift to the goddess, and was watched over by the three melodious nymphs. This tree had a descendant who had always desired and hoped to share the same destiny and be presented to a beautiful bride, for recently the gods had also introduced this custom among mortals. After long waiting in vain, it seemed that a maiden had been found to whom the young tree might turn his affection. She showed him favour and spent much time with him. But beside the fountain he had a proud neighbour, the laurel, the tree of the Muses, who aroused his jealousy; for it seemed to be stealing away the heart and mind of the young maiden, gifted as she was in many arts, and turning her away from the love of men. The myrtle tried in vain to console the lover, to teach him patience by her own example; in the end, the long absence of his beloved increased his grief and after he had pined for a time it proved fatal.

In summer the absent beloved returned, and her heart had happily changed. The village, the castle, the garden, all greeted her with the greatest joy. Roses and lilies, their colours glowing more brightly than ever, gazed up at her in rapture and modest humility, and all the bushes and trees waved her a welcome: but for one of them, alas, the noblest of them all, she had come too late. She found its crown withered, her fingers caressed its lifeless trunk and its dry rustling twigs. The tree no longer saw or recognized its protectress. How she wept, how tender a lament streamed from her lips and eyes!

From far off, Apollo hears his daughter's voice. He comes, he approaches her, and looks with pity on her sorrow. At once he touches the tree with his all-healing hands: it trembles inwardly, the dry sap in its bark flows with new strength, already it puts forth young leaves and white blossoms cover it in ambrosial abundance. Yes – for what limits are there to the power of the gods? – beautiful round fruit appears, three times three oranges, the number of the nine Muses, the sisters of the god; they grow and grow, their childlike green turning to an ever deeper gold. Phoebus[17] – for so the poem ended –

> Phoebus counts the fruit, he waters
> At the mouth, and gazes long
> At the precious tree, his daughter's
> Bridal gift. The god of song
>
> Plucks an orange nectar-filled,
> And divides it then and there:
> 'Here's a treat, my lovely child,
> You and I and Love shall share!'

The poet's audience rewarded him with a burst of rapturous applause, willingly overlooking his baroque conclusion which so completely nullified the heartfelt character of the piece as a whole.

Francesca, whose high-spirited native wit had already been stimulated more than once by conversational exchanges with her host or with Mozart, now seemed to recall by chance something she had forgotten, and hastened from the room: she returned with a large brown English engraving, glazed and framed, which had long hung unnoticed in a remote little study.

'So,' she exclaimed, setting up the picture at the end of the table, 'what I've always been told must be true after all: that there's nothing new under the sun! Here is a scene from the Golden Age, and haven't we just relived it today? I certainly hope Apollo will recognize himself in this situation.'

'Splendid!' cried Max triumphantly. 'Why, there he is, the beautiful god, in the very act of stooping pensively over the sacred waters. And not only that – look, don't you see, an old satyr hiding back there in the bushes, spying on him! Upon my word, I believe Apollo's just remembered a long forgotten little Arcadian dance, which Chiron[18] taught him to play on the zither when he was a child.'

'And so it is! What else can it be!' replied Francesca, applauding. She was standing behind Mozart, and turning to him she continued: 'Don't you also notice this branch loaded with fruit, hanging down to just within the god's reach?'

'Of course; it's the olive-tree sacred to him.'

'Not at all! Those are the finest oranges! He's just about to pick one in a fit of distraction!'

'On the contrary!' exclaimed Mozart, 'he's just about to stop this mischievous mouth with a thousand kisses!' So saying, he caught her by the arm and vowed he would not let her go again until she offered him her lips, which indeed she then did with little demur.

'Please tell us, Max,' said the Countess, 'what is written here under the picture.'

'It's some lines from a famous ode by Horace. The Berlin poet Ramler has just translated it wonderfully for us. It's quite inspired. How magnificent this one passage is:

> . . . he who on his shoulder
>   Carries a bow that is never idle;
>
> The Delos-born, who dwells in his Lycian woods
> And native grove, and on Pataranian shores;
>   He who plunges his locks of gold deep
>   Into Castalian streams, Apollo.'[19]

'Beautiful! Quite beautiful!' said the Count. Just one or two points that need explaining. For instance, ". . . carries a bow that is never idle". I suppose that must simply mean: who has always been a very hard-working fiddler. But by the way, my dear Mozart: you are sowing discord between two tender hearts.'

'I hope not – how so?'

'Eugenie is envious of her friend, and well she may be.'

'Aha! You have noticed my weakness already. But what does the bridegroom say?'

'I will turn a blind eye once or twice.'

'Very well; we shall use our opportunity. But don't be alarmed, Baron; there's no danger, unless this god will lend me his features and his long yellow hair. I wish he would! In exchange he could have Mozart's pigtail and its most handsome ribbon.'

'But Apollo,' laughed Francesca, 'would then have to work out a seemly way of plunging his new French hairstyle into the Castalian stream.'

Amid these and similar pleasantries the general merriment and high spirits continued to increase. The men, as the wine flowed, warmed to the occasion; a number of healths were drunk, and Mozart, as was his habit, began speaking in verse. In this he was backed up by the Lieutenant, and the Count tried his hand as well, occasionally with remarkable success. But such trifles are lost in the retelling, and scarcely bear repetition: for the very thing that made them irresistible at the time and place, the general festive mood, the brilliance and joviality of personal expression in words and looks, is missing.

Among others, a toast in the master's honour was proposed by the old lady, Francesca's aunt, promising him a further long series of immortal works. '*A la bonne heure*, and amen to that!' exclaimed Mozart, heartily clinking glasses with her. Whereupon the Count, with a powerful voice and accurate intonation, began an impromptu song of his own devising:

> May the gods inspire his heart
> To delightful works of art –

> *Max* (continuing):

> Of which Da Ponte and the clever
> Schikaneder[20] know nothing whatever –

> *Mozart:*

> Nor, God bless him, does the composer:
> He should know, and he's no wiser!

The Count:

As for that Italian fop
Signor Bonbonnière,[21] the wop,
The arch-crook, let's wish he may
Live on to hear them all one day!

Max:

May he live a hundred years, say I –

Mozart:

Or may the devil by that time fly –

All three (con forza):

Off with him and his works to we-know-
          where,
Our sweet-toothed Monsieur Bonbonnière!

The Count had by now got so much into the way of singing that this improvised trio soon developed from a repetition of its last four lines into a so-called finite canon, and Francesca's aunt had humour or self-assurance enough to join in with her frail soprano voice, adding a variety of suitable embellishments. Mozart promised afterwards that as soon as he had time he would elaborate this little jest into a musically correct composition, dedicated expressly to the present company; and this indeed he did later on after his return to Vienna.

Eugenie in the meantime had long been carefully studying her precious keepsake from the grove of the fierce Tiberius; the company now with one accord demanded to hear the duet sung by the composer and herself, and her uncle was happy at the chance to show off his voice again in the chorus. And so everyone rose from table and hastened into the big drawing-room next door where the piano stood.

Enchanted though everyone was by this exquisite piece, its very theme led them all, by an easy transition, to a high point of merrymaking at which the music as such was no longer of primary importance; and it was our friend himself who first gave the signal for this by jumping up from the piano, approaching Francesca, and as Max willingly reached for his violin, persuading her to dance a slow waltz with him. Their host was quick to extend a similar invitation to Mozart's wife. In a trice the servants, to make more room, had busily shifted all the movable furniture out of the way. By the end of it everyone had had to take their turn, and the old lady was by no means displeased when the gallant Lieutenant led her out to a minuet, indeed it had the effect of entirely rejuvenating her. Finally, as Mozart was dancing the last round with the bride-to-be, he was able to claim in full his promised right to her rosy lips.

Evening had fallen, the sun was about to set, and at last it was pleasant out of doors; the Countess therefore proposed to the ladies that they might like to take the air in the garden. The Count on the other hand invited the gentlemen to the billiard room, for it was well known that Mozart was very fond of the game. The company thus divided into two groups, and we for our part will follow the ladies.

After strolling up and down the main avenue once or twice they climbed a small rounded hill, half surrounded by a high vine-covered trellis, which offered a view of the open country, the village and the highroad. The last rays of the autumn sunlight were glowing red through the vines.

'Would this not be a quiet and pleasant place to sit,' said the Countess, 'if Madame Mozart were willing to tell us something about herself and her husband?'

Constanze was quite willing to do so, and they all sat down very comfortably on chairs which had been drawn up and placed in a circle.

'I will gladly oblige,' she said, 'with something you would have had to hear in any case, as I am planning a little jest in connection with it. I have taken it into my head to make the young Countess, as a happy memento of her betrothal day, a rather special kind of present, which is so far from being an object of luxury or fashion that only a knowledge of its history can make it halfway interesting.'

'Whatever can it be, Eugenie?' said Francesca. 'I think it must be a certain famous man's inkpot, at least.'

'Not a bad guess! You will see the treasure very shortly, it's packed in our trunk. Now I'll tell you my story, which with your permission shall go back a little way.

'The winter before last I was getting more and more worried about Mozart's state of health: he was feverish, and increasingly irritable and frequently depressed. His spirits rose sometimes when he was in company, often higher than was really natural, but at home would mostly be turned in on himself, brooding and sighing and complaining. The doctor recommended a diet and Pyrmont water and country walks. The patient paid little attention to this good advice; such a cure was inconvenient and time-consuming and ran clean contrary to his daily routine. So then the doctor put the fear of God into him, gave him a long lecture on the properties and circulation of human blood and the little round things in it, and on breathing and phlogiston – a whole lot of things you never heard of; and on what nature's intentions really are when we eat and drink and digest, which Mozart had been as innocent about until now as his little five-year-old son. And indeed, this lesson made a certain impression on him. The doctor had scarcely been gone half an hour when I found my husband in his room looking pensively but happily at a walking-stick, which he'd searched for in a cupboard among other old things and luckily found; I'd never have thought he'd even have remembered it. It had belonged once to my father – a fine cane with a big knob made of lapis lazuli. No one had ever seen Mozart with a walking-stick, and I couldn't help laughing.

' "You see," he cried, "I'm just about to throw myself whole-heartedly into my cure. I shall drink that water, take some open-air exercise every day, and use this stick to do so. And I've had a few ideas in this connection. It's not for nothing, I thought, that other people, respectable mature men, can't do without a walking-stick. Our neighbour the Commercial Councillor never crosses the street to visit his old crony without taking his stick with him. Professional men and officials, lawyers, merchants and their clients – when they take a walk out of town with their families on a Sunday, every one of them's accompanied by his well-used, honest cane. In particular I've often noticed those worthy citizens standing around in groups in front of St Stephen's Cathedral, having a bit of a gossip just before the sermon and the Mass begin: you can see it very well there, you can see every one of their quiet virtues, their industry and orderliness and equable temper and contentment, leaning, half sitting, well propped up as it were on their trusty sticks. In short, there must be something of a blessing and a special consolation in this age-old habit, rather tasteless though I must say it is. Believe it or not, I can hardly wait for my first constitutional outing with this good companion, my first walk over the bridge to the Rennweg! We've made each other's acquaintance now, and I hope we shall be partners for life."

'That partnership didn't last long. From their third outing together he returned without his good companion. Another was purchased, which kept faith for a little while longer, and it was certainly to this fancy for walking-sticks that I gave much of the credit for the fact that for three weeks Mozart persevered tolerably well in following his doctor's advice. And the consequent improvements were soon to be seen: we'd almost never known him so fresh, so cheerful and in such an equable temper. But alas, before long he went back to his old excesses, and I was in constant trouble with him about this. And then it happened that one evening, exhausted by the work of a busy day and when it was already late, he went out to a musical soirée to please a few inquisitive visitors – only for an hour, he vowed and swore to me. But it's on those very occasions, once he's settled at the piano and in the mood, that people most misuse his good nature; for there he sits, like the little man in a Montgolfier, hovering six miles above the earth where he can no longer hear bells chime. I sent our servant twice to him in the middle of the night, but it was no use, he couldn't get to his master. So at last my husband came home at three in the morning. I made up my mind that I would be seriously cross with him for the rest of the day.'

Madame Mozart here passed over certain details in silence. The fact is that another of the guests at that soirée would in all likelihood have been a young singer, a certain Signora Malerbi, to whom Constanze had good reason to object. This lady from Rome had been appointed at the Opera thanks to Mozart's intervention, and there was no doubt that it was largely by her coquettish wiles that she had won the master's favour. Some even said that she had had him seriously in tow for several months and led him a terrible dance. Whether this was entirely true or much exaggerated, it is certain that she later behaved with great insolence and ingratitude and would even make mocking remarks about her benefactor. It was entirely typical of her that she once described him outright to one of her more fortunate admirers as *un piccolo grifo raso*, a shaven little pig-snout. This witticism, worthy of the arts of Circe, was all the more wounding for containing, it must be admitted, a modicum of truth.[22]

On his way home from that same soirée, at which as it happened the singer had in any case failed to appear, one of his friends, in a convivial moment, indiscreetly let fall to the master her malicious remark. Mozart did not take this in good part, for it was in fact the first clear proof he had had of the complete heartlessness of his protégée. In sheer indignation he did not at first even notice the chilly reception he was given at his wife's bedside. Without pausing to think, he poured out his story of the insult, and from this candour it may no doubt be concluded that there was no great guilt on his conscience. She even felt rather sorry for him. But she had made up her mind, he was not to get away with it so easily. When he woke from a heavy sleep just after midday, he found that neither his little wife nor the two boys were at home, but that the table had been neatly laid for him with a solitary lunch.

Few things ever made Mozart so unhappy as when all was not going smoothly and well between him and his better half. And if only he had known what further burden of anxiety she had carried about with her for the last few days! It was indeed serious trouble, and as always she had been sparing him the knowledge of it for as long as possible. Their ready cash was all spent, and there was no immediate prospect of any further income. Although he was unaware of this domestic crisis, his heart was nevertheless despondent in a way that seemed in keeping with her state of constriction and helplessness. He had no appetite and no wish to stay indoors. He at once got fully dressed, if only to escape from the stifling atmosphere of the house. He left an open note for her with a few lines written in Italian: 'You have roundly rebuked me and it serves me right. But please, I beg you, forgive me, and be laughing again when I get back. I've a good mind to become a Carthusian and a Trappist; I promise you, I could cry my eyes out.' And off he went, taking his hat but leaving his stick behind; it had served its turn.

Having taken over our narrative from Constanze up to this point, let us continue it in the same fashion a little further.

Leaving his lodging by the market and turning right towards the Civic Arsenal, our good friend sauntered – it was a warm, rather overcast summer afternoon – in a pensive and leisurely manner across the so-called Hof or Court Square and then past the parish church of Our Lady in the direction of the Schottentor; here he walked up the Moelkerbastei on his left on to the fortifications and thereby avoided meeting several acquaintances who were just entering the city. Although unmolested by a sentry who paced silently to and fro between the cannon, he paused here only briefly to enjoy the fine view across the green expanse of the glacis, beyond the suburbs to the Kahlenberg and southwards towards the Styrian Alps. The tranquil beauty of the natural scene was out of keeping with his inner state. With a sigh he continued his walk, along the esplanade and then through the Alser district, without any particular destination in mind.

At the end of the Währinger Gasse there was an inn with a skittle-alley; its landlord, a ropemaker, was well known to passing neighbours and countrymen for the fine quality both of his wares and of his wine. The sound of bowling could be heard, but with a dozen guests at most little else was going on. A scarcely conscious impulse to forget himself for a while among simple and natural people moved the composer to join this company. At one of the tables, which were partly shaded by trees, he sat down beside an inspector of wells from Vienna and two other worthy citizens, ordered a glass and joined with a will in their very commonplace conversation, from time to time rising to walk about or watch the game in the skittle-alley.

Close to the latter, at one side of the house, was the rope-maker's open shop, a small room stuffed full of his wares, for in addition to the immediate products of his own craft there were a number of other things standing around or hanging up for sale: all kinds of wooden utensils for the kitchen or the cellar, farm implements, blubber and axle grease, and an assortment of seeds such as dill and caraway. A young girl, whose business it was to serve the guests as a waitress and also to look after the shop, was just dealing with a peasant who, holding his little son by the hand, had come in to buy a few things: a fruit measure, a brush, a whip. He would select one among many similar articles, examine it, put it down, pick up a second and a third and then revert irresolutely to the first, evidently unable to make up his mind. The girl left him several times to wait on customers, then came back, tirelessly attempting to ease his choice and make it acceptable to him, though without too much persuasive talk.

Mozart, sitting on a bench by the skittle-alley, watched and listened to all this with the greatest pleasure. And much as he appreciated the kind and sensible behaviour of the girl and the calm seriousness in her attractive features, it was the peasant who chiefly aroused his interest, and who now, after he had gone away finally satisfied, continued to give him food for thought. He had found himself fully identifying with the man, feeling how seriously he had taken his small piece of business, how anxiously and conscientiously he had considered and reconsidered the prices, although they differed by only a few pence. He thought of the man coming home to his wife, telling her what a good bargain he has made, and the children all watching for his knapsack to be opened in case there was something for them in it too; and his wife hurrying to serve him the light meal and the cool glass of home-brewed apple cider he has saved up all his appetite for till now!

If only one could be so happy, he reflected, so independent of other people, so entirely relying on Nature and her bounty, however hard one might have to work for it! And yet even if my art does impose a different task on me, one after all that I would not exchange for any other in the world: even so, why does this

mean that I must live in circumstances that are the very opposite
of such an innocent, simple existence? If only I had a small
property, a little house at the edge of a village in lovely country-
side, what a new lease of life that would be! Busy all morning
with my scores, and the rest of the time with my family; planting
trees, inspecting my fields, going out with the boys in autumn
to shake down the apples and pears; sometimes a trip into town
for a performance or whatever it might be, from time to time
inviting a friend or two home – how wonderful! Ah well, who
knows what may yet happen.

He went up to the shop, spoke kindly to the girl, and began
to take a closer look at her wares. Many of them were directly
associated with his idyllic daydream, and this gave the clean,
pale, polished look and even the smell of the various wooden
implements a particular appeal. It suddenly occurred to him to
buy a number of the things for his wife, choosing what he
thought she would like and find useful. The garden tools were
the first to catch his eye. About a year ago Constanze had in
fact, at his suggestion, rented a small allotment outside the
Kärntner Tor and was growing some vegetables on it; accord-
ingly he now judged that a large new rake, together with a
smaller one and a spade, would meet the case. As he then
considered further possibilities, it does great credit to his sense
of thrift that after that brief reflection, though unwillingly, he
resolved not to buy a butter-keg which greatly caught his fancy;
though he did decide in favour of a tall wooden vessel designed
for some uncertain purpose, with a lid and an attractive handle.
It was made from narrow staves of two kinds of wood, alter-
nately light and dark, tapering towards the top and well coated
with pitch on the inside. As indispensable kitchen equipment he
chose a fine selection of wooden spoons, rolling-pins, chopping-
boards, and plates in all sizes, as well as a very simply con-
structed salt container which could be hung on the wall.

Finally he looked long and hard at a stout stick and its
leather-covered handle properly studded with round brass nails.
Noticing that this too seemed to tempt her eccentric customer,
the young saleswoman remarked with a smile that it was not
really quite suitable for a gentleman.

'You are quite right, my dear,' he replied. 'Sticks like this are for butchers' journeymen; away with it, I will not have it. But please deliver to my house today or tomorrow all these other things we have chosen.' So saying, he told her his name and address. He then returned to his table to finish drinking; of his three companions only one, a master tinsmith, was still sitting there.

'Well, it's a lucky day for our waitress,' remarked the man. 'Her cousin allows her a penny or two in the florin for the sales in the shop.'

At this, Mozart was doubly glad of his purchases; but his interest in the girl's welfare was soon to increase still further. For when she approached again, the tinsmith called out to her: 'And how are things with you, Crescence? How's your locksmith? Won't he soon be working his own iron?'

'Oh, goodness me,' she answered as she hurried off, 'I think that iron's still growing back there in the mountain.'

'She's a good girl,' said the tinsmith. 'She kept house for her stepfather for years, and nursed him in his illness, and then when he was dead it came to light that he had spent all her money. Since then she's been in service with her kinsman, does all the work in the shop and in the inn and with the children. She's friendly with a fine young fellow and would like to marry him, the sooner the better; but there are difficulties there.'

'What difficulties? I suppose he has no money either?'

'They've both got savings, but not enough. And now the half share of a house, with a workshop, is coming up for auction soon; it would be easy for the ropemaker to lend them the balance of the purchase price, but of course he doesn't want to lose the girl. He has good friends in the city council and in the guild, so now the young fellow finds himself blocked at every turn.'

'Damnation!' exclaimed Mozart, quite startling the tinsmith, who looked about him to see if anyone was listening. 'And is there no one here who can speak up for what's right and just? No one to put the fear of God into that fellow? The scoundrels! Just wait, you'll get your come-uppance yet!'

The tinsmith, mortally embarrassed, tried ineptly to tone down what he had said, almost retracting it completely; but Mozart would not listen to him. 'Be ashamed of yourself to talk like that!' he said. 'That's how you contemptible wretches always behave if you ever have to stand up and be counted.' And with that he unceremoniously turned his back on the poltroon. But as he passed the waitress, who had her hands full with new guests, he murmured: 'Come early tomorrow; and give my greetings to your sweetheart. I hope things will turn out well for you both.' She was quite taken aback and had neither the time nor the presence of mind to thank him.

He set off first by the way he had come, walking more quickly than usual in the excitement to which the scene had roused him; but on reaching the glacis he took a detour and followed the city walls round in a wide half-circle at a more leisurely pace. Busily pondering the affairs of the unfortunate young couple, he thought in turn of a whole series of his acquaintances and patrons who might be able in one way or another to intervene in the matter. Since, however, it would be necessary to get further particulars from the girl before deciding on any action, he resolved to wait calmly until he heard them; and in the meantime his heart and mind, hastening ahead of his footsteps, were filled with the anticipation of getting home to his wife.

Inwardly he felt quite sure that she would welcome him affectionately and indeed joyfully, that she would kiss and embrace him on the very threshold, and longing quickened his pace as he entered the Kärntner Tor. Near it he heard his name called by the postman, who handed him a small but weighty package, addressed in an honest and meticulous hand which he instantly recognized. He stepped into the nearest shop with the messenger to sign for it; then, back in the street and unable to contain his impatience until he reached his house, he tore open the seals and devoured the letter half walking and half standing.

'I was sitting at my sewing-table,' continued Madame Mozart at this point in her narrative to the ladies, 'when I heard my husband coming up the stairs and asking the servant whether I was at home. His step and his voice seemed to me more sprightly and assured than I expected and than I really liked to hear. He went first to his room and then came straight to me. "Good evening!" he said. Rather abashed, I answered him without looking up. After pacing the room once or twice in silence, he put on a show of yawning, and took the fly-swatter from behind the door, a thing I had never before known him do. Muttering to himself: "All these flies again! Where on earth have they come from!" he began swatting as hard as he could in various places. The noise of this was something he never could stand, and I had never been allowed to do it in his presence. Hmm! I thought, so it's quite all right, is it, if one does it oneself, especially if one's the man! In any case I hadn't noticed any great number of flies. I was really vexed by his strange behaviour. "Six at one stroke!" he cried. "Do you want to look at them?" I didn't answer. Then he put something right down on my sewing-cushion, so that without raising my eyes from my work I couldn't help seeing it. It was nothing less than a little pile of gold, as many ducats as you can pick up with two fingers. And behind my back he went on playing the fool, delivering a swipe here and there and muttering as he did so: "Disgusting, useless, shameless brutes! Obviously the sole purpose of their existence – smack! – is to be swatted dead – slap! – And that's something I may say I'm quite good at. We read in natural history how amazingly these creatures multiply – smack, slap! – well, they get short shrift in my house. *Ah, maledette! disperate!* Here's another score of them! Here, do you want them?" And he came to me and did the same thing as before. Up to this point I had found it hard to keep a straight face, but now I could do so no longer, I burst out laughing, he caught me in his arms, and there the pair of us were, laughing and giggling our hearts out.

' "But where on earth did you get the money?" I asked, as he shook the rest of it out of the purse. "From Prince Esterhazy! Transmitted to me by Haydn![23] Just look at this letter!" I read:

Eisenstadt, etc.

My dear friend!

His Serene Highness, my most gracious master, has done me the great pleasure of entrusting to my hands these sixty ducats which I am to convey to you. Recently we again performed your quartets, and His Highness was so delighted and gratified by them as I think he scarcely can have been when he first heard them three months ago. The Prince remarked to me (I must give you his exact words): "When Mozart dedicated this work to you, he thought it was only you he honoured; but he will not object to my seeing it as a compliment to myself as well. Tell him that I think almost as highly of his genius as you do; and more than that he truly cannot ask." – To which I add: Amen! Does this content you?

Postscript: A word in your dear wife's ear: Please make sure that proper thanks are rendered without delay, preferably in person. We must make the most of this favourable wind.

'"Oh, you dear, dear man! You noblest of souls!" exclaimed Mozart over and over again, and it would be hard to say which delighted him the most, the letter or the Prince's approval or the money. As for me, I must say frankly that it was the money I was truly glad of at that particular time. We passed a very festive evening.

'As to the affair in the suburb, I heard nothing about it that evening or in the next few days, indeed the whole following week passed, no Crescence appeared, and my husband, caught up in the whirl of his own affairs, soon forgot all about the matter. One Saturday we had company, a musical soirée with Captain Wesselt, Count Hardegg and others. During an interval I was called to the door – and lo and behold, there was the whole kettle of fish! I went back in and asked him: "Did you order a whole lot of wooden goods in the Alservorstadt?" "My goodness gracious!" he exclaimed, "has a girl brought them? Ask her to come right in!" And so in she came in the most courteous manner, carrying a rake and a spade and a whole basketful of other things. She apologized for not having come before, saying she had forgotten the name of the street and had not been able to get proper directions until today. Mozart took all the things from her one after another, and with great satisfaction at once

handed them to me. I thanked him most warmly and appreciat-
ively for each and every item, though I could not imagine why
he had bought the garden tools. He said: "But they're for your
allotment by the Wien, of course!" "Oh, good heavens, we gave
that up long ago! There was always so much flood damage, and
nothing ever grew there anyway. I told you at the time and
you had no objection." "What! So the asparagus we ate last
spring –" "It was all from the market!" "Now look! If only I'd
known that! I only praised it to you to be nice to you, because I
felt really sorry for you, gardening away like that; those aspara-
guses were like skinny little pencils."

'The guests were greatly amused by this comical episode, and
I was immediately obliged to distribute some of the unwanted
articles to them as souvenirs. Mozart then questioned the girl
about her marriage plans, urging her to talk to us quite frankly
and assuring her that anything we might do for her and her
sweetheart would be done on the quiet, discreetly and without
making trouble for anyone. She answered with so much mod-
esty, circumspection and tact as to charm everyone present, and
in the end we let her go with very encouraging promises.

'"We must do something to help these young people," said
the Captain. "The intrigues of the guild are the least of the
problems; I know a man who will soon deal with that. What's
needed is a contribution towards the purchase of the house and
the furnishing of it and so forth. How would it be if we were to
announce a benefit concert in the Trattner Hall, with the entry
fee at the discretion of patrons?" This suggestion was warmly
supported. One of the gentlemen picked up the salt-cellar and
said: "Someone should introduce the concert with an elegant
little historical account describing Herr Mozart's shopping
expedition and explaining his philanthropic intentions, and this
splendid vessel should be placed on the table as a collecting-box,
with the pair of rakes crossed right and left behind it as a
decoration."

'This was not in fact done, but the concert did take place; the
profits were considerable, and various further contributions
followed, so that the fortunate pair ended up with a surplus;
the other obstacles were also soon overcome. The Dušeks[24] in

Prague, who are our closest friends there and with whom we shall be staying, got wind of the story, and Frau Dušek, who is a very charming and kind-hearted woman, asked me if she too might have some part of the collection as a curiosity. So of course I set aside the most suitable of the articles for her, and I have taken the present occasion to bring them with me. But since it has unexpectedly turned out that we were to make the acquaintance of a new and dear musical colleague who is just about to set up her own home, and who I am sure will not despise a humble piece of domestic equipment selected by Mozart himself, I shall divide my present in two, and you may have the choice between a very fine openwork chocolate whisk and the much-aforementioned salt-cellar, which the artist has permitted himself to decorate tastefully with a tulip. I would myself definitely recommend the latter piece: for salt, I believe, is a noble substance, symbolizing domestic bliss and hospitality, both of which we most heartily wish you may enjoy.'

This was the end of Constanze's narrative, and it may be imagined with what delight it was heard by the ladies and with what gratitude the gift was accepted. Back in the house with the men, there was presently further occasion for rejoicing when the wooden objects were displayed and the model of patriarchal simplicity formally presented. Eugenie's uncle promised that it would be accorded no less a place in the silver-cabinet of its new owner and her remotest descendants than that famous salt-cellar by the Florentine master occupied in the Ambras collection.[25]

It was now nearly eight o'clock, and tea was served. But our musical hero soon found himself pressingly reminded of his promise, made that afternoon, to acquaint the company more closely with the 'hell-fire story' which he had with him in his luggage under lock and key, though fortunately not too deeply buried. He consented without hesitation. It did not take long to summarize the plot of the opera, and presently the text stood open and the candles were alight at either side of the keyboard.

How we wish we could here convey to our readers at least a touch of that singular sensation which can strike us with such electrifying and spellbinding force even when one unrelated chord floats from an open window, when our hearing catches it as we pass, aware that it can only come from that unknown source; even a touch of that sweet perturbation which affects us as we sit in a theatre while the orchestra tunes, and wait for the curtain to rise! Is it not so? If, on the threshold of any sublime and tragic work of art, whether it be called *Macbeth* or *Oedipus* or anything else, we feel a hovering tremor of eternal beauty: where could this be more the case, or even as much the case, as in the present situation? Man simultaneously longs and fears to be driven out of his usual self, he feels that he will be touched by the infinite, by something that will seize his heart, contracting it even as it expands it, as it violently embraces his spirit. Add to this the awe inspired by consummate art, the thought that we are being permitted and enabled to enjoy a divine miracle, to assimilate it as something akin to ourselves – and such a thought brings with it a special emotion, indeed a kind of pride, which is perhaps the purest and most joyful feeling of which we are capable.

The fact, however, that the present company were now to make the acquaintance for the first time of a work that has been fully familiar to us since our youth, gave them a standpoint and a relationship to it that were infinitely different from ours. And indeed, apart from the enviable good fortune of having it communicated to them by its author in person, they were far less favourably placed than we are; for a clear and perfect appreciation was not really possible to any of those who heard it, and in more than one respect would not even have been possible if the whole opera could have been given to them in unabbreviated form.

Out of eighteen finished numbers the composer probably performed less than half (in the report on which our narrative is based the only one explicitly mentioned is the last piece in this series, the Sextet). It seems that he rendered most of them very freely, presenting extracts on the piano and singing occasional passages at random or when appropriate. Similarly, all we find on record about his wife is that she sang two arias. Since her voice is supposed to have been powerful as well as charming, we should like to think that these were Donna Anna's first ('Or sai chi l'onore') and one of Zerlina's two.

Strictly speaking, so far as intellect, insight and taste were concerned, Eugenie and her fiancé were the only members of that audience entirely after the maestro's own heart, and the former a great deal more than the latter. They both sat right at the back of the room, the young lady still as a statue and so absorbed in the music that even in the brief intervals during which the others discreetly applauded or involuntarily expressed their inner emotion in admiring murmurs, she was scarcely able to give any adequate response to her fiancé's remarks.

When Mozart had come to a conclusion with the glorious Sextet and conversation gradually revived, he seemed to take particular interest and pleasure in some of the Baron's observations. Discussion had touched on the end of the opera, and on the performance provisionally arranged for the beginning of November, and when someone remarked that certain parts of the Finale still represented an enormous task, the maestro smiled rather mysteriously. But Constanze, leaning over and addressing the Countess though talking loudly enough for her husband to hear, said:

'He still has something up his sleeve, and he's keeping it secret even from me.'

'My darling!' he replied, 'you are talking out of turn in mentioning that now. What if the mood were to take me to start composing again? And in fact I'm already itching to do so.'

'Leporello!' cried the Count, jumping merrily to his feet and beckoning to a servant. 'Wine! Three bottles of Sillery!'[26]

'Please, no! Enough is enough – my young gentleman still hasn't finished his last glass.'

'Good health to him, then – and let everyone have what he needs!'

'Oh God, now what have I done!' lamented Constanze, glancing at the clock. 'It's almost eleven and tomorrow morning we have to start first thing – whatever shall we do?'

'Dear lady, you just can't do it, you absolutely can't.'

'Sometimes,' began Mozart, 'things can happen in a strange way. What will my dear little wife say when she learns that the very piece of work she is about to hear was born into the world at this very hour of the night, and just before a proposed journey too?'

'Is it possible? When? You must mean three weeks ago, when you were just about to leave for Eisenstadt.'

'Exactly. And this was how it happened. I got home from dinner at Richter's by ten, when you were already fast asleep, and indeed I meant to go to bed early as I had promised, in order to be able to get up and into the carriage in good time next morning. Meanwhile Veit, as usual, had lit the candles on my desk; I mechanically put on my dressing-gown, and it occurred to me to take another look at my last piece of work. But, alas! oh, the confounded, untimely meddlings of women! You had tidied everything away, and packed the score – for I had to take it with me, of course, the Prince wanted to hear the music. And so I searched and grumbled and cursed, all in vain! But as I did so my eyes fell on a sealed envelope: from the Abbé, to judge by the dreadful spiky writing of the address – yes, indeed! He had sent me the rest of his revised text, which I wasn't expecting to see for another month. At once I sat down eagerly to read it, and was enchanted to find how well the strange fellow had understood my intentions. It was all much simpler, more concentrated and yet with more substance. Both the scene in the graveyard, and the Finale up to the death of the hero, had been much improved in every respect. (You excellent poet! I thought, now you have conjured up heaven and hell for me again, and you shall have your reward!) Now it is not normally my custom to write part of a composition in advance, however tempting it may be; this is a bad habit, and one often has to pay dearly for it. But exceptions can be made, and in short, that scene with the equestrian statue of the Commendatore, when the nocturnal prowler's laughter is suddenly interrupted by a ghastly voice from the grave of the murdered man – that scene had already gripped me. I struck one chord, and felt that I had knocked at the right door, that behind it they were all lying ready, the whole legion of terrors that are to be unleashed in the Finale. At first an Adagio came: in D minor, only four bars, then a second phrase with five – I do believe that this will be remarkably effective on the stage, with the most powerful of the wind instruments accompanying the voice. Meanwhile let's make what we can of it here: listen!'

Without further ado he extinguished the candles in the two chandeliers on either side of him, and through the dead silence of the room the fearful chant rang out: *Di rider finirai pria dell' aurora!*[27] As from some remote stellar region, from silver trumps the notes dropped, ice-cold, piercing the marrow and shivering the soul, down through the dark blue night.

'*Chi va là?*' demands Don Giovanni, '*chi va là?*' And then we hear it again, on a single repeated note as before, commanding the impious youth to leave the dead in peace.

And when the last reverberation of those deep-resounding notes had died away, Mozart continued: 'And now, as you may appreciate, it was impossible for me to stop. Once the ice has broken at even one point on the shore of a lake, we hear the whole surface splitting and cracking, right across to the furthest corner. Involuntarily I took up the same thread at a point further on, when Don Giovanni is sitting at supper, when Donna Elvira has just left and the ghost appears as invited. Listen to this!'

And now followed that whole long, terrifying dialogue which snatches even the soberest of listeners away to the border-line of human understanding and beyond it: away to where our eyes and ears apprehend the supernatural, and we are helplessly tossed to and fro from one extreme to another within our own hearts.

Estranged already from human utterance, the immortal tongue of the dead man deigns again to speak. Soon after his first dreadful greeting, as the half-transfigured visitant scorns the earthly food they offer him, how strange and uncanny is his voice as it moves with irregular strides up and down the rungs of a ladder woven from air! He demands swift resolve to repentance and penance: the time of grace for the spirit is short, long, long, long is the journey! And now as Don Giovanni in monstrous self-will defies the eternal ordinances, desperately struggling against the growing onslaught of the infernal powers, resisting and writhing and finally perishing, though still sublime in every gesture – whose heart is not moved, who would not be shaken to the innermost core with simultaneous ecstasy and terror? It is with a similar feeling of astonishment that we watch the magnificent spectacle of a violent natural force, the burning of some splendid ship. Involuntarily we feel a kind of sympathy with this blind greatness, and share its agony as it whirls towards its self-destruction.

The composer had finished. For a while no one dared to be the first to break the general silence. Finally, still scarcely able to breathe, the Countess ventured: 'Tell us, please tell us something about how you felt when you put down your pen that night!'

As if waking from a private reverie, he looked at her with a smile, quickly collected his thoughts and said, half to the lady and half to his wife: 'Well, I suppose my head did feel a bit dizzy. I had sat by the open window writing the whole of that desperate *dibattimento*, down to the chorus of demons at the end, in a single flush of inspiration; I had finished it, and after a brief rest I rose from my chair, meaning to go to your room and chatter with you for a moment until I calmed down. But suddenly an unwelcome thought stopped me where I stood.' (Here he lowered his eyes for a moment or two, and when he continued there was a scarcely perceptible tremor of emotion in his voice.) 'I said to myself: Suppose you were to sicken and die this very night, suppose you had to abandon your score at this point – would you rest at peace in your grave? I stared at the wick of the candle in my hand and at the mounds of wax that had dripped from it. The thought gave me a momentary pang of grief. Then I reflected again: Suppose another man later, sooner or later, perhaps even some sort of Italian, were commissioned to finish the opera? And suppose he found it, with the exception of one passage, all neatly put together from the Introduction to the seventeenth number, all healthy ripe fruit shaken down into the tall grass for him to pick up? And suppose he still felt rather daunted by this central part of the Finale – and were then unexpectedly to find that big stumbling-block more or less already removed: what a laugh he would secretly have then! Perhaps he would be tempted to cheat me of the honour due to me. But I think he'd burn his fingers over that; I'd still have a few good friends who know my handiwork and would honestly make sure I got the credit. So now I left my study, looking up to thank God with all my heart, and thanking your good genius as well, my dear little wife, for holding his hands gently above your brow for so long, making you sleep on and on like a little rat, unable to call out to me even once. But when I finally did get to you and you asked me what time it was, I brazenly swore a couple of hours off your age, for it was in fact nearly four o'clock. So now you understand why you couldn't dig me out of bed at six, and why the coachman had to be sent home and told to come back next day.'

'Of course!' retorted Constanze, 'but my clever husband need not imagine that I was so stupid as to notice nothing! That was certainly no good reason for not saying a word to me about the fine progress you had made!'

'And that wasn't the reason either.'

'I know – you wanted to keep your treasure a secret for the time being.'

'All I can say,' exclaimed their good-humoured host, 'is that I'm delighted we shan't need to hurt the noble feelings of a Viennese coachman if Herr Mozart absolutely refuses to get out of bed tomorrow morning. Unharness the horses again, Hans – it's always a very painful order to give.'

This indirect request by the Count that the Mozarts should prolong their visit was one in which all the rest of those present most heartily joined, and the travellers were now obliged to expound very serious reasons for not doing so; but as a compromise it was gladly agreed that they would not leave too early, and that the company would have the pleasure of taking breakfast together.

The party continued for a while with everyone moving around and talking in groups. Mozart was looking about him, evidently hoping for some further conversation with the young bride; but as she was momentarily absent, he artlessly addressed the question he had intended for her directly to Francesca who was standing near by: 'So what, on the whole, is your opinion of our *Don Giovanni*? Can you prophesy some success for it?'

'I will answer that,' she replied laughingly, 'in the name of my cousin, as well as I can: it is my humble opinion that if *Don Giovanni* does not turn the head of everyone who hears it, then the Lord God will simply shut up his music shop till further notice and announce to mankind –' – 'And give mankind', her uncle corrected her, 'a bagpipes to play with, and harden their hearts till they turn to worshipping idols!'

'God forbid!' laughed Mozart. 'But indeed: in the next sixty or seventy years, long after I am gone, many a false prophet will arise.'[28]

Eugenie reappeared with Max and the Baron, the conversation took a new turn and again became serious and significant, so that before the company dispersed the composer's hopes had been pleasurably encouraged by many flattering and perceptive remarks.

The party did not break up till long after midnight; no one noticed until then how tired they all were.

At ten o'clock on the following morning (a day of equally fine weather) a handsome coach, packed with the luggage of the two Viennese guests, had appeared in the courtyard. The Count was standing by it with Mozart just before the horses were brought out, and asked him how he liked it.

'Very much; it looks extremely comfortable.'

'Well, then, do me the pleasure of keeping it as a souvenir from me.'

'What, are you serious?'

'But most certainly!'

'Holy Sixtus and Calixtus! Constanze!' he called up to the window at which she and the others stood looking out, 'I'm to be given the coach! From now on you'll be travelling in your own coach!'

He embraced his chuckling benefactor, walked round his new property inspecting it from all sides, opened the door, jumped in and called out: 'I feel as noble and rich as Chevalier Gluck![29] My, how they'll stare at this in Vienna!' – 'I hope,' said the Countess, 'that on your way back from Prague we shall see your carriage again, with triumphal garlands hanging all over it!'

Not long after this happy scene the much-lauded carriage did in fact set off with the departing pair, and headed for the

highway at a brisk trot. The Count's horses were to take them
as far as Wittingau, where post-horses were to be hired.

When our home has been temporarily enlivened by the presence
of goodhearted and admirable visitors, and when like a breath
of spiritual fresh air they have renewed and quickened our very
being, so that we have enjoyed the giving of hospitality as never
before, their departure always fills us with a certain *malaise*, at
any rate for the rest of the day and if we are again thrown back
entirely on our own company.

  This at least was not the case with our friends at the castle.
To be sure, Francesca's parents and her old aunt now also
departed; but Francesca herself and Eugenie's fiancé, and Max
of course, stayed on. It is Eugenie that we here chiefly have in
mind, for she had been moved more deeply than any of the
others by so rare and wonderful an experience, and it might be
thought that there was nothing she lacked, nothing to grieve or
sadden her. Her pure happiness with the man she truly loved, a
happiness which had been given its formal confirmation only
today, must surely have eclipsed all other feelings; or rather, the
noblest and finest emotions that could touch her heart must
surely have mingled and united with that abundant joy. And
this no doubt would have been true had she been able, yesterday
and today, to live only for the present moment, and now only
for its pure retrospective enjoyment. But that evening, as she
had listened to Mozart's wife telling her story, she had, despite
all her delight in his charm, been secretly touched by a certain
anxiety on his behalf. And all the time he was playing, despite
all the indescribable beauty of the music and through all its
mysterious terror, this apprehension lived on in the depths of
her consciousness, till in the end she was startled and shocked
to hear him mention his own similar forebodings. The convic-
tion, the utter conviction grew upon her that here was a man
rapidly and inexorably burning himself out in his own flame;
that he could be only a fleeting phenomenon on this earth,
because the overwhelming beauty that poured from him would
be more than the earth could really endure.

  She had gone to bed on the previous evening with this and

many other thoughts touching and stirring her heart, and with the music of *Don Giovanni* haunting her inner ear as a ceaseless throng of manifold sound. It had been almost daybreak when she wearily fell asleep.

But now the three ladies were sitting in the garden with their needlework, the men were keeping them company, and since Mozart was naturally the first and sole topic of conversation, Eugenie made no secret of her apprehensions. None of the others was in the least inclined to share them, although the Baron understood them perfectly. In a happy hour, in a mood of quite unmixed human gratitude, we usually find ourselves rejecting strongly any idea of misfortune or unhappiness that does not immediately concern us at the time. The most telling counter-arguments were laughingly advanced to her, especially by her uncle, and how gladly she drank them all in! They fell little short of truly convincing her that she was taking too gloomy a view.

A few moments later, as she passed through the large room upstairs which had just been cleaned and set in order again and whose green damask curtains, now drawn, admitted only a soft twilight, she paused sorrowfully by the piano. Remembering who had sat there only a few hours ago, she felt certain she must be dreaming. She looked long and pensively at the keys which *he* had been the last to touch, then gently closed the lid and removed the key, jealously resolved that for some time to come no other hand should open it again. As she left, she casually put a few volumes of songs back in their place; an old sheet fell out of one of them, it was a copy of a little Bohemian folk-song, one that Francesca had once often sung, indeed she had no doubt sung it herself. She picked it up and looked at it with emotion. In such a mood as hers the most natural coincidence easily becomes an oracle. But however she understood it, its contents were such that, as she reread these simple verses, hot tears fell from her eyes.

> In the woods, who knows where,
> Stands a green fir-tree;
> A rosebush, who can tell,

Blooms in what garden?
Already they have been chosen –
Oh soul, remember! –
To take root on your grave,
For they must grow there.

Out on the meadow two
Black steeds are grazing,
And homewards to the town
They trot so sprightly.
They will be walking when
They draw your coffin;
Who knows but that may be
Even before they shed
That iron on their hooves
That glints so brightly.

Selected Poems

An einem Wintermorgen, vor Sonnenaufgang

O flaumenleichte Zeit der dunkeln Frühe!
Welch neue Welt bewegest du in mir?
Was ists, daß ich auf einmal nun in dir
Von sanfter Wollust meines Daseins glühe?

Einem Kristall gleicht meine Seele nun,
Den noch kein falscher Strahl des Lichts getroffen;
Zu fluten scheint mein Geist, er scheint zu ruhn,
Dem Eindruck naher Wunderkräfte offen,
Die aus dem klaren Gürtel blauer Luft
Zuletzt ein Zauberwort vor meine Sinne ruft.

Bei hellen Augen glaub ich doch zu schwanken;
Ich schließe sie, daß nicht der Traum entweiche.
Seh ich hinab in lichte Feenreiche?
Wer hat den bunten Schwarm von Bildern und Gedanken
Zur Pforte meines Herzens hergeladen,
Die glänzend sich in diesem Busen baden,
Goldfarbnen Fischlein gleich im Gartenteiche?

Ich höre bald der Hirtenflöten Klänge,
Wie um die Krippe jener Wundernacht,
Bald weinbekränzter Jugend Lustgesänge;
Wer hat das friedenselige Gedränge
In meine traurigen Wände hergebracht?

Und welch Gefühl entzückter Stärke,
Indem mein Sinn sich frisch zur Ferne lenkt!
Vom ersten Mark des heutgen Tags getränkt,
Fühl ich mir Mut zu jedem frommen Werke.

1824–1838

On a Winter Morning before Sunrise

Oh dark dawn time, oh light-as-down dawn light!
What have you done to me, what sudden glow
Of gentle joy in living moves me so,
What new world stirs within me at this sight?

My soul is like a crystal, though I seem
Untouched by day's false brightness yet; my mind,
Still as still water, moving like a stream,
Is opened at some magical command
To nearby powers of wonder: from that ring
Of clear blue sky they are called, my senses visiting.

My eyes are wide and yet I sway with sleep;
I close them, lest this precious dream should fade.
Into what faery realms do I gaze so deep?
These many-coloured images and thoughts, who bade
Them come to me, bright presences, what made
Them plunge and glide into this heart of mine,
As in the garden pond gold fishes swim and shine?

Two musics, now the shepherds piping clear
As round the manger on that wondrous night,
Now the glad songs of vine-crowned youth I hear;
But through my poor walls who has brought them here,
This peaceful throng, these envoys of delight?

How I am strengthened, and with what new joy
I steer my thoughts upon a distant course!
I drink the morning marrow's earliest force,
My will grows bold to every good employ.

Die Seele fliegt, so weit der Himmel reicht,
Der Genius jauchzt in mir! Doch sage,
Warum wird jetzt der Blick von Wehmut feucht?
Ists ein verloren Glück, was mich erweicht?
Ist es ein werdendes, was ich im Herzen trage?
– Hinweg, mein Geist! hier gilt kein Stillestehn:
Es ist ein Augenblick, und Alles wird verwehn!

Dort, sieh, am Horizont lüpft sich der Vorhang schon!
Es träumt der Tag, nun sei die Nacht entflohn;
Die Purpurlippe, die geschlossen lag,
Haucht, halbgeöffnet, süße Atemzüge:
Auf einmal blitzt das Aug, und, wie ein Gott, der Tag
Beginnt im Sprung die königlichen Flüge!

Peregrina

I

Der Spiegel dieser treuen, braunen Augen
Ist wie von innerm Gold ein Widerschein
Tief aus dem Busen scheint ers anzusaugen,
Dort mag solch Gold in heilgem Gram gedeihn.
In diese Nacht des Blickes mich zu tauchen,
Unwissend Kind, du selber lädst mich ein –
Willst, ich soll kecklich mich und dich entzünden,
Reichst lächelnd mir den Tod im Kelch der Sünden!

II

Aufgeschmückt ist der Freudensaal.
Lichterhell, bunt, in laulicher Sommernacht
Stehet das offene Gartengezelte.
Säulengleich steigen, gepaart,

My soul flies up, far as the endless skies,
The spirit exults in me! But say,
What softening sadness still makes moist my eyes?
Do I recall a lost content, or does one rise
Still unborn in my heart? – Up, my soul, and away!
Let me not linger here: a moment made
What I have seen, and now it all must fade.

There, on the horizon, look, the curtain lifts at last!
The day is dreaming that the night has passed:
His crimson lips lay closed, but now, half parted,
Breathe out a sweetest fragrance; suddenly
The great eye flashes: like a god, oh see,
The day leaps forth, his royal flight has started!

Peregrina

I

The surface of your eyes, so dark and true,
Mirrors the gold that seems to live who knows
How deep within, drawn from the heart of you,
The holy sorrow where such treasure grows.
Into this night, so innocently, your wild
Sweet gaze invites me: I must dive and drown,
We both must drink sin's deadly chalice down,
Set on fire by your smile, oh artless child!

II

The festive room is adorned and ready.
Brightly lit, many-coloured, the garden pavilion
Stands open in the mild summer night.
Rising like columns, in pairs,

Grün-umranket, eherne Schlangen
Zwölf, mit verschlungenen Hälsen
Tragend und stützend das
Leicht gegitterte Dach.

Aber die Braut noch wartet verborgen
In dem Kämmerlein ihres Hauses.
Endlich bewegt sich der Zug der Hochzeit,
Fackeln tragend,
Feierlich stumm.
Und in der Mitte,
Mich an der rechten Hand,
Schwarz gekleidet, geht einfach die Braut
Schön gefaltet ein Scharlachtuch
Liegt um den zierlichen Kopf geschlagen.
Lächelnd geht sie dahin; das Mahl schon duftet.

Später im Lärmen des Fests
Stahlen wir seitwärts uns beide
Weg, nach den Schatten des Gartens wandelnd
Wo im Gebüsche die Rosen brannten,
Wo der Mondstrahl um Lilien zuckte,
Wo die Weymouthsfichte mit schwarzem Haar
Den Spiegel des Teiches halb verhängt.

Auf seidnem Rasen dort, ach, Herz am Herzen,
Wie verschlangen, erstickten meine Küsse den
        scheueren Kuß!
Indes der Springquell, unteilnehmend
An überschwänglicher Liebe Geflüster,
Sich ewig des eigenen Plätscherns freute;
Uns aber neckten von fern und lockten
Freundliche Stimmen,
Flöten und Saiten umsonst.

Ermüdet lag, zu bald für mein Verlangen,
Das leichte, liebe Haupt auf meinem Schoß.

Green foliage clinging to them, twelve brazen
Serpents, with necks intertwined,
Bear and support
The lightly trellised roof.

But hidden in her house, in her little room,
The bride is still waiting.
At last the wedding procession sets forth,
Carrying torches,
Solemnly silent.
And in the midst,
Myself at her right hand,
The bride walks simply, clothed in black;
She wears a scarlet cloth,
Beautifully folded, round her dainty head.
Smiling she walks; the scent of the meal is on the air
    already.

Later, amid the noisy festivities,
The two of us stole away from the others,
Wandering off into the shadows of the garden,
Where the roses burned in the bushes,
Where the moon's rays gleamed on the lilies,
Where the Weymouth fir half covers the surface
Of the pond with its dark hair.

There on the silk-smooth lawn, oh heart against heart,
How my kisses devoured and smothered her more
    bashful kiss!
While the fountain, ignoring
The susurration of extravagant love,
Took delight in its own eternal murmur;
But we were teased by distant friendly
Voices, flutes and violins,
Which enticed us in vain.

In weariness, too soon for my desire,
Her dear head then lay lightly in my lap.

Spielender Weise mein Aug auf ihres drückend
Fühlt ich ein Weilchen die langen Wimpern,
Bis der Schlaf sie stillte,
Wie Schmetterlingsgefieder auf und nieder gehn.

Eh das Frührot schien,
Eh das Lämpchen erlosch im Brautgemache,
Weckt ich die Schläferin,
Führte das seltsame Kind in mein Haus ein.

III

Ein Irrsal kam in die Mondscheingärten
Einer einst heiligen Liebe.
Schaudernd entdeckt ich verjährten Betrug.
Und mit weinendem Blick, doch grausam,
Hieß ich das schlanke,
Zauberhafte Mädchen
Ferne gehen von mir.
Ach, ihre hohe Stirn,
War gesenkt, denn sie liebte mich;
Aber sie zog mit Schweigen
Fort in die graue
Welt hinaus.

Krank seitdem,
Wund ist und wehe mein Herz
Nimmer wird es genesen!
Als ginge, luftgesponnen, ein Zauberfaden
Von ihr zu mir, ein ängstig Band,
So zieht es, zieht mich schmachtend ihr nach!
– Wie? wenn ich eines Tags auf meiner Schwelle
Sie sitzen fände, wie einst, im Morgen-Zwielicht,
Das Wanderbündel neben ihr,
Und ihr Auge, treuherzig zu mir aufschauend,
Sagte, da bin ich wieder
Hergekommen aus weiter Welt!

And as I playfully pressed my eye on hers
I felt for a little while her long lashes,
Till sleep stilled them,
Fluttering up and down like moth-feathers.

Before dawn broke,
Before the lamp went out in the bridal chamber,
I woke the sleeper,
The strange child, and took her into my house.

III

A madness broke into the moonlit gardens
Of a love that had once been sacred.
With horror I discovered a betrayal of years ago.
And with tears in my eyes, but cruelly,
I banished the slender
Enchanting girl
Far from my presence.
Alas, her noble head
Was bowed, for she loved me;
But in silence she left me
And away into the grey
World she went.

Since then my heart
Has been sick and wounded and sore.
It will never heal again!
As if between her and me there were a magic thread
Spun from the air, a fearful bond,
I am drawn, drawn after her in longing!
– How would it be if one day I found her
Sitting on my threshold as once she did, in the morning
Dusk, with her bundle by her,
And her eyes, looking up to me with kind affection,
Were to say: Here I am again,
Coming back to you from the wide world!

IV

Warum, Geliebte, denk ich dein
Auf einmal nun mit tausend Tränen,
Und kann gar nicht zufrieden sein,
Und will die Brust in alle Weite dehnen?

Ach, gestern in den hellen Kindersaal,
Beim Flimmer zierlich aufgesteckter Kerzen,
Wo ich mein selbst vergaß in Lärm und Scherzen,
Tratst du, o Bildnis mitleid-schöner Qual;
Es war dein Geist, er setzte sich ans Mahl,
Fremd saßen wir mit stumm verhaltnen Schmerzen;
Zuletzt brach ich in lautes Schluchzen aus,
Und Hand in Hand verließen wir das Haus.

V

Die Liebe, sagt man, steht am Pfahl gebunden,
Geht endlich arm, zerrüttet, unbeschuht;
Dies edle Haupt hat nicht mehr, wo es ruht,
Mit Tränen netzet sie der Füße Wunden.

Ach, Peregrinen hab ich so gefunden!
Schön war ihr Wahnsinn, ihrer Wange Glut,
Noch scherzend in der Frühlingsstürme Wut,
Und wilde Kränze in das Haar gewunden.

Wars möglich, solche Schönheit zu verlassen?
– So kehrt nur reizender das alte Glück!
O komm, in diese Arme dich zu fassen!

Doch weh! o weh! was soll mir dieser Blick?
Sie küßt mich zwischen Lieben noch und Hassen,
Sie kehrt sich ab, und kehrt mir nie zurück.

IV

Oh why, beloved, suddenly
And with a thousand tears of comfortless
Grief, do I now remember you, and press
My yearning heart out to infinity?

Yesterday, with those children, in that bright-
Lit room, the lovely candles all alight,
As I forgot myself in noise and fun –
Oh beauty, torment and compassion! you
Appeared, your ghost had joined the feast; we two
Sat strangely, dumbly suffering as one,
Until I sobbed aloud in anguish, and
We left the house together, hand in hand.

V

Love is tied to a stake, and full of cares,
Ragged, unshod and destitute, they say;
Her noble head she has nowhere to lay,
Her wounded feet she washes with her tears.

Oh, thus I found my Wanderer, so she appears!
Still beautiful, flushed, with her wits astray,
And in the spring storms' raging still at play;
Wild garlands wound about her head she wears.

Oh how could I forsake such beauty, how
That joy of long ago, so sweet returning?
Come to me, let my arms heal my heart's yearning!

But what is this? Alas, what frowning brow!
She kisses me, with love and hate still burning;
She turns away, she is lost for ever now.

Gesang zu Zweien in der Nacht

Sie: Wie süß der Nachtwind nun die Wiese streift,
Und klingend jetzt den jungen Hain durchläuft!
Da noch der freche Tag verstummt,
Hört man der Erdenkräfte flüsterndes Gedränge,
Das aufwärts in die zärtlichen Gesänge
Der reingestimmten Lüfte summt.

Er: Vernehm ich doch die wunderbarsten Stimmen,
Vom lauen Wind wollüstig hingeschleift,
Indes, mit ungewissem Licht gestreift,
Der Himmel selber scheinet hinzuschwimmen.

Sie: Wie ein Gewebe zuckt die Luft manchmal,
Durchsichtiger und heller aufzuwehen;
Dazwischen hört man weiche Töne gehen
Von selgen Feen, die im blauen Saal
Zum Sphärenklang,
Und fleißig mit Gesang,
Silberne Spindeln hin und wieder drehen.

Er: O holde Nacht, du gehst mit leisem Tritt
Auf schwarzem Samt, der nur am Tage grünet,
Und luftig schwirrender Musik bedienet
Sich nun dein Fuß zum leichten Schritt,
Womit du Stund um Stunde missest,
Dich lieblich in dir selbst vergissest –
Du schwärmst, es schwärmt der Schöpfung Seele mit!

Two Voices in the Night

She: How sweetly through the fields the night wind blows,
Through the young grove how sweet its music goes!
The insolent day still finds no speech,
And we can hear the earthly powers, their whispering
    throng
Resound, rise up to where in delicate song,
The breaths of heaven blend each with each.

He: Surely I hear strange voices, wondrously
Borne on by the mild wind's voluptuous flight:
And all the while, streaked with uncertain light,
The sky itself seems floating far and free.

She: Shaken sometimes, the woven sheet of air
Waves out more radiant, more diaphanous,
And as it spreads, soft tones drift down to us
From the blue vault: blest elfin spirits there
As heaven's spheres outring
Tirelessly sing,
While to and fro their silver spindles pass.

He: Dear night, with gentle tread you walk upon
Black velvet, velvet green again by day,
And now your feet to murmuring music play,
Notes light as air that move you lightly on
Spanning the hours, lost in your sole
Self's magic, while creation's soul
Dances your dream, dreams your oblivion.

Um Mitternacht

Gelassen stieg die Nacht ans Land,
Lehnt träumend an der Berge Wand,
Ihr Auge sieht die goldne Waage nun
Der Zeit in gleichen Schalen stille ruhn;
  Und kecker rauschen die Quellen hervor,
   Sie singen der Mutter, der Nacht, ins Ohr
     Vom Tage,
   Vom heute gewesenen Tage.

Das uralt alte Schlummerlied,
Sie achtets nicht, sie ist es müd;
Ihr klingt des Himmels Bläue süßer noch,
Der flüchtgen Stunden gleichgeschwungnes Joch.
  Doch immer behalten die Quellen das Wort,
   Es singen die Wasser im Schlafe noch fort
     Vom Tage,
   Vom heute gewesenen Tage.

In der Frühe

Kein Schlaf noch kühlt das Auge mir,
Dort gehet schon der Tag herfür
An meinem Kammerfenster.
Es wühlet mein verstörter Sinn
Noch zwischen Zweifeln her und hin
Und schaffet Nachtgespenster.
– Ängste, quäle
Dich nicht länger, meine Seele!
Freu dich! schon sind da und dorten
Morgenglocken wach geworden.

At Midnight

The night has come ashore; so still
She broods in dreams on height and hill;
She watches now how motionless they are,
The equal scales hung from time's golden bar;
   And they bubble more boldly, the mountain springs,
   To the night, to their mother, their water sings
     Of the day,
   Of the day that has been today.

The age-old wearying lullaby
She does not heed; the deep blue sky
Is the still sweeter music she enjoys,
The fleeting hours' tranquil equipoise.
   But the springs are talking and have not done,
   They babble in sleep as their waters run,
     Of the day,
   Of the day that has been today.

In the Early Morning

No slumber soothes my burning eyes,
And at my window, in the skies,
The day's already bright.
Torn to and fro in its debates
My busy doubting mind creates
Dark phantoms of the night.
– Oh my soul, now cease
This self-torment, be at peace
And rejoice! now here, now there, the morning
Bells chime out, from their own sleep returning.

Fußreise

Am frischgeschnittnen Wanderstab
Wenn ich in der Frühe
So durch Wälder ziehe,
Hügel auf und ab:
Dann, wie's Vögelein im Laube
Singet und sich rührt,
Oder wie die goldne Traube
Wonnegeister spürt
In der ersten Morgensonne:
So fühlt auch mein alter, lieber
Adam Herbst- und Frühlingsfieber,
Gottbeherzte,
Nie verscherzte
Erstlings-Paradieseswonne.

Also bist du nicht so schlimm, o alter
Adam, wie die strengen Lehrer sagen;
Liebst und lobst du immer doch,
Singst und preisest immer noch,
Wie an ewig neuen Schöpfungstagen,
Deinen lieben Schöpfer und Erhalter.

Möcht es dieser geben,
Und mein ganzes Leben
Wär im leichten Wanderschweiße
Eine solche Morgenreise!

Frühlingsgefühl

Frühling läßt sein blaues Band
Wieder flattern durch die Lüfte;
Süße, wohlbekannte Düfte
Streifen ahnungsvoll das Land.
Veilchen träumen schon,

A Journey on Foot

My wanderer's staff's fresh-hewn again
And the day is breaking
And my way I'm taking
Over the hills, through wood and glen:
And as birds that sing
As they flutter in the trees,
As they fly and take their ease,
Or as grapes in morning sun
Feel their golden joy begun,
So too my dear old sinful Adam, given
New strength from heaven,
Feels the autumn or the spring
Like an unlost ardour burning,
Eden's first delight returning.

Well, old Adam, tell your moral teacher
That you're really not so bad a creature,
For you still give thanks and praise
And sing with loving heart and true,
As if creation were for ever new,
To the good Maker who preserves your days.

May He grant it so
That the whole of life may be
(Though sweating slightly as I go)
A morning walk like this for me!

Intimation of Spring

Now again the earth with new
Long-familiar fragrance brings
Its sweet presage, and the spring's
Sky-borne banner flutters blue.
Violets wake today

Wollen balde kommen.
– Horch, von fern ein leiser Harfenton!
Frühling, ja du bists!
Dich hab ich vernommen!

Im Frühling

Hier lieg ich auf dem Frühlingshügel:
Die Wolke wird mein Flügel,
Ein Vogel fliegt mir voraus.
Ach, sag mir, all-einzige Liebe,
Wo du bleibst, daß ich bei dir bliebe!
Doch du und die Lüfte, ihr habt kein Haus.

Der Sonnenblume gleich steht mein Gemüte offen,
Sehnend,
Sich dehnend
In Lieben und Hoffen.
Frühling, was bist du gewillt?
Wann werd ich gestillt?

Die Wolke seh ich wandeln und den Fluß,
Es dringt der Sonne goldner Kuß
Mir tief bis ins Geblüt hinein;
Die Augen, wunderbar berauschet,
Tun, als schliefen sie ein,
Nur noch das Ohr dem Ton der Biene lauschet.
Ich denke dies und denke das,
Ich sehne mich, und weiß nicht recht, nach was:
Halb ist es Lust, halb ist es Klage;
Mein Herz, o sage,
Was webst du für Erinnerung
In golden grüner Zweige Dämmerung?
– Alte unnennbare Tage!

Dreaming their time is near.
– Oh listen: soft harp-music far away!
Spring, yes, I have heard you
Coming, you are here!

In the Spring

Here on the hill in spring I am lying:
With a cloud I am flying,
A bird soars ahead of me through
The sky. Oh my only love, tell me where,
Where *you* are, that I may be there!
But you have no homing-place, the winds and you.

Like a sunflower my soul has opened wide,
Longing,
Outreaching
In love and hope. Oh spring,
What is your will, when shall
My thirst be satisfied?

I see the cloud drifting, the river flowing,
And deep into my veins I feel
The golden kisses of the sun are going;
My eyes, bound by a spell,
Are drunken and seem to slumber,
Only my ears still listen to the bee's murmur.
My thoughts turn this way and the other way,
I yearn, and yet for what I cannot say:
It is half joy, it is half woe.
Oh, does my heart not know
What memories it weaves
Into this twilight of the gold-green leaves?
– The nameless days of long ago!

Besuch in Urach

Nur fast so wie im Traum ist mirs geschehen,
Daß ich in dies geliebte Tal verirrt.
Kein Wunder ist, was meine Augen sehen,
Doch schwankt der Boden, Luft und Staude schwirrt,
Aus tausend grünen Spiegeln scheint zu gehen
Vergangne Zeit, die lächelnd mich verwirrt;
Die Wahrheit selber wird hier zum Gedichte,
Mein eigen Bild ein fremd und hold Gesichte!

Da seid ihr alle wieder aufgerichtet,
Besonnte Felsen, alte Wolkenstühle!
Auf Wäldern schwer, wo kaum der Mittag lichtet
Und Schatten mischt mit balsamreicher Schwüle.
Kennt ihr mich noch, der sonst hieher geflüchtet,
Im Moose, bei süß-schläferndem Gefühle,
Der Mücke Sumsen hier ein Ohr geliehen,
Ach, kennt ihr mich, und wollt nicht vor mir fliehen?

Hier wird ein Strauch, ein jeder Halm zur Schlinge,
Die mich in liebliche Betrachtung fängt;
Kein Mäuerchen, kein Holz ist so geringe,
Daß nicht mein Blick voll Wehmut an ihm hängt:
Ein jedes spricht mir halbvergeßne Dinge;
Ich fühle, wie von Schmerz und Lust gedrängt
Die Träne stockt, indes ich ohne Weile,
Unschlüssig, satt und durstig, weiter eile.

Hinweg! und leite mich, du Schar von Quellen,
Die ihr durchspielt der Matten grünes Gold!
Zeigt mir die ur-bemoosten Wasserzellen,
Aus denen euer ewigs Leben rollt,
Im kühnsten Walde die verwachsnen Schwellen,
Wo eurer Mutter Kraft im Berge grollt,

Urach Revisited

To this beloved valley once again
Somehow I have wandered: or is it a dream?
The ground, the breeze, the bushes – my eyes see plain
This is no miracle, yet they all seem
To move and murmur. Bygone days remain
Green-mirrored, myriadfold: their smiling stream
Bemuses. Truth itself's a poem here
And my own face a vision strange and dear.

Here you all are, ancient and ever-new,
Bare sunlit hills uprearing, summits made
For cloud-thrones, woods where scarcely noon breaks
    through,
Where balmy warmth mingles with deepest shade:
Do you still know me, who once fled to you,
Whose heavy head sweet-slumbrously was laid
Here in cool moss to hear the insects humming –
Do you know me, and shrink not at my coming?

Here every shrub and blade of grass ensnares
My heart to muse on it; no little wall,
No clump of trees, but with nostalgic tears
My gaze must linger on it; none too small
But speaks to me of half-forgotten years;
To mingled pain and joy I am in thrall,
And dry-eyed, restless, with irresolute will
I hasten on, full-fed and thirsting still.

You thousand streams that wander through the gold-
Green meadows, come, now lead me! Show me where
From ancient mossy springs your life has rolled
Eternally: from hidden thresholds there
In wildest woods, your mother has of old
Muttered her strength in its deep mountain lair

Bis sie im breiten Schwung an Felsenwänden
Herabstürzt, euch im Tale zu versenden.

O hier ists, wo Natur den Schleier reißt!
Sie bricht einmal ihr übermenschlich Schweigen;
Laut mit sich selber redend will ihr Geist,
Sich selbst vernehmend, sich ihm selber zeigen.
– Doch ach, sie bleibt, mehr als der Mensch, verwaist,
Darf nicht aus ihrem eignen Rätsel steigen!
Dir biet ich denn, begierge Wassersäule,
Die nackte Brust, ach, ob sie dir sich teile!

Vergebens! und dein kühles Element
Tropft an mir ab, im Grase zu versinken.
Was ists, das deine Seele von mir trennt?
Sie flieht, und möcht ich auch in dir ertrinken!
Dich kränkts nicht, wie mein Herz um dich entbrennt,
Küssest im Sturz nur diese schroffen Zinken;
Du bleibest, was du warst seit Tag und Jahren,
Ohn eingen Schmerz der Zeiten zu erfahren.

Hinweg aus diesem üppgen Schattengrund
Voll großer Pracht, die drückend mich erschüttert!
Bald grüßt beruhigt mein verstummter Mund
Den schlichten Winkel, wo sonst halb verwittert
Die kleine Bank und wo das Hüttchen stund;
Erinnrung reicht mit Lächeln die verbittert
Bis zur Betäubung süßen Zauberschalen;
So trink ich gierig die entzückten Qualen.

Hier schlang sich tausendmal ein junger Arm
Um meinen Hals mit inngem Wohlgefallen.
O säh ich mich, als Knaben sonder Harm,
Wie einst mit Necken durch die Haine wallen!
Ihr Hügel, von der *alten* Sonne warm,
Erscheint mir denn auf keinem von euch allen
Mein Ebenbild, in jugendlicher Frische
Hervorgesprungen aus dem Waldgebüsche?

Till out and over cliff-sides it is spent
And hurled, as to the valley you are sent.

Oh, it is here that nature parts her veil!
Her superhuman silence breaks, as she
Speaks to her spirit, tells herself a tale,
Hears herself, shows what she herself would see –
Yet she, more desolate than man, must fail
Still to escape from her own mystery!
Come then, impetuous waterfall! My heart
I bare to you, now let it burst apart

And take you in! In vain – you trickle down
Past me, your cool flood soaks into the grass.
What separates our souls? I long to drown
In yours, yet heedless of my love, alas,
You flee from me; from the cliff's jagged crown
You fall, and merely kiss it as you pass;
And still the same as days and years ago,
No sorrow at the flux of time you know.

Hence! this great splendour weighs upon my mind
And heart, this shady valley, this lush wood!
With dumb relief that simple place I'll find
Where, weather-worn, so long ago they stood:
The little bench, the hut. How well combined
These smiling memories are! Their sweetness would
Make drunk, their gall enchants; this pleasing cup
Of pain, how eagerly I drink it up!

A thousand times some youthful arm, with joy
Unfeigned, would here embrace me. Ah, could I
But see myself again, an artless boy
Wandering and sporting in these woodlands! Why,
You hills, when the same sun you can enjoy,
Warm then as now, can you not show me my
Young image, fresh as once it was and sprightly,
Out of the undergrowth still leaping lightly?

O komm, enthülle dich! dann sollst du mir
Mit Freundlichkeit ins dunkle Auge schauen!
Noch immer, guter Knabe, gleich ich dir,
Uns beiden wird nicht voreinander grauen!
So komm und laß mich unaufhaltsam hier
Mich deinem reinen Busen anvertrauen! –
Umsonst, daß ich die Arme nach dir strecke,
Den Boden, wo du gingst, mit Küssen decke!

Hier will ich denn laut schluchzend liegen bleiben,
Fühllos, und alles habe seinen Lauf! –
Mein Finger, matt, ins Gras beginnt zu schreiben:
Hin ist die Lust! hab alles seinen Lauf!
Da, plötzlich, hör ichs durch die Lüfte treiben,
Und ein entfernter Donner schreckt mich auf;
Elastisch angespannt mein ganzes Wesen
Ist von Gewitterluft wie neu genesen.

Sieh! wie die Wolken finstre Ballen schließen
Um den ehrwürdgen Trotz der Burgruine!
Von weitem schon hört man den alten Riesen,
Stumm harrt das Tal mit ungewisser Miene,
Der Kuckuck nur ruft sein einförmig Grüßen
Versteckt aus unerforschter Wildnis Grüne, –
Jetzt kracht die Wölbung, und verhallet lange,
Das wundervolle Schauspiel ist im Gange!

Ja nun, indes mit hoher Feuerhelle
Der Blitz die Stirn und Wange mir verklärt,
Ruf ich den lauten Segen in die grelle
Musik des Donners, die mein Wort bewährt:
O Tal! du meines Lebens andre Schwelle!
Du meiner tiefsten Kräfte stiller Herd!
Du meiner Liebe Wundernest! ich scheide,
Leb wohl! – und sei dein Engel mein Geleite!

O come, reveal yourself to me! You will
Look kindly into my dark eyes, for you
And I, dear youth, are like each other still;
No need for shrinking fear between us two.
Here let me pour out my whole heart, and spill
My soul in yours, for yours is clear and true!
– How vainly I reach out for what is gone,
How vainly kiss the ground you walked upon!

Here then I'll lie and sob aloud, prostrate,
Insensate, and let all things take their course.
My weak hand scribbles in the grass: 'Too late
For happiness! All things must take their course.'
Then suddenly I hear the winds debate,
And distant thunder startles me: new force
Invigorates me, in this air my whole
Being revives, this storm shall heal my soul!

Look, the clouds cluster darkly all about
That ruined tower's venerable pride!
Far off we hear the ancient giant's shout;
Uncertainly the valley waits, tongue-tied;
Only the cuckoo's same two notes call out
From the green trackless thicket where they hide –
Now heaven's vault cracks with long re-echoing din:
Now the marvellous spectacle can begin!

And now, as I can feel my face and brow
Transfigured by the lightning's brilliant flame,
I call aloud a blessing, and hear how
The thunder's song repeats it in my name:
Oh valley, second birthplace, then as now
Home of my deepest strength, and still the same
Nest of all love, all magic – stay beside
Me as I leave you, oh angelic guide!

Nimmersatte Liebe

So ist die Lieb! So ist die Lieb!
Mit Küssen nicht zu stillen:
Wer ist der Tor und will ein Sieb
Mit eitel Wasser füllen?
Und schöpfst du an die tausend Jahr,
Und küssest ewig, ewig gar,
Du tust ihr nie zu Willen.

Die Lieb, die Lieb hat alle Stund
Neu wunderlich Gelüsten;
Wir bissen uns die Lippen wund,
Da wir uns heute küßten.
Das Mädchen hielt in guter Ruh,
Wie's Lämmlein unterm Messer;
Ihr Auge bat: nur immer zu,
Je weher, desto besser!

So ist die Lieb, und war auch so,
Wie lang es Liebe gibt,
Und anders war Herr Salomo,
Der Weise, nicht verliebt.

Das verlassene Mägdlein

Früh, wann die Hähne krähn,
Eh die Sternlein verschwinden,
Muß ich am Herde stehn,
Muß Feuer zünden.

Schön ist der Flammen Schein,
Es springen die Funken;
Ich schaue so drein,
In Leid versunken.

Love Insatiable

For such is love, and such is love:
Mere kisses cannot still it;
What fool draws water in a sieve
And hopes that he will fill it?
Draw for a thousand centuries,
Kiss her with an eternal kiss:
Her want will still outwill it.

Love finds new fancies day by day
And curious delighting:
Her lips and mine are sore with play
Of kissing and of biting.
She, like a little slaughtered lamb,
Bore it with silent ardour,
And her eyes told me: here I am,
Come, hurt me, hurt me harder!

For such is love, and always so
It was, and so will be;
The wise King Solomon long ago
Loved just like you and me.

The Forsaken Girl

At cockcrow, with the stars
Not faded away,
I'm up and at the hearth;
The fire's to lay.

The flames make a fine blaze,
The sparks are leaping.
I'm heartsore as I gaze
And still half sleeping.

The Forsaken Lassie

The first cocks craw, the stars
Slowly awa are gyan.
An I maun tend the hearth
In this cauld dawn.

Flames mak a bonny bleeze,
Sparks upward flyin.
I stand an stand an gaze.
Dooncast an sighin.

Plötzlich, da kommt es mir,
Treuloser Knabe,
Daß ich die Nacht von dir
Geträumet habe.

Träne auf Träne dann
Stürzet hernieder;
So kommt der Tag heran –
O ging er wieder!

An die Geliebte

Wenn ich, von deinem Anschaun tief gestillt,
Mich stumm an deinem heilgen Wert vergnüge,
Dann hör ich recht die leisen Atemzüge
Des Engels, welcher sich in dir verhüllt.

Und ein erstaunt, ein fragend Lächeln quillt
Auf meinem Mund, ob mich kein Traum betrüge,
Daß nun in dir, zu ewiger Genüge,
Mein kühnster Wunsch, mein einzger, sich erfüllt?

Von Tiefe dann zu Tiefen stürzt mein Sinn,
Ich höre aus der Gottheit nächtger Ferne
Die Quellen des Geschicks melodisch rauschen.

Betäubt kehr ich den Blick nach oben hin,
Zum Himmel auf – da lächeln alle Sterne;
Ich kniee, ihrem Lichtgesang zu lauschen.

Sudden the memory comes:
Last night, my lover,
I saw you in my dreams;
You love another.

Oh, now they tumble down,
Tears hot and burning.
I wish the day were gone
And not returning!

O faithless lad, noo sudden
The memory gleams:
Yestreen ye cam unbidden
Intae ma dreams.

Doon drap the tears than,
Fast they doon fa.
So the day nears, an
Oh, gin 'twere awa!

To My Beloved

Veiled in your flesh, angelic life shines through,
Whose gentle sighing breath I seem to hear
When speechlessly, as if in sacred fear,
I gaze upon your face, and ever new,

Such joy fulfils me. Can it be in you
(My puzzled smile still wonders if a mere
Dream has deceived my heart) that now, that here,
My boldest wish, my only wish, comes true?

Oh then from deep to deep I plunge, I sense
The darkness of the godhead, where from far
The streams of destiny are murmuring

Melodiously; dazed, I look up, the immense
Night sky is smiling, and from every star
A music shines: I kneel to hear them sing.

Gesang Weylas

Du bist Orplid, mein Land!
Das ferne leuchtet;
Vom Meere dampfet dein besonnter Strand
Den Nebel, so der Götter Wange feuchtet.

Uralte Wasser steigen
Verjüngt um deine Hüften, Kind!
Vor deiner Gottheit beugen
Sich Könige, die deine Wärter sind.

Verborgenheit

Laß, o Welt, o laß mich sein!
Locket nicht mit Liebesgaben,
Laßt dies Herz alleine haben
Seine Wonne, seine Pein!

Was ich traure weiß ich nicht,
Es ist unbekanntes Wehe;
Immerdar durch Tränen sehe
Ich der Sonne liebes Licht.

Oft bin ich mir kaum bewußt,
Und die helle Freude zücket
Durch die Schwere, so mich drücket
Wonniglich in meiner Brust.

Laß, o Welt, o laß mich sein!
Locket nicht mit Liebesgaben,
Laßt dies Herz alleine haben
Seine Wonne, seine Pein!

The Song of Weyla

You are Orplid, my land,
Oh far-off light!
The faces of the gods grow fresh and bright
With sea-mist-moisture from your sunlit strand.

Ancient waters renew,
Rising about your limbs, their youth once more,
My child! Kings bow before
Your godhead, and attend on you.

Seclusion

World, oh world, oh let me be!
Let these love-gifts not entice me;
Solitary heart, suffice me
With your pain, your ecstasy!

Why I grieve I do not know:
When the sun's dear light appears
I must gaze at it through tears;
What is this mysterious woe?

Often, in my half-unknowing,
Sudden joy will flash and start
Through my heaviness of heart,
Like a sweet contentment flowing.

World, oh world, oh let me be!
Let these love-gifts not entice me;
Solitary heart, suffice me
With your pain, your ecstasy!

An eine Äolsharfe

Tu semper urges flebilibus modis
Mysten ademptum: nec tibi Vespero
Surgente decedunt amores,
Nec rapidum fugiente Solem.

Horaz

Angelehnt an die Efeuwand
Dieser alten Terrasse,
Du, einer luftgebornen Muse
Geheimnisvolles Saitenspiel,
Fang an,
Fange wieder an
Deine melodische Klage!

Ihr kommet, Winde, fern herüber,
Ach! von des Knaben,
Der mir so lieb war,
Frisch grünendem Hügel.
Und Frühlingsblüten unterweges streifend,
Übersättigt mit Wohlgerüchen,
Wie süß bedrängt ihr dies Herz!
Und säuselt her in die Saiten,
Angezogen von wohllautender Wehmut,
Wachsend im Zug meiner Sehnsucht,
Und hinsterbend wieder.

Aber auf einmal
Wie der Wind heftiger herstößt,
Ein holder Schrei der Harfe
Wiederholt, mir zu süßem Erschrecken,
Meiner Seele plötzliche Regung;
Und hier – die volle Rose streut, geschüttelt,
All ihre Blätter vor meine Füße!

To an Aeolian Harp

In plangent tones you mourn him continually,
Your dead lost Mystes; while still the evening star
  shines forth, while the swift dawn pursues it,
    Your love undimmed evermore laments him.

Horace

Leaning against the ivy-covered
Wall of this old terrace,
Mysterious instrument of a Muse
Born in the air, oh begin to sing,
Begin,
Once more begin to utter
Your melodious lament!

Oh winds, you are blowing,
Alas, from the freshly green
Grave-mound of the boy
I have loved so much.
And caressing spring blossoms on your way here,
Saturated with their fragrance,
How sweetly you besiege my heart!
And into these strings you murmur,
Drawn by sorrow's euphonious music,
Waxing in the movement of my heart's desire
And once more dying away.

But suddenly,
On a stronger gust of the wind,
How beautifully the harp cries out,
To my sweet alarm repeating
My soul's sudden emotion;
And look – the full-blown rose is shaken
And scatters all its petals at my feet!

Storchenbotschaft

Des Schäfers sein Haus und das steht auf zwei Rad,
Steht hoch auf der Heiden, so frühe, wie spat;
Und wenn nur ein mancher so'n Nachtquartier hätt!
Ein Schäfer tauscht nicht mit dem König sein Bett.

Und käm ihm zu Nacht auch was Seltsames vor,
Er betet sein Sprüchel und legt sich aufs Ohr;
Ein Geistlein, ein Hexlein, so lustige Wicht',
Sie klopfen ihm wohl, doch er antwortet nicht.

Einmal doch, da ward es ihm wirklich zu bunt:
Es knopert am Laden, es winselt der Hund;
Nun ziehet mein Schäfer den Riegel – ei schau!
Da stehen zwei Störche, der Mann und die Frau.

Das Pärchen, es machet ein schön Kompliment,
Es möchte gern reden, ach, wenn es nur könnt!
Was will mir das Ziefer? – ist so was erhört?
Doch ist mir wohl fröhliche Botschaft beschert?

Ihr seid wohl dahinten zu Hause am Rhein?
Ihr habt wohl mein Mädel gebissen ins Bein?
Nun weinet das Kind und die Mutter noch mehr,
Sie wünschet den Herzallerliebsten sich her?

Und wünschet daneben die Taufe bestellt:
Ein Lämmlein, ein Würstlein, ein Beutelein **Geld**?
So sagt nur, ich käm in zwei Tag oder drei,
Und grüßt mir mein Bübel und rührt ihm den Brei!

News from the Storks

The shepherd-lad's shelter, on two wheels it stands,
Day and night, away up on the wide open lands.
There's not many, he thinks, have a lodging so fine;
Let the king keep his palace, this little hut's mine!

And if he hears something go bump in the night,
He just says his prayers and then curls up tight.
A ghoulie or ghostie may knock on his wall,
But such comical gentry he heeds not at all.

One night, though, it's too much, it's really too bad!
Something's scratching the shutters, the dog's going mad.
So my shepherd unbolts them, and what does he see
But two storks standing there, man and wife,
        goodness me!

The couple, they make him a most polite bow,
And they surely would speak if they only knew how.
What can the brutes want? What a very queer thing!
But perhaps it's a message, some good news they bring?

So you come from the Rhine? from my sweetheart? –
        It's true!
You've been pecking her leg, there's a present from you!
And now the brat's yelling, she's crying as well;
My darling, she wants me, and sends you to tell!

The christening feast she'll be thinking about:
Lamb, sausages, money – a bagful, no doubt.
I'll be back in three days, tell her that's what I said;
Greet my little one from me, make sure he gets fed!

Doch halt! warum stellt ihr zu zweien euch ein?
Es werden doch, hoff ich, nicht Zwillinge sein? –
Da klappern die Störche im lustigsten Ton,
Sie nicken und knicksen und fliegen davon.

Jägerlied

Zierlich ist des Vogels Tritt im Schnee,
Wenn er wandelt af des Berges Höh:
Zierlicher schreibt Liebchens liebe Hand,
Schreibt ein Brieflein mir in ferne Land'.

In die Lüfte hoch ein Reiher steigt,
Dahin weder Pfeil noch Kugel fleugt:
Tausendmal so hoch und so geschwind
Die Gedanken treuer Liebe sind.

Schön-Rohtraut

Wie heißt König Ringangs Töchterlein?
    Rohtraut, Schön-Rohtraut.
Was tut sie denn den ganzen Tag,
Da sie wohl nicht spinnen und nähen mag?
    Tut fischen und jagen.
O daß ich doch ihr Jäger wär!
Fischen und jagen freute mich sehr.
    – Schweig stille, mein Herze!

Und über eine kleine Weil,
    Rohtraut, Schön-Rohtraut,
So dient der Knab auf Ringangs Schloß
In Jägertracht und hat ein Roß,
    Mit Rohtraut zu jagen.
O daß ich doch ein Königssohn wär!
Rohtraut, Schön-Rohtraut lieb ich so sehr.
    – Schweig stille, mein Herze!

But stop! why have two of you come here? – Oh, God!
Surely – surely you didn't bring twins? – And they nod,
The storks nod and they curtsey and merrily thrash
With their wings, and fly off and are gone in a flash.

A Huntsman's Song

Daintily a bird's claw prints the snows
As upon the mountain heights it goes:
Daintily my darling's little hand
Writes to greet me in a far-off land.

High the heron soars into the blue
Where no shot nor arrow can pursue:
And a thousand times so swift and high
To their goal the thoughts of true love fly.

Sweet-Rohtraut

King Ringang's daughter, oh what is her name?
    Rohtraut, Sweet-Rohtraut.
And how does she pass the live-long day?
Neither sewing nor spinning, so they say.
    She goes fishing and hunting.
Oh, her hunting-squire if I could but be!
Fishing and hunting, what joy for me!
    – Be silent, my heart!

And after and after a little while,
    Rohtraut, Sweet-Rohtraut,
The boy has a horse and a huntsman's gear
And serves King Ringang in the castle here,
    And rides with Rohtraut.
Oh, a prince, a prince if I could but be!
For I love Sweet-Rohtraut so tenderly.
    – Be silent, my heart!

Einsmals sie ruhten am Eichenbaum,
    Da lacht Schön-Rohtraut:
Was siehst mich an so wunniglich?
Wenn du das Herz hast, küsse mich!
    Ach! erschrak der Knabe!
Doch denket er: mir ists vergunnt,
Und küsset Schön-Rohtraut auf den Mund.
    – Schweig stille, mein Herze!

Darauf sie ritten schweigend heim,
    Rohtraut, Schön-Rohtraut;
Es jauchzt der Knab in seinem Sinn:
Und würdst du heute Kaiserin,
    Mich sollts nicht kränken:
Ihr tausend Blätter im Walde wißt,
Ich hab Schön-Rohtrauts Mund geküßt!
    – Schweig stille, mein Herze!

Abschied

Unangeklopft ein Herr tritt abends bei mir ein:
'Ich habe die Ehr, Ihr Rezensent zu sein.'
Sofort nimmt er das Licht in die Hand,
Besieht lang meinen Schatten an der Wand,
Rückt nah und fern: 'Nun, lieber junger Mann,
Sehn Sie doch gefälligst mal Ihre Nas so von der
    Seite an!
Sie geben zu, daß das ein Auswuchs is.'
– Das? Alle Wetter – gewiß!
Ei Hasen! ich dachte nicht,
All mein Lebtage nicht,
Daß ich so eine Weltsnase führt im Gesicht!!

Der Mann sprach noch verschiednes hin und her,
Ich weiß, auf meine Ehre, nicht mehr;
Meinte vielleicht, ich sollt ihm beichten.
Zuletzt stand er auf; ich tat ihm leuchten.

They rested under an oak one day,
   And she laughed, Sweet-Rohtraut:
Come, little soft-eyes, why do you stare?
Be bold and kiss me now if you dare!
   Oh, how the boy trembled!
But: I have her leave! to himself he said,
And he kissed Sweet-Rohtraut's lips so red.
   – Be silent, my heart!

Then they rode home with never a word,
   Rohtraut, Sweet-Rohtraut;
And with joy his thoughts were leaping still:
Let them make her an empress now if they will,
   I'll not be minding!
You thousand leaves in the forest can say
Sweet-Rohtraut's lips I have kissed today!
   – Be silent, my heart!

Good Riddance

Unannounced, one evening, in came a visitor:
'I have the honour to be your critic, sir.'
At once he took the lamp in his hand
And my shadow on the wall for a time he scanned,
From close, from a distance. 'Young man, you must
   admit:
Your nose – now please, just take a sideways look at it:
That nose is an excrescence, by your leave.'
– What? Now, by God, I do believe
You're right! Just fancy! How could one suppose,
Never in my life did I suppose,
That my face possessed so monstrous a nose!

The man said a few other things as well;
What they were, truly I now can't tell;
He expected a confession, I don't doubt.
Then he got up to go; I lighted him out.

Wie wir nun an der Treppe sind,
Da geb ich ihm, ganz froh gesinnt,
Einen kleinen Tritt,
Nur so von hinten aufs Gesäße, mit –
Alle Hagel! ward das ein Gerumpel,
Ein Gepurzel, ein Gehumpel!
Dergleichen hab ich nie gesehn,
All mein Lebtage nicht gesehn
Einen Menschen so rasch die Trepp hinabgehn!

And when the two of us reached the stair,
My high spirits were such that then and there
A parting present from me he got:
Just a little kick on a posterior spot –
Oh, my goodness me, what a tumbling,
What a totter and a clatter and a rumbling!
I never have seen, I do declare,
Never in my life, I do declare,
A man get so quickly to the bottom of a stair!

1837–1863

Gebet

Herr! schicke, was du willt,
Ein Liebes oder Leides;
Ich bin vergnügt, daß beides
Aus Deinen Händen quillt.

Wollest mit Freuden
Und wollest mit Leiden
Mich nicht überschütten!
Doch in der Mitten
Liegt holdes Bescheiden.

Johann Kepler

Gestern, als ich vom nächtlichen Lager den Stern mir in
    Osten
  Lang betrachtete, den dort mit dem rötlichen Licht,
Und des Mannes gedachte, der seine Bahnen zu messen,
  Von dem Gotte gereizt, himmlischer Pflicht sich ergab,
Durch beharrlichen Fleiß der Armut grimmigen Stachel
  Zu versöhnen, umsonst, und zu verachten bemüht:
Mir entbrannte mein Herz von Wehmut bitter; ach!
    dacht ich,
  Wußten die Himmlischen dir, Meister, kein besseres Los?
Wie ein Dichter den Helden sich wählt, wie Homer von
    Achilles'
  Göttlichem Adel gerührt, schön im Gesang ihn erhob,
Also wandtest du ganz nach jenem Gestirne die Kräfte,
  Sein gewaltiger Gang war dir ein ewiges Lied.

1837–1863

A Prayer

Lord, send what is thy will,
Blessing or pain to me:
Since both must come from thee,
I love thy bounty still.

I ask not too much woe,
Not too much joy to fill
My heart to overflow:
Contentment sweet and wise
Midway between them lies.

Johann Kepler

Last night, lying in bed and gazing long at that eastern
   Star, the one with the red tinge, I remembered the man
Who devoted himself to the task of measuring its courses
   (For by behest of the gods such a high duty was his).
Under the furious goad of poverty, tireless he laboured
   To appease it, or hold hunger in scorn, but in vain.
Bitter the sorrow that burned in my heart for him: Master,
     I wondered,
   Could the immortals not grant you a more merciful fate?
Even as a poet chooses a hero, as Homer was touched by
   Noble Achilles, and raised him to the skies in his verse,
So you turned to that planet the whole of your genius, its
     mighty
   Circuit became your theme, ever your song and your joy.

Doch so bewegt sich kein Gott von seinem goldenen Sitze,
　　Holdem Gesange geneigt, den zu erretten, herab,
Dem die höhere Macht die dunkeln Tage bestimmt hat,
　　Und euch Sterne berührt nimmer ein Menschengeschick;
Ihr geht über dem Haupte des Weisen oder des Toren
　　Euren seligen Weg ewig gelassen dahin!

An den Schlaf

Somne levis! quanquam certissima mortis imago,
　　Consortem cupio te tamen esse tori.
Alma quies, optata, veni! nam sic sine vita
　　Vivere, quam suave est, sic sine morte mori!

Schlaf! süßer Schlaf! obwohl dem Tod wie du nichts
　　　gleicht,
　　Auf diesem Lager doch willkommen heiß ich dich!
Denn ohne Leben so, wie lieblich lebt es sich!
　　So weit vom Sterben, ach, wie stirbt es sich so leicht!

Bei Tagesanbruch

'Sage doch, wird es denn heute nicht Tag? es dämmert so
　　　lange,
　　Und schon zu Hunderten, horch! singen die Lerchen
　　　im Feld.'
Immer ja saugt ihr lichtbegieriges Auge die ersten
　　Strahlen hinweg, und so wächset nur langsam der Tag.

Yet there's no god, though he love sweet poetry, who from
    his golden
  Seat will arise and come down, rescuer-like, to befriend
One whom a higher decree has condemned to a lifetime of
    dark days.
  When were the stars ever moved by a mere human distress?
They pass by, high over the heads of the wise and the foolish,
  Unperturbed in their calm, blest on their infinite way.

To Sleep

Kindly sleep, close kinsman to death and so close in his likeness,
  Nevertheless I desire you as a friend for my bed.
Come, oh beloved repose! for such life without life is so gentle,
  And to be dead yet alive, what can compare with such joy!

Sleep, gentle sleep! though closely you resemble death,
Upon my bed I still desire your company.
Come! for how sweet it is, that quiet lifeless life!
And when death is not death, how willingly we die!

At Daybreak

  'Tell me, why does the day not break? So long it's been
    dawning,
    And I hear larks in the fields, hundreds already in song.'
  Larks' eyes long for the light, and they greedily drink in
    the sun's first
    Rays as it rises: their thirst hinders the coming of day.

Märchen vom sichern Mann

Soll ich vom sicheren Mann ein Märchen erzählen, so höret!
– Etliche sagen, ihn habe die steinerne Kröte geboren.
Also heißet ein mächtiger Fels in den Bergen des
    Schwarzwalds,
Stumpf und breit, voll Warzen, der haßlichen Kröte
    vergleichbar.
Darin lag er und schlief bis nach den Tagen der Sündflut.
Nämlich es war sein Vater ein Waldmensch, tückisch und
    grausam,
Allen Göttern ein Greul und allen Nymphen gefürchtet.
Ihm nicht durchaus gleich ist der Sohn, doch immer ein
    Unhold;
Riesenhaft an Gestalt, von breitem Rücken und Schultern.
Ehmals ging er fast nackt, unehrbarlich; aber seit Menschen-
Denken im rauh grauhärenen Rock, mit schrecklichen
    Stiefeln.
Grauliche Borsten bedecken sein Haupt und es starret der Bart
    ihm.
(Heimlich besucht ihn, heißt es, der Igelslocher Balbierer
In der Höhle, woselbst er ihm dient wie der sorgsame
    Gärtner,
Wenn er die Hecken stutzt mit der unermeßlichen Schere.)
Lauter Nichts ist sein Tun und voll von törichten Grillen:
Wenn er herniedersteigt vom Gebirg bei nächtlicher Weile,
Laut im Gespräch mit sich selbst, und oft ingrimmigen
    Herzens
Weg- und Meilenzeiger mit *einem* gemessenen Tritt knickt
(Denn die hasset er bis auf den Tod, unbilligerweise);

The Tale of the Safe and Sound Man

Now I will tell you a tale of the Safe and Sound Man, if
    you'll listen.
– Who was his mother? The great Stone Toad, according to
    some folk.
That is the name of a mighty great rock in the Black Forest
    mountains,
Stumpy and broad, full of warts, like the ugly old toad it
    resembles.
Deep inside it he lay, and slept till the Flood was well over.
As for his father, well, he was a wood-demon, wild and
    malicious;
All the gods thought him a monster, and nymphs fled from
    him in terror.
Our man's not quite as bad, but a desperate rascal for all that:
He's gigantic of stature, broad-backed and with great broad
    shoulders.
Once, most improperly, he went about almost naked, but
    now since
Time immemorial he wears his grey hairy coat and his
    fearsome
Boots. His head bristles with dirty grey thatch, and his beard
    is a thicket.
(Some say the barber from Igelsloch comes and secretly trims it,
Visiting him in his cave, as a careful gardener will visit
Hedges to keep them neat, with enormous shears for the
    clipping.)
Idly he spends his time, in the foolish pranks of his whimsy:
As when he clambers down from his mountain heights after
    nightfall,
Muttering aloud to himself; and often, enraged by the
    signposts
Or the milestones he sees (for he hates such things, very oddly),
Knocks them all flat with a single kick well aimed and delivered.

Oder auch wenn er zur Winterzeit ins beschneiete Blachfeld
Oft sich der Länge nach streckt und, aufgestanden, an
     seinem
Konterfei sich ergötzt, mit bergerschütterndem Lachen.

Aber nun lag er einmal mittags in seiner Behausung,
Seinen geliebtesten Fraß zu verdaun, saftstrotzende Rüben,
Zu dem geräucherten Speck, den die Bauern ihm bringen
     vertragsweis;
Plötzlich erfüllete wonniger Glanz die Wände der Höhle:
Lolegrin stand vor ihm: der liebliche Götterjüngling,
Welcher ein Lustigmacher bestellt ist seligen Göttern,
(Sonst nur auf Orplid gesehn, denn andere Lande vermied er)
Weylas schalkischer Sohn, mit dem Narrenkranz um die
     Schläfe,
Zierlich aus blauen Glocken und Küchenschelle geflochten.
Er nun redte den Ruhenden an mit trüglichem Ernste:
'Suckelborst, sicherer Mann, sei gegrüßt! und höre
     vertraulich
Was die Himmlischen dir durch meine Sendung entbieten.
– Sämtlich ehren sie deinen Verstand und gute Gemütsart
Sowie deine Geburt: es war dein Vater ein Halbgott
Und desgleichen auch hielten sie dich stets; aber in *einem*
Bist du ihnen nicht recht; das sollt du jetzo vernehmen.
Bleibe nur, Lieber, getrost so liegen – ich setze bescheiden
Mich auf den Absatzrand hier deines würdigen Stiefels,
Der wie ein Felsblock ragt, und unschwer bin ich zu tragen.

Siehe, Serachadan zeugete dich mit der Riesenkröte,
Seine unsterbliche Kraft in ihrem Leibe verschließend,
Da sie noch lebend war; doch gleich nach ihrer Empfängnis

Or when the snow falls deep on the wintry fields, he will
 sometimes
Lie full length in it, get up again and look down at his
 imprint,
Greatly delighted to see it, his laughter shaking the mountains.

One afternoon, then, he lay in his lair, digesting his luncheon,
Full of his favourite fodder, the fattest and juiciest turnips
Well mixed with the smoked bacon that farmers bring him
 by contract,
When of a sudden the walls of his cave grew wondrously radiant:
Lolegrin stood there before him, the charmer, the beautiful
 god-boy,
Who to the blessèd gods is appointed as their entertainer
(Once he lived only in Orplid, for other lands he avoided),
Weyla's mischievous son; on his head was the jester's garland,
Prettily woven from wild anemone-flowers and blue bells.
He, with a serious air, thus addressed the recumbent colossus:
'Greetings, O Suckelborst, Safe and Sound Man! You must
 now listen closely
To what the heavenly gods by my mission and errand would
 tell you.
– They all respect you for your good sense and your good
 disposition,
And indeed for your birth: for yours was a half-divine father,
And in their eyes you too are a demigod. Only in one point
They are not satisfied with you; and now I shall tell you what
 that is.
But, my dear fellow, remain lying down – I'll be modestly seated
Here on the edge of the heel of your worthy boot, for it juts up
Just like a mountain rock; I am light, and shall not be a burden.

Hear me! Serachadan fathered you on the Great Toad, his
 immortal
Strength was stored in her body while she still lived, but no
 sooner
Had he begotten you thus and no sooner had she then
 conceived you,

Ward sie verwandelt in Stein und hauchte dein Vater den
    Geist aus.
Aber du schliefest im Mutterleib neun Monde und drüber,
Denn im zehnten kamen die großen Wasser auf Erden;
Vierzig Tage lang strömte der Regen und vierzig Nächte
Auf die sündige Welt, so Tiere wie Menschen ersäufend;
Eine einzige See war über die Lande ergossen,
Über Gebirg und Tal, und deckte die wolkigen Gipfel.
Doch du lagest zufrieden in deinem Felsen verborgen,
So wie die Auster ruht in festverschlossenen Schalen
Oder des Meeres Preis, die unbezahlbare Perle.
Götter segneten deinen Schlaf mit hohen Gesichten,
Zeigten der Schöpfung Heimliches dir, wie alles geworden:
Erst, wie der Erdball, ganz mit wirkenden Kräften
    geschwängert,
Einst dem dunkelen Nichts entschwebte, zusamt den
    Gestirnen;
Wie mit Gras und Kraut sich zuerst der Boden begrünte,
Wie aus der Erde Milch, so sie hegt im inneren Herzen,
Wurde des Fleisches Gebild, das zarte, darinnen der Geist
    wohnt,
Tier- und Menschengeschlecht, denn erdgeboren sind beide.
Zudem sang dir dein Traum der Völker späteste Zukunft,
So wie der Throne Wechselgeschick und der Könige Taten,
Ja, du sahst den verborgenen Rat der ewigen Götter.
Solches vergönnten sie dir, auf daß du, ein herrlicher Lehrer

Than she was changed into stone, and he gave up the ghost
  at the same time.
But you slept on in the womb nine months and more, for
  the tenth month,
That was when mighty waters came down on the earth to
  engulf it;
Forty days long did the rain stream down and forty nights also,
Down on the sinful world; man and beast were drowned in
  the deluge.
There was a single great sea overwhelming the earth's lands,
  rising
Over the mountains and valleys, the cloudy peaks were all
  covered.
But you still lay there contented, concealed in the rock of
  your fastness,
Just like an oyster lying enclosed in its shell very firmly,
Or as the prize of the ocean, the pearl beyond price, remains
  hidden.
Lofty visions were sent by the gods to your sleep as you lay
  there,
Blessing your innermost eye with creation's secrets: they
  showed you
First how the globe of the earth long ago, all pregnant with
  active
Powers, floated free from the darksome void, all the stars
  coming with it,
And how its soil was covered with grass and the green
  vegetation;
How from the milk that the earth secretes in its innermost centre
Flesh grew into its delicate shape, which the spirit inhabits,
Human and animal kinds, for they all were born as the earth's
  gifts.
And in your dream-song you learnt the remotest future of
  peoples,
Likewise the deeds of kings and the changing fates of their
  kingdoms;
Yes, and you saw the eternal gods in their high secret council.
Such great privileges did they grant you, to make you a famous

Oder ein Seher, die Wahrheit wiederum andern verkündest;
Nicht den Menschen sowohl, die da leben und wandeln auf
    Erden –
Ihnen ja dient nur wenig zu wissen, – ich meine die Geister
Unten im Schattengefild, die alten Weisen und Helden,
Welche da traurig sitzen und forschen das hohe Verhängnis,
Schweigsam immerdar, des erquicklichen Wortes entbehrend.
Aber vergebens harren sie dein, dieweil du ja gänzlich
Deines erhabnen Berufs nicht denkst. Laß, Alter, mich offen
Dir gestehen, so, wie du es bisher getrieben, erscheinst du
Weder ein Halbgott, noch ein Begeisteter, sondern ein
    Schweinpelz.
Greulichem Fraß nachtrachtest du nur und sinnest auf Unheil;
Steigest des Nachts in den Fluß, bis über die Kniee gestiefelt,
Trennest die Bänder los an den Flößen und schleuderst die
    Balken
Weit hinein in das Land, den ehrlichen Flößern zum Torten.
Taglang trollest du müßig umher im wilden Gebirge,
Ahmest das Grunzen des Keulers nach und lockest sein
    Weibchen,
Greifest, wenn sie nun rennt durch den Busch, die Sau bei den
    Ohren,
Zwickst die wütende, grausam an ihrem Geschreie dich
    weidend.
Siehe, dies wissen wir wohl, denn jegliches sehen die Götter.
Aber du reize sie länger nicht mehr! es möchte dich reuen.
Schmeidige doch ein weniges deine borstige Seele!
Suche zusammen dein Wissen und lichte die rußigen
    Kammern
Deines Gehirns und besinne dich wohl auf alles und jedes,
Was dir geoffenbart; dann nimm den Griffel und zeichn es

Teacher or seer, who in time would pass these truths on
    to others;
Not so much to mankind, the earth-dwellers who walk on
    the earth's ways –
Little use they have for knowledge – I mean the spirits who
    dwell down
Under the earth in the fields of shadows, old sages and heroes
Sitting there sadly and pondering the world's high destiny, silent
Ever and speechless, for the refreshment of words is denied
    them.
But in vain they await you, for you have forgotten entirely
Your sublime calling, you give it no thought. Old fellow, if I
    may
Speak to you frankly, your life hitherto has been
    un-demigodlike,
And unlike that of a seer: you have lived like a slubberdegullion.
Beastly fodder is all you eat, all you do is make mischief:
Wading at night in the river for instance, with thigh-length
    boots on,
Undoing ropes from the loaded rafts, and picking up logs and
Hurling them far from the water, to spoil honest lumbermen's
    business.
All day long you go sauntering idly about in the mountains,
Grunting like the wild boar, to entice his mate from him,
    then you
Grab the sow by the ears when she comes running up
    through the bushes,
Cruelly tweaking the furious beast and enjoying her squealing.
Yes, we know all about this; for nothing escapes the gods'
    notice.
But now I warn you, provoke them no longer, or you may
    regret it.
Come, take your unkempt nature in hand and refine it a little!
Gather your wits, and let some light into the sooty recesses
Of your brain, and take cognizance now of each thing and all
    things
That were revealed to you; then take a stylus and write it down
    nicely,

Fein mit Fleiß in ein Buch, damit es daure und bleibe;
Leg den Toten es aus in der Unterwelt! Sicherlich weißt du
Wohl die Pfade dahin und den Eingang, welcher dich nicht
    schreckt,
Denn du bist ja der sichere Mann mit den wackeren Stiefeln.
Lieber, und also scheid ich. Ade! wir sehen uns wieder.'

Sprach es, der schelmische Gott, und ließ den Alten alleine.
Der nun war wie verstürzt und stand ihm fast der Verstand
    still.
Halblaut hebt er zu brummen erst an und endlich zu fluchen,
Schandbare Worte zumal, gottloseste, nicht zu beschreiben.
Aber nachdem die Galle verraucht war und die Empörung,
Hielt er inne und schwieg; denn jetzo gemahnte der Geist ihn,
Nicht zu trotzen den Himmlischen, deren doch immer die
    Macht ist,
Sondern zu folgen vielmehr. Und alsbald wühlt sein
    Gedanke
Rückwärts durch der Jahrtausende Wust, bis tief wo er
    selber
Noch ein Ungeborener träumte die Wehen der Schöpfung,
(Denn so sagte der Gott und Götter werden nicht lügen).
Aber da deucht es ihm Nacht, dickfinstere; wo er
    umhertappt,
Nirgend ist noch ein Halt und noch kein Nagel geschlagen,
Anzuhängen die Wucht der wundersamen Gedanken,
Welche der Gott ihm erregt in seiner erhabenen Seele;
Und so kam er zu nichts und schwitzete wie ein Magister.
Endlich ward ihm geschenkt, daß er flugs dahin sich
    bedachte:
Erst ein Buch sich zu schaffen, ein unbeschriebenes, großes,

Diligently, in a book, that it may be preserved and recorded.
Tell the whole tale to the dead in the underworld! You know
    the way there,
I'll be bound, and you know the entrance, and it will not
    scare you,
For you are, after all, the Safe and Sound Man with the
    big boots.
Now, my dear fellow, I'll leave you. Goodbye, until our next
    meeting!'

Roguishly thus the god spoke, and left our friend to his own
    thoughts.
As for him, his mind boggled and nearly came to a standstill.
Under his breath he grumbled at first, and then he yelled curses,
Uttered most godless and shameful words, which we cannot
    repeat here.
But when he had given vent to his gall, and puffed all his
    rage out,
He fell silent: the spirit within him admonished and warned him
Not to defy the immortals, for power is always on their side,
But to obey them rather. And straightway, burrowing
    backwards
Through the wastes of the ages, his thought returned to the
    deep point
Where he himself, still unborn, had dreamt the pains of creation
(For so the god had said, and the words of a god must be
    truthful).
But when he got there, all seemed dark, and he groped in a
    thick night,
Finding no place of support, no nail driven in where he
    might now
Hang up the weight of the wondrous thoughts that once had
    possessed him
When his exalted soul had been stirred by the god's inspiration;
So there he sat nonplussed, like a dominie sweating his
    brains out.
But, enlightened at last, he resolved of a sudden as follows:
First, he must make a book for himself, blank pages to write on,

Seinen Fäusten gerecht und wert des künftigen Inhalts.
Wie er solches erreicht, o Muse, dies hilf mir verkünden!

Längst war die Sonne hinab, und Nacht beherrschte den
    Erdkreis
Seit vier Stunden, da hebt der sichere Mann sich vom Lager,
Setzet den runden Hut auf das Haupt und fasset den Wander-
Stab und verlässet die Höhle. Gemächlich steigt er
    bergaufwärts,
Redt mit sich selber dabei und brummt nach seiner
    Gewohnheit.

Aber nun hub sich der Mond auch schon in leuchtender
    Schöne
Rein am Forchenwalde herauf und erhellte die Gegend,
Samt der Höhe von Igelsloch, wo nun Suckelborst anlangt.
Kaum erst hatte der Wächter die zwölfte Stunde gerufen,
Alles ist ruhig im Dorf und nirgend ein Licht mehr zu sehen,
Nicht in den Kunkelstuben gesellig spinnender Mägdlein,
Nicht am einsamen Stuhle des Webers oder im Wirtshaus,
Mann und Weib im Bette, die Last des Tages verschlafend.

Suckelborst tritt nun sacht vor die nächstgelegene Scheuer,
Misset die zween Torflügel, die Höhe sowohl wie die Breite,
Still mit zufriedenem Blick (auch waren sie nicht von den
    kleinsten,
Aber er selbst war größer denn sie, dieweil er ein Riese).
Schloß und Riegel betrachtet er wohl, kneipt dann mit dem
    Finger
Ab den Kloben und öffnet das Tor und hebet die Flügel

Big enough for his great fists, and worthy of what he would
    write there.
Teach me, O Muse, now to tell how this great task was
    accomplished.

Long past sunset it was, and the land had been covered in
    darkness
Now for four hours, when the Safe and Sound Man rose up
    from his couch; he
Put on his great round hat, and left his cave with his walking-
Stick in his hand. With commodious pace he made his way
    downhill,
Talking the while to himself and muttering as was his custom.

Now the moon had risen as well in its radiant beauty
Over the Forchenwald, and was shedding its light on the region
And on the hill where Igelsloch stands, just as Suckelborst got
    there.
All was silent now, the night-watchman had scarcely called
    midnight,
And there was not a light to be seen as the whole village
    slumbered,
Not in the parlours where chattering girls had sat over their
    spinning,
Not by the weaver's lonely loom, and not in the tavern;
Man and wife were in bed, sleeping off the burdens of daytime.

Suckelborst now took a look at the first barn door that he
    came to,
Eyed it with silent approval to measure it heightwise
    and widthwise
(And we must add that these double doors were nothing if
    not big,
But he was bigger than they were, because, you see, he was a
    giant).
Having inspected the lock and the bolt, he then with his finger
Nipped off the hook and opened the door and lifted its
    two wings

Leicht aus den Angeln und lehnt an die Wand sie
    übereinander.
Alsbald schaut er sich um nach des Nachbars Scheuer und
    schreitet
Zu demselben Geschäft und raubet die mächtigen Tore
Stellt zu den vorigen sie an die Wand und also fort macht er
Weiter im Gäßchen hinauf, bis er dem fünften und sechsten
Bauern auf gleiche Weise die Tenne gelüftet. Am Ende
Überzählt er die Stücke: es waren gerade ein Dutzend
Blätter, und fehlte nur noch, daß er mit sauberen Stricken
Hinten die Öhre der Angeln verband, da war es ein
    Schreibbuch
Gar ein stattliches; doch dies blieb ein Geschäft für daheime.
Also nimmt er es unter den Arm, das Werk, und trollt sich.

Unterdes war aufschauernd vom Schlaf der schnarchenden
    Bauern
Einer erwacht und hörte des schwer Entwandelnden Fußtritt.
Hastig entrauscht er dem Lager und stößt am niedrigen
    Fenster
Rasch den Schieber zurück und horcht und sieht mit
    Entsetzen
Rings im mondlichen Dorf der Scheuern finstere Rachen
Offen stehn; da fährt er voll Angst in die lederne Hose
(Beide Füße verkehrt, den linken macht er zum rechten)
Rüttelt sein Weib und redet zu ihr die eifrigen Worte:
'Käthe! steh auf! Der sichere Mann – ich hab ihn
    vernommen –
Hat wie der Feind im Flecken hantiert und die Scheuern
    geplündert!
Schau im Hause mir nach und im Stall! ich laufe zum
    Schulzen.'

Easily out of their hinges and leaned them against the stone
    wall, one
Over the other. Proceeding at once to the neighbouring
    barn, he
Did the same job, purloined the great doors, and leaned them
    together
With the others against the wall. And thus he continued
Right up the village street, until in the same manner five or
Six of the farmers had had their threshing-floors aired. In
    conclusion
Our friend counted his spoils, and there were exactly a dozen
Leaves; now all that was left to be done was to tie them
    up neatly,
Roping the eyes of the hinges together to make a most handsome
Exercise-book. But that was a job better done back at home; so,
Picking his work up and tucking it under one arm, off he trotted.

Meanwhile one of the snoring peasants, upstartled from
    deep sleep,
Opened his eyes and heard a thump-thump as of footsteps
    departing.
Quickly he jumped out of bed and in haste undid the low
    window,
Listened and looked out, and to his horror and great
    consternation
Saw the black gaping wide-open barns all over the moonlit
Village. Then straight into his leather breeches he jumped in
    a panic
(Putting them on wrong way round, mistaking his left for his
    right foot),
Woke up his wife and in words of great agitation addressed her:
'Käthe, get up! It's the Safe and Sound Man – I heard him,
    that devil –
He's paid a visit, he's raided the village, the barns are all
    plundered!
You go and look round the house and the stable! I'm off to
    the mayor.'

Also stürmt er hinaus. Doch tut er selber im Hof erst
Noch einen Blick in die Ställe, ob auch sein Vieh noch
      vorhanden;
Aber da fehlte kein Schweif, und es muht ihm entgegen
      die Schecke,
Meint, es wär Fütternszeit; er aber enteilt in die Gasse,
Klopft unterwegs dem Büttel am Laden und ruft ihm das
      Wort zu:
'Michel, heraus! mach Lärm! Der sichere Mann hat den
      Flecken
Heimgesucht und die Scheuern erbrochen und übel
      gewirtschaft't!'
Solches noch redend hinweg schon lief er und weckte den
      Schultheiß,
Weckte den Bürgermeister und andere seiner Gefreundte.
Alsbald wurden die Straßen lebendig, es staunten die Männer,
Stießen Verwünschungen aus, im Chor lamentierten die
      Weiber,
Jeder durchmusterte seinen Besitz, und wenig getröstet,
Als kein größerer Schaden herauskam, fielen mit Unrecht
Über den Wächter die grimmigsten her und schrieen: 'Du
      Schlafratz!
Du keinnütziger Tropf!' und ballten die bäurischen Fäuste,
Ihn zu bläuen, und nahmen auch nur mit Mühe Vernunft an.
Endlich zerstreuten sie sich zur Ruhe; doch stellte der
      Schultheiß
Wachen noch aus für den Fall, daß der Unhold noch einmal
      käme.

Suckelborst hatte derweil schon wieder die Höhle gewonnen,
Welche von vorn gar weit und hoch in den Felsen sich wölbte.
Duftende Kiefern umschatteten, riesige, dunkel den Eingang.
Hier denn leget er nieder die ungeheuren Tore,
Und sich selber dazu, des goldenen Schlafes genießend.

And off he rushed; though not without taking a good look
    himself out-
Side in the yard, at the stables and byres, and counting his
    livestock.
But not a head was missing; the spotted cow mooed at him,
    thinking
It must be feeding-time. So into the street he now hurried,
Knocked as he passed on the bailiff's shutter and shouted to
    rouse him:
'Michel, get up and raise the alarm! The Safe and Sound
    Man has
Raided the village and broken the barn doors and done us
    a mischief!'
Still so shouting, he hurried on further and wakened the mayor,
Wakened the burgomaster and other friends in the village.
Soon the streets were a-swarm with people, the men in
    amazement
Stood there exclaiming and cursing, the women lamented in
    chorus.
Each man checked his own property, but they then took little
    comfort
Finding they'd suffered no further loss, and some of the angriest
Turned on the night watchman very unfairly, yelling 'You dozy
Lieabed, useless tramp that you are!' and clenching their rustic
Fists at him, and it was hard to persuade them to come to
    their senses.
Finally they dispersed and went back to bed, but the mayor
Put some more watchmen in place, just in case the monster
    should come back.

Suckelborst had in the meantime regained his cavernous
    dwelling;
Wide and high at the front its entrance gaped in the cliff face,
Shaded by tall odoriferous pine-trees, dark and gigantic.
Here he laid down the enormous doors, and lay down himself
    too,
And for a while the pleasures of golden slumber possessed him.

Aber sobald die Sonne nur zwischen den Bäumen
    hereinschien,
Gleich an die Arbeit machet er sich, die Tore zu heften.
Saubere Stricke schon lagen bereit, gestohlene freilich;
Und er ordnet die Blätter mit sinnigen Blicken und füget
Vorn und hinten zur Decke die schönsten (sie waren des
    Schulzen,
Künstlich über das Kreuz mit roten Leisten beschlagen).
Aber auf einmal jetzt, in des stattlichen Werkes Betrachtung,
Wächst ihm der Geist, und er nimmt die mächtige Kohle vom
    Boden,
Legt vor das offene Buch sich nieder und schreibet aus
    Kräften,
Striche, so grad wie krumm, in unnachsagbaren Sprachen,
Kratzt und schreibt und brummelt dabei mit zufriedenem
    Nachdruck.
Anderthalb Tag arbeitet er so, kaum gönnet er Zeit sich,
Speise zu nehmen und Trank, bis die letzte Seite gefüllt ist,
Endlich am Schluß denn folget das Punktum, groß wie ein
    Kindskopf.
Tief aufschnaufend erhebet er sich, sein Buch zuschmetternd.

Jetzo, nachdem er das Herz sich gestärkt mit reichlicher
    Mahlzeit,
Nimmt er den Hut und den Stock und reiset. Auf einsamen
    Pfaden
Stets gen Mitternacht läuft er, denn dies ist der Weg zu
    den Toten.
Schon mit dem siebenten Morgen erreicht er die finstere
    Pforte.
Purpurn streifte soeben die Morgenröte den Himmel,
Welche den lebenden Menschen das Licht des Tages
    verkündet
Als er hinabwärts stieg, furchtlos, die felsigen Hallen.
Aber er hatte der Stunden noch zweimal zwölfe zu wandeln
Durch der Erde gewundenes Ohr, wo ihn Lolegrin heimlich

But when the sun came peeping between the branches at
    daybreak,
He fell at once to his task of binding the barn-doors together.
Fine lengths of rope (all stolen of course) he had lying ready;
Carefully he put the pages in order, and then for a binding
Fitted the mayor's great doors, front and back, for they were
    the finest
(They had a cross, and were bordered with red; very handsome
    they were too).
But all at once, as he gazed at his handiwork with admiration,
He was moved in the spirit, and seizing a large piece of
    charcoal,
Lay down in front of the great open book, and set to work
    writing:
Straight strokes, crooked strokes, words in strange languages
    no man can mimic,
All this he scratched and scribbled and scrawled, contentedly
    burbling.
Thus he toiled for a day and a half, and scarcely took time off
Even to eat or to drink, till he'd filled the last of the pages.
Finally, right at the end, came a full stop, big as a child's head.
With a deep snuffle he rose to his feet then, banging his book
    shut.

And, having strengthened his heart first of all with abundant
    refreshment,
He took his hat and his stick and set off. On untravelled
    pathways
Ever towards midnight he went, for that is the way to the
    dead folk.
Seven days only it took till he reached the portal of darkness.
Just as the rose-red dawn was touching the sky, giving notice
To living men of the light of the day, just then he descended
Fearlessly into its depths, with the halls of rock all about him.
But there was further to go, still twice twelve hours to be
    wandered
Through the earth's labyrinthine ear, with the elf-god in secret

Führete, bis er die Schatten ersah, die, luftig und schwebend
Dämmernde Räume bewohnen, die Bösen sowohl wie die
  Guten.

Vorn bei dem Eingang sammelte sich unliebsames Kehricht
Niederen Volks: trugsinnende Krämer und Kuppler und
  Metzen,
Lausige Dichter dabei und unzählbares Gesindel.
Diese, zu schwatzen gewohnt, zu Possen geneigt und zu
  Händeln,
Mühten vergebens sich ab, zu erheben die lispelnde Stimme –
Denn hellklingendes Wort ist nicht den Toten verliehen –
Und so winkten sie nur mit heftig bewegter Gebärde,
Stießen und zerrten einander als wie im Gewühle des
  Jahrmarkts.
Weiter dagegen hinein sah man ruhmwürdige Geister,
Könige, Helden und Sänger, geschmückt mit ewigem
  Lorbeer;
Ruhig ergingen sie sich und saßen, die einen zusammen,
Andre für sich, und es trennte die weit zerstreueten Gruppen
Hügel und Fels und Gebüsch und die finstere Wand der
  Zypressen.

Kaum nun war der sichere Mann in der Pforte erschienen,
Aufrecht die hohe Gestalt, mit dem Weltbuch unter dem
  Arme,
Sieh, da betraf die Schatten am Eingang tödliches Schrecken.
Auseinander stoben sie all, wie Kinder vom Spielplatz,
Wenn es im Dorfe nun heißt: 'Der Hummel ist los!' und 'da
  kommt er!'
Doch der sichere Mann, vorschreitend, winkete gnädig
Ringsumher, da kamen sie näher und standen und gafften.

Suckelborst lehnet nunmehr sein mächtiges Manuskriptum
Gegen den niedrigen Hügel, den rundlichen, welchem genüber
Er selbst Platz zu nehmen gedenkt auf moosigem Felsstück.

Leading him, till he beheld the shades, who hover like air-shapes
There in those twilit spaces, the good and the evil together.

Outside the entrance, the low-born trash, the contemptible
    sweepings
Had piled up: cunning fraudulent merchants, whoremongers
    and harlots,
Lousy poets likewise, and uncountable similar riff-raff.
These were the chatterers, lovers of jests and pickers of quarrels;
Ever they struggle in vain to raise their lisping and twittering
Voices – for clear-spoken words are a gift not granted to
    dead folk.
So all they did was to mop and to mow with vehement gestures,
Pushing and dragging each other about like a mob in the market.
But further in could be seen many worthy and notable spirits,
Kings and heroes and bards all crowned with the evergreen
    laurel;
Calmly they walked about, some strolling or sitting together,
Others apart by themselves, and the wide-scattered groups were
    divided
By rocky hills, by the bushes, by cypresses darkly surrounding.

Scarcely the Safe and Sound Man had appeared at the portal,
    his upright
Figure so tall as under his arm he carried the World Book,
When a most mortal panic beset those shades by the entrance,
And they took to their heels in every direction, like village
Children when somebody cries 'The bull's broken out!' and 'It's
    coming!'
But the Safe and Sound Man walked on, making gestures of
    kindly
Reassurance all round, so they all drew near and stood staring.

Thereupon Suckelborst took his enormous manuscript,
    propped it
On the side of a round low hill, and over against this
He had selected a moss-covered rock on which to be seated.

Doch erst leget er Hut und Stock zur Seite bedächtig,
Streicht mit der breiten Hand sich den beißenden Schweiß von
    der Stirne,
Räuspert sich, daß die Hallen ein prasselndes Echo
    versenden,
Sitzet nieder sodann und beginnt den erhabenen Vortrag.
Erst, wie der Erdball, ganz mit wirkenden Kräften
    geschwängert,
Einst dem dunkelen Nichts entschwebte zusamt den
    Gestirnen,
Wie mit Gras und Kraut sich zuerst der Boden begrünte,
Wie aus der Erde Milch, so sie hegt im inneren Herzen,
Wurde des Fleisches Gebild, das zarte, darinnen der Geist
    wohnt,
Tier- und Menschengeschlecht, denn erdgeboren sind beide.

Solches, nach bestem Verstand und soweit ihn der Dämon
    erleuchtet,
Lehrte der Alte getrost, und still aufhorchten die Schatten.
Aber es hatte der Teufel, das schwarze, gehörnete Scheusal,
Sich aus fremdem Gebiet des unterirdischen Reiches
Unberufen hier eingedrängt, neugierig und boshaft,
Wie er wohl manchmal pflegt, wenn er Kundschaft suchet und
    Kurzweil.
Und er stellte sich hinter den Sprechenden, ihn zu verhöhnen,
Schnitt Gesichter und reckte die Zung und machete Purzel-
Bäum, als ein Aff, und reizte die Seelen beständig zu lachen.
Wohl bemerkt' es der sichere Mann, doch tat er nicht also,
Sondern er redete fort, in würdiger Ruhe beharrend.

Indes trieb es der andere nur um desto verwegner,
Schob am Ende den Schwanz, den gewichtigen, langen, dem
    Alten
Sacht in die Hintertasche des Rocks, als wenn es ihn fröre:

First, however, he carefully laid his hat and his stick down,
Wiped with his great broad hand the prickling sweat from his
    forehead,
Cleared his throat (which in the great halls made an echo like
    thunder),
Then sat down, and boldly began his grandiose discourse.
First how the globe of the earth long ago, all pregnant with
    active
Powers, floated free from the darksome void, all the stars
    coming with it,
And how its soil was covered with grass and the green
    vegetation;
How from the milk that the earth secretes in its innermost centre
Flesh grew into its delicate shape, which the spirit inhabits,
Human and animal kinds, for they all were born as the earth's
    gifts.

Thus, to the best of his knowledge and moved by the god's
    inspiration,
Our friend taught, and the shades gave heed, attentive and
    silent.
But, as it chanced, the Devil, that black and horny old monster,
Had arrived from a different part of the underworld and slipped
In uninvited, as often he does with inquisitive malice
When he is out and about exploring or seeking amusement.
He now took up his position behind the speaker, to mock him,
Pulling faces and sticking his tongue out, and like a monkey
Turning somersaults, setting the spirits off into the giggles.
And the Safe and Sound Man took good note of this, but he
    pretended
Not to, and went on talking, preserving a dignified patience.

Meanwhile the other continued his pranks and waxed all
    the bolder,
Finally slipping his long heavy tail surreptitiously into
Suckelborst's back coat pocket, as if his cold tail needed
    warming:

Plötzlich da greifet der sichere Mann nach hinten, gewaltig
Mit der Rechten erfaßt er den Schweif und reißet ihn
    schnellend
Bei der Wurzel heraus, daß es kracht – ein gräßlicher Anblick.
Laut aufbrüllet der Böse, die Tatzen gedeckt auf die Wunde,
Dreht im rasenden Schmerz wie ein Kreisel sich, schreiend und
    winselnd,
Und schwarz quoll ihm das Blut wie rauchendes Pech aus der
    Wunde;
Dann, wie ein Pfeil zur Seite gewandt, mit Schanden entrinnt er
Durch die geschwind eröffnete Gasse der staunenden Seelen,
Denn nach der eigenen Hölle verlangt ihn, wo er zu Haus
    war;
Und man hörte noch weit aus der Ferne des Flüchtigen
    Wehlaut.

Aber es standen die Scharen umher von Grausen gefesselt,
Ehrfurchtsvoll zum sicheren Mann die Augen erhoben.
Dieser hielt noch und wog den wuchtigen Schweif in den
    Händen,
Den bisweilen ein zuckender Schmerz noch leise bewegte.
Sinnend schaut' er ihn an und sprach die prophetischen
    Worte:
'Wie oft tut der sichere Mann dem Teufel ein Leides?
Erstlich heute, wie eben geschehn, ihr saht es mit Augen;
Dann ein zweites, ein drittes Mal in der Zeiten Vollendung:
Dreimal rauft der sichere Mann dem Teufel den Schweif aus.
Neu zwar sprosset hervor ihm derselbige, aber nicht ganz
    mehr;
Kürzer gerät er, je um ein Dritteil, bis daß er welket.
Gleichermaßen vergeht dem Bösen der Mut und die Stärke,

And at that moment the Safe and Sound Man reached back with
    his right hand,
Powerfully seized the great tail and, suddenly jerking it,
    pulled it
Out by the roots with a snap and a bang, and that was a dreadful
Sight. The Evil One howled, he covered the wound with his
    two paws,
Spinning round, maddened with pain, like a top, and shrieking
    and whimpering,
While from the wound, like black smoking pitch, his
    sticky blood bubbled;
Then he was off like an arrow and ignominiously fleeing
Past the astonished shades, who made way for him hastily as he
Bolted back to his own part of Hell and home to headquarters;
And as he fled, they could still hear his wailing far off in the
    distance.

But the hosts of the dead stood around, dumbstricken with
    horror,
Gazing up at the Safe and Sound Man in respectful amazement.
He was still holding and guessing the weight of the severed
    appendage,
Which still twitched in his hands, recalling the pain it had
    suffered.
Pensively he surveyed it, and spoke with prophetical utterance:
'How many times shall the Safe and Sound Man do the Devil
    a mischief?
This was the first occasion, today, as your eyes have just
    witnessed,
And in the fullness of years there will be a second and
    third time:
Thrice the Safe and Sound Man shall tear out the tail of
    the Devil.
It will grow back on his rump, to be sure, but no longer
    completely:
It will be one third shorter each time, and at last it will wither.
So too the spirit and strength of the Evil One shall diminish.

Kindisch wird er und alt, ein Bettler, von allen verachtet.
Dann wird ein Festtag sein in der Unterwelt und auf der
    Erde;
Aber der sichere Mann wird ein lieber Genosse den Göttern.'

Sprach es, und jetzo legt' er den Schweif in das Buch als ein
    Zeichen,
Sorgsam, daß oben noch just der haarige Büschel heraussah,
Denn er gedachte für jetzt nicht weiter zu lehren, und basta
Schmettert er zu den Deckel des ungeheueren Werkes,
Faßt es unter den Arm, nimmt Hut und Stock und empfiehlt
    sich.

Unermeßliches Beifallklatschen des sämtlichen Pöbels
Folgte dem Trefflichen nach, bis er ganz in der Pforte
    verschwunden,
Und es rauschte noch lang und tosete freudiger Aufruhr.

Aber Lolegrin hatte, der Gott, das ganze Spektakel
Heimlich mit angesehn und gehört, in Gestalt der Zikade
Auf dem hangenden Zweig der schwarzen Weide sich wiegend.
Jetzo verließ er den Ort und schwang sich empor zu den Göttern,
Ihnen treulich zu melden die Taten des sicheren Mannes
Und das himmlische Mahl mit süßem Gelächter zu würzen.

He shall grow childish and old, like a beggar, and all shall
    despise him.
Then shall a feast-day be held in the underworld and on
    the earth too;
But the high gods shall welcome the Safe and Sound Man
    and befriend him.'

Thus he spoke, and with care laid the tail in his book as a
    bookmark,
Letting its hairy tassel just peep from the top of the pages,
For he was minded now to cut short his lecture, and *basta!*
With a great bang he clapped shut the mighty tome, then he
    placed it
Under his arm, took his hat and his stick, took his leave
    and departed.

Thunderous acclamation, unending applause from the
    whole mob
Followed our excellent friend, till he'd quite disappeared
    through the doorway,
And an uproar of pleasure continued for long and resounded.

But the god Lolegrin, he all the while had secretly watched and
Heard this great spectacle, for he had taken a grasshopper's
    likeness,
And on a dark willow-tree's hanging twig he was perching
    and rocking.
Now he in turn departed, and soared aloft to the high gods,
Bringing them faithful report of the Safe and Sound Man and
    his doings,
Such as would spice their ambrosial feast with the sweetest of
    laughter.

Waldplage

Im Walde deucht mir alles miteinander schön
Und nichts Mißliebiges darin, so vielerlei
Er hegen mag; es krieche zwischen Gras und Moos
Am Boden, oder jage reißend durchs Gebüsch,
Es singe oder kreische von den Gipfeln hoch
Und hacke mit dem Schnabel in der Fichte Stamm,
Daß lieblich sie ertönet durch den ganzen Saal.
Ja machte je sich irgend etwas unbequem,
Verdrießt es nicht, zu suchen einen andern Sitz
Der schöner bald, der allerschönste, dich bedünkt.
Ein einzig Übel aber hat der Wald für mich,
Ein grausames und unausweichliches beinah.
Sogleich beschreib ich dieses Scheusal, daß ihrs kennt;
Noch kennt ihrs kaum, und merkt es nicht, bis unversehns
Die Hand euch und, noch schrecklicher, die Wange schmerzt.
Geflügelt kommt es, säuselnd, fast unhörbarlich;
Auf Füßen, zweimal dreien, ist es hoch gestellt
(Deswegen ich in Versen es zu schmähen auch
Den klassischen Senarium mit Fug erwählt);
Und wie es anfliegt, augenblicklich lässet es
Den langen Rüssel senkrecht in die zarte Haut;
Erschrocken schlagt ihr schnell darnach, jedoch umsonst,
Denn, graziöser Wendung, schon entschwebet es.
Und alsobald, entzündet von dem raschen Gift
Schwillt euch die Hand zum ungestalten Kissen auf,
Und juckt und spannt und brennet zum Verzweifeln euch
Viel Stunden, ja zuweilen noch den dritten Tag.
So unter meiner Lieblingsfichte saß ich jüngst –
Zur Lehne wie gedrechselt für den Rücken, steigt
Zwiestämmig, nah dem Boden, sie als Gabel auf –
Den Dichter lesend, den ich jahrelang vergaß:
An Fanny singt er, Cidly und den Züricher See
Die frühen Gräber und des Rheines goldnen Wein
(O sein Gestade brütet jenes Greuels auch
Ein größeres Geschlechte noch und schlimmres aus,

The Woodland Pest

Forests delight me, everything is beautiful
In them, their various creatures crawling in the grass
And moss, or rushing headlong through the undergrowth,
Are none of them displeasing to me, whether they
Sing or screech loud and high among the branches, or
Attack the trunks of fir-trees with their beaks, until
Sweet music echoes all about the spacious hall.
And even should some thing or other chance to irk,
Then it's no problem to seek out another spot,
More beautiful perhaps than any found before.
But there's one terror that the forest holds for me,
One cruel thing, and almost unavoidable.
I will describe this monster now, that you may know
It better: hitherto you scarcely did, until
A sudden pain attacked your hand or, worse, your face.
It comes on wings, its buzzing one can hardly hear;
High on its feet, twice three of them, long-legged it stands
(So that, to abuse the creature well, I judged
It right to choose this classical six-footed line);
And when it comes, immediately it drives its long
Proboscis vertically through one's tender skin;
Startled, one strikes at it in haste, but all in vain,
For with a graceful motion it has winged its way
Far hence. And now at once its venom, quick to act,
Inflames one's hand, which like an ugly cushion swells,
Itches and smarts and burns and plagues one to despair
For many an hour, and sometimes even for three days.
Under my favourite fir-tree lately thus I sat –
Twin-trunked and forking upwards near the ground, it seems
Expressly crafted for one's back to lean against –
Reading a poet I had left for many years
Unread: the bard of Fanny, Cidly, of the Lake
Of Zürich, early graves and golden Rhenish wine
(Now that's a river where these horrors also breed,
A bigger, fiercer species too, as well I know,

Ich kenn es wohl, doch höflicher dem Gaste wars.) –
Nun aber hatte geigend schon ein kleiner Trupp
Mich ausgewittert, den geruhig Sitzenden;
Mir um die Schläfe tanzet er in Lüsternheit.
Ein Stich! der erste! er empört die Galle schon.
Zerstreuten Sinnes immer schiel ich übers Blatt.
Ein zweiter macht, ein dritter, mich zum Rasenden.
Das holde Zwillings-Nymphenpaar des Fichtenbaums
Vernahm da Worte, die es nicht bei mir gesucht;
Zuletzt geboten sie mir flüsternd Mäßigung:
Wo nicht, so sollt ich meiden ihren Ruhbezirk.
Beschämt gehorcht ich, sinnend still auf Grausamtat.
Ich hielt geöffnet auf der flachen Hand das Buch,
Das schwebende Geziefer, wie sich eines naht',
Mit raschem Klapp zu töten. Ha! da kommt schon eins!
'Du fliehst! o bleibe, eile nicht, Gedankenfreund!'
(Dem hohen Mond rief jener Dichter zu dies Wort.)
Patsch! Hab ich dich, Canaille, oder hab ich nicht?
Und hastig – denn schon hatte meine Mordbegier
Zum stillen Wahnsinn sich verirrt, zum kleinlichen –
Begierig blättr' ich: ja, da liegst du plattgedrückt,
Bevor du stachst, nun aber stichst du nimmermehr,
Du zierlich Langgebeinetes, Jungfräuliches!
– Also, nicht achtend eines schönen Buchs Verderb
Trieb ich erheitert lange noch die schnöde Jagd,
Unglücklich oft, doch öfter glücklichen Erfolgs.
So mag es kommen, daß ein künftger Leser wohl
Einmal in Klopstocks Oden, nicht ohn einiges
Verwundern, auch etwelcher Schnaken sich erfreut.

An Philomele

Tonleiterähnlich steiget dein Klaggesang
Vollschwellend auf, wie wenn man Bouteillen füllt:
    Es steigt und steigt im Hals der Flasche –
        Sieh, und das liebliche Naß schäumt über.

Though they were more polite then to their visitor).
But now a little troop, a fiddling band of them,
Had sniffed me out as I sat there so peacefully;
And round my brows they danced with lustful appetite.
A prick! the first! Enough to bring my dander up.
My eyes, distracted, were still squinting at the book.
A second prick! a third! Now I was in a rage,
And the twin maidens, gentle nymphs of that twin tree,
Heard me use words they never would have thought I
     knew;
Till in the end they quietly bade me moderate
My tongue, or forthwith quit their peaceable domain.
In shamefaced silence then I planned a deed of dread.
Flat open on one hand I held my book of verse
Ready, should they approach, to clap those hovering bugs
To death between its pages. Ha! here's one of them!
'Thou fleest! oh hasten not away, pale friend of thought!'
(Thus had my poet once invoked the lofty moon).
Smack! Have I caught you, villainous fiend, or did I miss?
In eager haste – for my insecticidal lust
Had now degenerated into insane spite –
I turned the pages: yes! There you lie squashed, in time
To stop you stinging; now you'll never sting again,
You dainty long-legged, maidenheaded creature you!
– Thus, disregardful of a fine book's ruin, I
Continued long and cheerfully my horrid hunt,
Unlucky sometimes, lucky oftener than not.
So it may well be that some future reader of
The *Odes* of Klopstock will be pleasantly surprised
To find some bugs among the bard's immortal lines.

To the Nightingale

How splendidly its musical scale it mounts,
Your song of grief, upsurging like bottled wine:
     Up through the tapering neck it rises
          And overflows, the sweet foaming nectar!

O Sängerin, dir möcht ich ein Liedchen weihn,
Voll Lieb und Sehnsucht! aber ich stocke schon;
  Ach, mein unselig Gleichnis regt mir
    Plötzlich den Durst und mein Gaumen lechzet.

Verzeih! im Jägerschlößchen ist frisches Bier
Und Kegelabend heut: ich versprach es halb
  Dem Oberamtsgerichtsverweser,
    Auch dem Notar und dem Oberförster.

Auf eine Christblume

I

Tochter des Walds, du Lilienverwandte,
So lang von mir gesuchte, unbekannte,
Im fremden Kirchhof, öd und winterlich
Zum erstenmal, o schöne, find ich dich!

Von welcher Hand gepflegt du hier erblühtest,
Ich weiß es nicht, noch wessen Grab du hütest;
Ist es ein Jüngling, so geschah ihm Heil,
Ists eine Jungfrau, lieblich fiel ihr Teil.

Im nächtgen Hain, von Schneelicht überbreitet,
Wo fromm das Reh an dir vorüberweidet,
Bei der Kapelle, am kristallnen Teich,
Dort sucht ich deiner Heimat Zauberreich.

Schön bist du, Kind des Mondes, nicht der Sonne;
Dir wäre tödlich andrer Blumen Wonne,
Dich nährt, den keuschen Leib voll Reif und Duft,
Himmlischer Kälte balsamsüße Luft.

Oh songstress, I would write a whole song for you,
All love and longing: but I am now stuck fast.
　My luckless simile has made me
　　Suddenly thirsty, with dry tongue drooping.

Excuse me! There's cool beer at the hunting-lodge;
They're playing bowls tonight. I half said I'd come;
　The county registrar expects me,
　　Likewise the notary and the game warden.

To a Christmas Rose

I

Oh lovely flower, so long unknown to me
And so long sought, which now at last I see
In this strange churchyard winter-dark and wild:
The lily's sister and the forest's child!

To blossom here, who tended you so well?
And whose grave do you watch? I cannot tell:
A boy's perhaps, whose burial you have blessed,
Or a maiden's; what grace befriends her rest!

I sought it in the grove, by the snow's light,
Where gentle deer graze past you in the night,
There by the chapel, by the pond's crystal face:
The magic kingdom of your native place.

Moon-daughter! In the sun's warm rays that give
Joy to all other flowers, you could not live;
Chaste frost-filled fragrance, you must drink your fill
From this balm-laden air's celestial chill.

In deines Busens goldner Fülle gründet
Ein Wohlgeruch, der sich nur kaum verkündet;
So duftete, berührt von Engelshand,
Der benedeiten Mutter Brautgewand.

Dich würden, mahnend an das heilge Leiden,
Fünf Purpurtropfen schön und einzig kleiden:
Doch kindlich zierst du, um die Weihnachtszeit,
Lichtgrün mit einem Hauch dein weißes Kleid.

Der Elfe, der in mitternächtger Stunde
Zum Tanze geht im lichterhellen Grunde
Vor deiner mystischen Glorie steht er scheu
Neugierig still von fern und huscht vorbei.

II

Im Winterboden schläft, ein Blumenkeim,
Der Schmetterling, der einst um Busch und Hügel
In Frühlingsnächten wiegt den samtnen Flügel;
Nie soll er kosten deinen Honigseim.

Wer aber weiß, ob nicht sein zarter Geist,
Wenn jede Zier des Sommers hingesunken,
Dereinst, von deinem leisen Dufte trunken,
Mir unsichtbar, dich blühende umkreist?

Die schöne Buche

Ganz verborgen im Wald kenn ich ein Plätzchen, da stehet
    Eine Buche, man sieht schöner im Bilde sie nicht.
Rein und glatt, in gediegenem Wuchs erhebt sie sich einzeln,
    Keiner der Nachbarn rührt ihr an den seidenen Schmuck.
Rings, soweit sein Gezweig der stattliche Baum ausbreitet,
    Grünet der Rasen, das Aug still zu erquicken, umher;

Deep in your golden heart so delicate
An odour lurks, scarcely articulate:
Was the blest Mother's bridal robe, touched by
The angel, scented so ineffably?

Five crimson drops, the holy Passion's trace,
No more than these, would match your lovely face;
Yet childlike, with a breath, a hint of green,
Your white dress flushes for this Christmas scene.

A little midnight elf is on his way
To join some starlit dance: not far away
He spies your mystic glory, is held fast
A moment in shy wonder, and darts past.

II

The butterfly that sleeps, a flower's seed
In wintry earth, will float on velvet wing
Round hill and bush in coming nights of spring,
But never shall he taste your nectar's mead.

And yet, who knows? Unseen by eyes like mine,
When summer's beauty all has gone to ground,
Perhaps his spirit still shall hover round
Your fragrant blossom, drunk as if on wine.

The Beautiful Beech-Tree

Hidden away in the forest I know a place where a beech-tree
    Stands, so lovely a tree never a painter could match.
Pure, smooth, solidly grown, in single splendour it rises,
    Free of its neighbours, for none touches its silken attire.
Round about, and as far as this great tree spreads out its
      branches,
    There is greensward, a still circle refreshes the eye,

Gleich nach allen Seiten umzirkt er den Stamm in der Mitte
   Kunstlos schuf die Natur selber dies liebliche Rund.
Zartes Gebüsch umkränzet es erst; hochstämmige Bäume,
   Folgend in dichtem Gedräng, wehren dem himmlischen
      Blau.
Neben der dunkleren Fülle des Eichbaums wieget die Birke
   Ihr jungfräuliches Haupt schüchtern im goldenen Licht.
Nur wo, verdeckt vom Felsen, der Fußsteig jäh sich
      hinabschlingt,
   Lässet die Hellung mich ahnen das offene Feld.
– Als ich unlängst einsam, von neuen Gestalten des Sommers
   Ab dem Pfade gelockt, dort im Gebüsch mich verlor,
Führt' ein freundlicher Geist, des Hains auflauschende
      Gottheit,
   Hier mich zum erstenmal, plötzlich, den Staunenden, ein.
Welch Entzücken! Es war um die hohe Stunde des Mittags,
   Lautlos alles, es schwieg selber der Vogel im Laub.
Und ich zauderte noch, auf den zierlichen Teppich zu treten;
   Festlich empfing er den Fuß, leise beschritt ich ihn nur.
Jetzo gelehnt an den Stamm (er trägt sein breites Gewölbe
   Nicht zu hoch), ließ ich rundum die Augen ergehn,
Wo den beschatteten Kreis die feurig strahlende Sonne,
   Fast gleich messend umher, säumte mit blendendem Rand.
Aber ich stand und rührte mich nicht; dämonischer Stille,
   Unergründlicher Ruh lauschte mein innerer Sinn.
Eingeschlossen mit dir in diesem sonnigen Zauber-
   Gürtel, o Einsamkeit, fühlt ich und dachte nur dich!

Göttliche Reminiszenz

Πάντα δι' αὐτοῦ ἐγένετο.
(Joh. 1:3)

Vorlängst sah ich ein wundersames Bild gemalt,
Im Kloster der Kartäuser, das ich oft besucht.
Heut, da ich im Gebirge droben einsam ging,
Umstarrt von wild zerstreuter Felsentrümmersaat,

Equal in all directions surrounding the trunk in the centre;
  Artless Nature itself fashioned this ring of delight.
Tender shrubs enwreath it at first, then taller trees follow,
  Thickly crowding, and these block out the blue of the sky.
Here by the oak's dark fullness the slender birch-tree is shyly
  Rocking its virginal head, high in the gold of the day.
Only up there, where the cliff-hidden footpath comes winding
      down steeply,
  Is there a clearing, a gap hinting at wide open land.
– Not long ago, all alone, new shapes of summer enticed me
  Off the path, and I strayed into the bushes; a sprite
Friendly to man, the listening god of the grove, must have
      led me;
  Suddenly, for the first time, here in amazement I stood,
And in rapture! It was the high hour of noon, and about me
  All was silent, no bird sang in the foliage, and I
Scarcely dared walk on that delicate carpet, which festively
      welcomed
  My still hesitant foot; gently and softly I trod.
Now, as against the tree-trunk I leaned (for its canopy arches
  Not too proudly) I gazed round me: the circle of shade
Under the fiery sun was bordered with dazzling brightness,
  Measured, as near as could be, equal from centre to edge.
And I stood on and listened unstirring: daemonic silence,
  Fathomless stillness spoke clear to my innermost sense.
Deep-enclosed in this sunlit zone of enchantment, I had no
  Feeling, oh Solitude! here I had no thought but of you.

Divine Remembrance

All things were made by him.
(John 1:3)

I saw a painting once, a wondrous work it was,
In a Carthusian monastery I know well.
Today again, my solitary mountain walk
High among rigid scattered rubble of wild rocks

Trat es mit frischen Farben vor die Seele mir.
An jäher Steinkluft, deren dünn begraster Saum,
Von zweien Palmen überschattet, magre Kost
Den Ziegen beut, den steilauf weidenden am Hang,
Sieht man den Knaben Jesus sitzend auf Gestein;
Ein weißes Vlies als Polster ist ihm unterlegt.
Nicht allzu kindlich deuchte mir das schöne Kind;
Der heiße Sommer, sicherlich sein fünfter schon,
Hat seine Glieder, welche bis zum Knie herab
Das gelbe Röckchen decket mit dem Purpursaum,
Hat die gesunden, zarten Wangen sanft gebräunt;
Aus schwarzen Augen leuchtet stille Feuerkraft,
Den Mund jedoch umfremdet unnennbarer Reiz.
Ein alter Hirte, freundlich zu dem Kind gebeugt,
Gab ihm soeben ein versteinert Meergewächs,
Seltsam gestaltet, in die Hand zum Zeitvertreib.
Der Knabe hat das Wunderding beschaut, und jetzt,
Gleichsam betroffen, spannet sich der weite Blick,
Entgegen dir, doch wirklich ohne Gegenstand,
Durchdringend ewge Zeiten-Fernen, grenzenlos:
Als wittre durch die überwölkte Stirn ein Blitz
Der Gottheit, ein Erinnern, das im gleichen Nu
Erloschen sein wird; und das welterschaffende,
Das Wort von Anfang, als ein spielend Erdenkind
Mit Lächeln zeigts unwissend dir sein eigen Werk.

Auf einer Wanderung

In ein freundliches Städtchen tret ich ein,
In den Straßen liegt roter Abendschein.
Aus einem offnen Fenster eben,
Über den reichsten Blumenflor
Hinweg, hört man Goldglockentöne schweben,
Und eine Stimme scheint ein Nachtigallenchor,
Daß die Blüten beben,
Daß die Lüfte leben,
Daß in höherem Rot die Rosen leuchten vor.

Has brought its lively colours back before my mind.
Beside a stony chasm, edged with scanty green
Where, shaded by two palm-trees, goats that graze on this
Precipitous slope enjoy a meagre nourishment,
It shows the Christ-Child, seated there on barren stone;
A soft white fleece is cushion for his tender limbs.
A little less than childlike looks this lovely boy;
Hot summers (five of them he must have seen by now)
Have gently browned his healthy skin, his delicate cheeks,
His arms and legs which to the knees are covered by
A little yellow tunic, purple at the hem.
Out of his dark eyes glows a quiet inward fire,
Yet a strange nameless charm hovers about his lips.
An aged friendly shepherd, stooping over him,
Has given him a plaything curiously shaped,
A petrifact from the sea's depths. The boy has held
This wonder in his hand and looked at it,
And now his gaze seems startled, widened into thought,
Staring at me, yet actually objectless,
Piercing eternal distances of infinite time:
As if there flickered on his clouded brow a flash
Of divine consciousness, an inkling that must fade
In the same instant; and the Maker of the worlds,
The Word in the Beginning, as an earthly child at play,
Smiling and all unwitting, shows me His own work.

A Walk in the Country

A little town: how kindly it greets
My coming! The late sun gleams in the streets.
A window is open, and over
A wealth of flowers, like bells
Of gold I hear these pure notes hover:
One voice alone like a choir of nightingales.
How the blossoms quiver,
How the breezes stir,
How the red of the roses glows, grows rosier!

Lang hielt ich staunend, lustbeklommen.
Wie ich hinaus vors Tor gekommen
Ich weiß es wahrlich selber nicht.
Ach hier, wie liegt die Welt so licht!
Der Himmel wogt in purpurnem Gewühle,
Rückwärts die Stadt in goldnem Rauch;
Wie rauscht der Erlenbach, wie rauscht im Grund die
    Mühle!
Ich bin wie trunken, irrgeführt –
O Muse, du hast mein Herz berührt
Mit einem Liebeshauch!

Am Rheinfall

Halte dein Herz, o Wanderer, fest in gewaltigen Händen!
    Mir entstürzte vor Lust zitternd das meinige fast.
Rastlos donnernde Massen auf donnernde Massen geworfen,
    Ohr und Auge, wohin retten sie sich im Tumult?
Wahrlich, den eigenen Wutschrei hörete nicht der Gigant hier,
    Läg er, vom Himmel gestürzt, unten am Felsen gekrümmt!
Rosse der Götter, im Schwung, eins über dem Rücken des
    andern,
    Stürmen herunter und streun silberne Mähnen umher;
Herrliche Leiber, unzählbare, folgen sich, nimmer dieselben,
    Ewig dieselbigen – wer wartet das Ende wohl aus?
Angst umzieht dir den Busen mit eins, und, *wie* du es denkest,
    Über das Haupt stürzt dir krachend das Himmelsgewölb!

Long I stood amazed, dazed with delight.
Through the town gate I went on my way,
How I got there, how can I say?
Oh the world here, how it is bathed in light!
The sky drifts, a chaos of crimson; I gaze
Back at the town and its golden haze,
And I hear the mill-wheel in the valley, the murmuring
    stream
By the alders. I am drunken, lost in this dream –
Oh Muse, by your breath, by a word
Of love, how my heart is stirred!

The Falls of the Rhine

Hold your heart fast, oh wayfarer, now, and with mighty hands
    clutch it!
  Mine so shuddered with joy, almost it dropped from
    my grasp.
Thundering masses, ceaselessly hurled on thundering masses:
  How shall our eyes and our ears flee such a tumult as this?
Truly, if there were a giant cast down from the sky to this
        cliff's base,
  Lying there twisted, the yell of his own rage he'd not hear.
Down storm steeds of the gods, swinging down, overleaping
    each other;
  See how their silvery manes shake as they scatter like spray!
Splendid these bodies, a countless succession, and never the
    same ones,
  Though they are ever the same – when shall this endlessness
    end?
Suddenly fear encircles one's soul, and at the thought's instant
  Over one's head the immense vault of the sky crashes down!

Erbauliche Betrachtung

Als wie im Forst ein Jäger, der, am heißen Tag
Im Eichenschatten ruhend, mit zufriednem Blick
Auf seine Hunde niederschaut, das treue Paar,
Das, Hals um Hals geschlungen, brüderlich den Schlaf,
Und schlafend noch des Jagens Lust und Mühe teilt:
So schau ich hier an des Gehölzes Schattenrand
Bei kurzer Rast auf meiner eignen Füße Paar
Hinab, nicht ohne Rührung; in gewissem Sinn
Zum ersten Mal, so alt ich bin, betracht ich sie,
Und bin fürwahr von ihrem Dasein überrascht,
Wie sie, in Schuhn bis überm Knöchel eingeschnürt,
Bestäubt da vor mir liegen im verlechzten Gras.

Wie manches Lustrum, ehrliche Gesellen, schleppt
Ihr mich auf dieser buckeligen Welt umher,
Gehorsam eurem Herren jeden Augenblick,
Tag oder Nacht, wohin er nur mit euch begehrt.
Sein Wandel mochte töricht oder weislich sein,
Den besten Herrn, wenn man euch hörte, trugt ihr stets.
Ihr seid bereit, den Unglimpf, der ihm widerfuhr,
– Und wäre sein Beleidiger ein Reichsbaron –
Alsbald zu strafen mit ergrimmtem Hundetritt
(Doch hiefür hat er selber zu viel Lebensart).
Wo war ein Berg zu steil für euch, zu jäh ein Fels?
Und glücklich immer habt ihr mich nach Haus gebracht;
Gleichwohl noch nie mit einem Wörtchen dankt ich euch,
Vom Schönsten was mein Herz genoß erfuhrt ihr nichts!

Wenn, von der blausten Frühlingsmitternacht entzückt,
Oft aus der Gartenlaube weg vom Zechgelag
Mein hochgestimmter Freund mich noch hinausgelockt,
Die offne Straße hinzuschwärmen raschen Gangs,
Wir Jünglinge, des Jugendglückes Übermaß
Als baren Schmerz empfindend, ins Unendliche
Die Geister hetzten, und die Rede wie Feuer troff,

An Edifying Meditation

Even as a huntsman, sheltered from the midday heat
By shady oak-trees, gazes down well satisfied
At his two hounds, a faithful pair, fraternally
Sharing, with neck and neck entwined, each other's sleep,
And even in sleep the joy and labour of the chase:
Even so do I here, at the forest's shady edge,
Taking a brief rest, gaze down at my own two feet
With some emotion; and indeed, in a certain sense,
Old as I am, I see them now for the first time,
And their existence is a real surprise to me:
Laced up in boots beyond the ankle, there they lie
Down there before me, dusty in the withered grass.

How many five-times-twelvemonths, honest fellows, you
Have dragged me with you round about this bumpy world,
Always obedient to your master's every wish,
By day or night, wherever he might care to go!
He might walk wisely or unwisely, but you bore
Your master lovingly and well in either case;
And you have been prepared, were insult done to him,
– Even if the offender were a baron of the realm –
At once to mete sound punishment out as to a dog
(Had not good breeding taught him it is rude to kick).
Where was there hill too high or cliff too steep for you?
And always you have brought me home successfully,
Although you never got from me one word of thanks
Or ever learnt the joy of which my heart was full!

Often, at midnight, tempted by spring's bluest sky,
When from the leafy garden where we had caroused
My friend's high mood enticed me, and on the open road
We two went wandering abroad at a wild pace
– Young as we were, feeling youth's joy as keenly as
If it were pain, driving our minds beyond the edge
Of thought, and casting fiery words about, till we

Bis wir zuletzt an Kühnheit mit dem sichern Mann
Wetteiferten, da dieser Urwelts-Göttersohn
In Flößerstiefeln vom Gebirg zum Himmel sich
Verstieg und mit der breiten Hand der Sterne Heer
Zusammenstrich in einen Habersack und den
Mit großem Schnaufen bis zum Rand der Schöpfung trug
Den Plunder auszuschütteln vor das Weltentor –
Ach, gute Bursche, damals wart ihr auch dabei,
Und wo nicht sonst, davon ich jetzo schweigen will!

Bleibt mir getreu, und altert schneller nicht als ich!
Wir haben, hoff ich, noch ein schön Stück Wegs vor uns;
Zwar weiß ichs nicht, den Göttern sei es heimgestellt.
Doch wie es falle, laßt euch nichts mit mir gereun.
Auf meinem Grabstein soll man ein Paar Schuhe sehn,
Den Stab darüber und den Reisehut gelegt,
Das beste Sinnbild eines ruhenden Wandersmanns.
Wer dann mich segnet, der vergißt auch eurer nicht.
Genug für jetzt! denn dort seh ichs gewitterschwer
Von Mittag kommen, und mich deucht, es donnert schon.
Eh uns der Regen übereilt, ihr Knaben, auf!
Die Steig hinab! zum Städtchen langt sichs eben noch.

Inschrift auf eine Uhr mit den drei Horen

Βάρδισται μακάρων Ὧραι Φίλαι –
Theokrit

Am langsamsten von allen Göttern wandeln wir,
Mit Blätterkronen schön geschmückte, schweigsame.
Doch wer uns ehrt und wem wir selber günstig sind,
Weil er die Anmut liebet und das heilge Maß,
Vor dessen Augen schweben wir im leichten Tanz
Und machen mannigfaltig ihm den langen Tag.

Grew bold as that great giant of the primal world,
The Safe and Sound Man, that descendant of the gods,
Who from the mountains climbed to heaven in raftsman's boots
And with his huge hand swept the host of stars into
A haversack, which then he humped with huff and puff
Right to creation's furthest limits, where he tipped
The whole lot out like rubbish through the world's front door –
Oh my dear lads, at all these times you too were there,
And elsewhere too, at places I'll not mention now!

Keep faith with me, keep pace with me in growing old!
We have, I hope, together still a fair way to go;
How far I cannot tell, on the gods' lap it lies.
But long or short, you two have nothing to regret.
Upon my tombstone shall be engraved a pair of boots,
And over them my stout stick and my travelling-hat;
The best of symbols for a wanderer laid to rest.
Then passers-by may bless me, not forgetting you.
Enough! for I can see approaching from the south
Some stormy weather, thunder too I think I hear.
Come, lads! let's not be overtaken by the rain.
Come, down the path! There's still just time to reach the town.

Inscription on a Clock
with the Three Hour-Goddesses

Dear Hours, more slow to move than all the gods –
                                        Theocritus

Fair-garlanded, most leisurely of deities,
Slowly and silently we move upon our way.
But he who honours us, who loves the sacred laws
Of grace and moderation, him we favour most:
Before his eyes we hover in an airy dance
Making his long day various and beautiful.

Auf eine Lampe

Noch unverrückt, o schöne Lampe, schmückest du,
An leichten Ketten zierlich aufgehangen hier,
Die Decke des nun fast vergeßnen Lustgemachs.
Auf deiner weißen Marmorschale, deren Rand
Der Efeukranz von goldengrünem Erz umflicht,
Schlingt fröhlich eine Kinderschar den Ringelreihn.
Wie reizend alles! lachend, und ein sanfter Geist
Des Ernstes doch ergossen um die ganze Form –
Ein Kunstgebild der echten Art. Wer achtet sein?
Was aber schön ist, selig scheint es in ihm selbst.

Der alte Turmhahn

Idylle

Zu Cleversulzbach im Unterland
Hundertunddreizehn Jahr ich stand,
Auf dem Kirchenturn ein guter Hahn,
Als ein Zierat und Wetterfahn.
In Sturm und Wind und Regennacht
Hab ich allzeit das Dorf bewacht.
Manch falber Blitz hat mich gestreift,
Der Frost mein' roten Kamm bereift,
Auch manchen lieben Sommertag,
Da man gern Schatten haben mag,
Hat mir die Sonne unverwandt
Auf meinen goldigen Leib gebrannt.
So ward ich schwarz für Alter ganz,
Und weg ist aller Glitz und Glanz.
Da haben sie mich denn zuletzt
Veracht't und schmählich abgesetzt.
Meinthalb! so ist der Welt ihr Lauf,

On a Lamp

Beautiful lamp, left hanging here so gracefully,
Unmoved, chained lightly to this ceiling which you still
Adorn, here in the half-forgotten summer-room!
Round your white marble bowl, which at its edge is
    wreathed
With green and golden ivy-leaves of bronze, a crowd
Of children happily are dancing hand in hand.
What great enchantment! Smiling, yet the entire form
Immersed somehow in a gentle air of seriousness –
A shape of truest art. Who pays it any heed?
But blest within itself beauty still seems to shine.

The Auld Steeplecock

An Idyll

In my country tounie in Buchan here	
I steed for a hunner an thirteen year,	
A trusty cock an weather-vane	
Hynd up on the kirk-tooer aa ma lane,	far up, all alone
Watchin ower aa in dark an licht,	
In storm an weend an rainy nicht.	
The lichtnin's scufft me, mony's the time,	brushed
The frost haes croont ma heid wi rime.	
On mony a bonny simmer's day,	
Fan wiser fowk in the shade wid stay,	when
The saen has baeten wi pooer oontault	sun; untold power
On my gowden body, an niver devault.	never let up
Noo age has turnt me black as the crook,	pot-hook
Aa my weel-faurt grandeur it took.	well-favoured good looks
Sae noo my time o eese is past.	usefulness
It's come tae this: at the verra last	
I'm disrespeckit an ootcast.	
Aweel, the wordle gyangs that gate.	that's the way of the world

Jetzt tun sie einen andern 'nauf.
Stolzier, prachtier und dreh dich nur!
Dir macht der Wind noch andre Cour.

Ade, o Tal, du Berg und Tal!
Rebhügel, Wälder allzumal!
Herzlieber Turn und Kirchendach,
Kirchhof und Steglein übern Bach!
Du Brunnen, dahin spat und früh
Öchslein springen, Schaf' und Küh,
Hans hinterdrein kommt mit dem Stecken,
Und Bastes Evlein auf dem Schecken!
– Ihr Störch und Schwalben, grobe Spatzen,
Euch soll ich nimmer hören schwatzen!
Lieb deucht mir jedes Drecklein itzt,
Damit ihr ehrlich mich beschmitzt.
Ade, Hochwürden, Ihr Herr Pfarr,
Schulmeister auch, du armer Narr
Aus ist, was mich gefreut so lang,
Geläut und Orgel, Sang und Klang.

Von meiner Höh so sang ich dort,
Und hätt noch lang gesungen fort,
Da kam so ein krummer Teufelshöcker,
Ich schätz, es war der Schieferdecker,
Packt mich, kriegt nach manch hartem Stoß
Mich richtig von der Stange los.
Mein alt preßhafter Leib schier brach,
Da er mit mir fuhr ab dem Dach
Und bei den Glocken schnurrt hinein;
Die glotzten sehr verwundert drein,
Regt' ihnen doch weiter nicht den Mut,
Dachten eben, wir hangen gut.

Jetzt tät man mich mit altem Eisen
Dem Meister Hufschmied überweisen;
Der zahlt zween Batzen und meint Wunder,
Wieviel es wär für solchen Plunder.

They're pittan anither in my place.
– Aye, prink an swank an turn, ma loon!   my boy
The wind'll seen gie ye a gey roch wooin.   soon; pretty rough
                                                                  [wooing

Sae fare-ye-weel, ma hill an glen,
Corn-rigs an wids an aa that I ken!   woods
Kirk-tooer, reef wi slates weel-worn,
Kirkyaird an briggie ower the burn,
The water-troch, far aye at lowsin-   where; at the end of the
time come sheep an kye an owsen,   kine and oxen [working day
Jock wi's staff ahin them, guidin,
Dod's lassie on the pownie ridin!
Ye birdies, swallas, sparras, niver-
mair sall I hear yer clash-ma-claiver;   chatter
I'll miss ilk honest birdie-drap
Ye iver keest upon ma tap.   head
Fare-ye-weel, minister, nay, Moderator!
Fare-ye-weel, dominie (puir fuil crayter)!   poor silly chap
Bells, organ, psalms an hymns an aa,
Aa my pleasure's weed awaa.   taken away

I jyn't in the singin fae my hicht,   from my height
An fain haed aye sung on; an I micht –
But a crookit humpbackit chiel appeart   fellow
(The slater, I jaloust an feart),   suspected
Laid haans on me, ryv't me aff my pole   wrenched
(Mony's the dunt I haed tae thole),   thump; bear
An nearly brak my puir auld benes
As he clumb aff the reef's slate-stenes
An jinkit in the bells atween   dodged
That hardly could believe their een
An niver even gaed a myaout –   uttered a peep
'As lang's we're aa richt here', they thocht.

Sae here's me noo, consignt, tae sell
Wi ither auld iron tae Smiddy Will.   Smithy
He peyt twa shillins an thocht it dear
For siccan a eeseless heap o gear.   such a useless

Und also ich selben Mittag
Betrübt vor seiner Hütte lag.
Ein Bäumlein – es war Maienzeit –
Schneeweiße Blüten auf mich streut,
Hühner gackeln um mich her,
Unachtend, was das für ein Vetter wär.
Da geht mein Pfarrherr nun vorbei,
Grüßt den Meister und lächelt: Ei,
Wärs so weit mit uns, armer Hahn?
Andrees, was fangt Ihr mit ihm an?
Ihr könnt ihn weder sieden noch braten,
Mir aber müßt es schlimm geraten,
Einen alten Kirchendiener gut
Nicht zu nehmen in Schutz und Hut.
Kommt! tragt ihn mir gleich vor ins Haus,
Trinket ein kühl Glas Wein mit aus.

Der rußig Lümmel, schnell bedacht,
Nimmt mich vom Boden auf und lacht.
Es fehlt' nicht viel, so tat ich frei
Gen Himmel einen Freudenschrei.
Im Pfarrhaus ob dem fremden Gast
War groß und klein erschrocken fast;
Bald aber in jedem Angesicht
Ging auf ein rechtes Freudenlicht.
Frau, Magd und Knecht, Mägdlein und Buben,
Den großen Göckel in der Stuben
Mit siebenfacher Stimmen Schall
Begrüßen, begucken, betasten all.
Der Gottesmann drauf mildiglich
Mit eignen Händen trägt er mich
Nach seinem Zimmer, Stiegen auf,
Nachpolteret der ganze Hauf.

Hier wohnt der Frieden auf der Schwell!
In den geweißten Wänden hell
Sogleich empfing mich sondre Luft,
Bücher- und Gelahrtenduft,

An aa that aifterneen I lay
Ootside his hoosie richt dowie an wae.   melancholy and sad
A wee tree shook its blossam doon
An happit me ower wi snaa-fite bloom;   covered; snow-white
Clockin hens scrattit roon aboot me
An cair't nae a doit fa the stranger micht be.   didn't give a damn
Weel, by cam the Minister, the man imsel,
Nods tae the smith an syne says: 'Well,   then
Poor old cock, are you over the hill?
What do you plan to do with him, Will?
I doubt if he'd do to roast or boil!
But it surely would look very disloyal
If I failed him and left him in the lurch,
This faithful servant of the Church.
He should be in the Manse. Come, carry him thither,
And we two shall take a dram together!'

Weel, he didnae haiver, the brooky-faced chiel –   hesitate; sooty
He shoodert me, leuch, weel-pleast wi the deal.   shouldered;
I wiz that kinechtit, it wiz fairly a wonner   delighted [laughed
I didnae skreich 'Thank-Ye' tae Him Up Yonner.
Syne up at the Manse, baith great an smaa
Got a gey bring-up fan the guest they saa;   quite a shock
But it didnae tak lang or ilka face   before each
Wi a lichtsome hairty smile wiz graced.
Mistress, sairvint-lass, grieve, an littlans,   farm bailiff
Aa saiven o them (an the cat an her kittlans)
Aa thrang in the parlour, they tit an they powk   tug; poke
An they gowp dumfoonert at the muckle tin cock.   gape
But the Man o God in his chairity   [dumbfounded
In his haans up the stairs he cairrit me,
Up till his study, wi aa the kin-
abrich o them breenging ahin.   clan; bustling behind

Sic lichtsome sweet contentment dwalls
Atween the clean fite-washen walls!   whitewashed
An comin ben, fit my neb assails   entering; what my nose
Is a hale jingbang o unco smells –   variety; unusual

Gerani- und Resedaschmack,
Auch ein Rüchlein Rauchtabak.
(Dies war mir all noch unbekannt.)
Ein alter Ofen aber stand
In der Ecke linkerhand.

Recht als ein Turn tät er sich strecken
Mit seinem Gipfel bis zur Decken,
Mit Säulwerk, Blumwerk, kraus und spitz –
O anmutsvoller Ruhesitz!
Zu öberst auf dem kleinen Kranz
Der Schmied mich auf ein Stänglein pflanzt'.

Betrachtet mir das Werk genau!
Mir deuchts ein ganzer Münsterbau;
Mit Schildereien wohl geziert,
Mit Reimen christlich ausstaffiert.
Davon vernahm ich manches Wort,
Dieweil der Ofen ein guter Hort
Für Kind und Kegel und alte Leut
Zu plaudern, wann es wind't und schneit.

Hier seht ihr seitwärts auf der Platten
Eines Bischofs Krieg mit Mäus und Ratten,
Mitten im Rheinstrom sein Kastell.
Das Ziefer kommt geschwommen schnell,
Die Knecht nichts richten mit Waffen und Wehr,
Der Schwänze werden immer mehr:
Viel Tausend gleich in dicken Haufen
Frech an der Mauer auf sie laufen,
Fallen dem Pfaffen in sein Gemach;
Sterben muß er mit Weh und Ach,
Von den Tieren aufgefressen,
Denn er mit Meineid sich vermessen.

Buiks an lear an flooers an a sype   learning; flowers; a hint
O bogie-roll fae the guid man's pipe   strong tobacco
(I niver haed kent the like afore).
But losh! in the ingle, left fae the door   good Lord
– An Deil kens foo in the name o Creation   how
Sicalike thing fae the German nation
Iver stravaigit ower lan an sea   ever wandered
Tae grace a Scots manse wi its company* –
There steed a dutch-til't stove, the hicht
O the waa, like a tooer, an unco sicht   wall
Wi its pillars an picters an flooers an aa
As fit for a laird's hoose as iver I saw.
An on the croon o't, richt at the tap,
Wi care on a pole Smiddy Will set me up.

Tak a richt look at this til't stove! Tae me
It's as grand as the gran'est toon's-kirk could be.
Some tiles wi picters is ornimentit,
Ithers wi godly proverbs paintit
(Come time I made sense o the guid words printit)
For siccan a stove is a quaiet repair   refuge
For aa Jock Tamson's bairns an mair   all humanity
On a coorse cauld nicht tae sit an news   cruel; gossip
Fan the weend an the snaa blaa roon the hoose.

See bi the bink here the tale oonforgotten   hob
O Hatto the Bishop*, the mice an the rottans,   rats
His ilant castle on the River Rhine,
The vermin sweemin tae far he's lyin;   where
His men can naither attack nor defen'
For the thrang o the crayters will niver en'.
They come in their hunners, aye thoosans, they rin
Stracht up the waa wi nae fear o the men,
An intae the chamber an yokit on the priest,   attacked
An he skirlt oot o him as they jyn't in the feast   screamed
Till there wisnae a smick o him left on the fleir,   scrap
An that's fit he got for bein a leear.   what; liar

– Sodann König Belsazers seinen Schmaus.
Weiber und Spielleut, Saus und Braus;
Zu großem Schrecken an der Wand
Rätsel schreibt eines Geistes Hand.

– Zuletzt da vorne stellt sich für
Sara lauschend an der Tür,
Als der Herr mit Abraham
Vor seiner Hütte zu reden kam,
Und ihme einen Sohn versprach.
Sara sich Lachens nicht entbrach,
Weil beide schon sehr hoch betaget.
Der Herr vernimmt es wohl und fraget:
Wie, lachet Sara? glaubt sie nicht,
Was der Herr will, leicht geschicht?
Das Weib hinwieder Flausen machet,
Spricht: Ich habe nicht gelachet.
Das war nun wohl gelogen fast,
Der Herr es doch passieren laßt,
Weil sie nicht leugt aus arger List,
Auch eine Patriarchin ist.

Seit daß ich hier bin dünket mir
Die Winterszeit die schönste schier.
Wie sanft ist aller Tage Fluß
Bis zum geliebten Wochenschluß!
– Freitag zu Nacht, noch um die Neune,
Bei seiner Lampen Trost alleine,
Mein Herr fangt an sein Predigtlein
Studieren; anderst mags nicht sein;
Eine Weil am Ofen brütend steht,
Unruhig hin und dannen geht:
Sein Text ihm schon die Adern reget;
Drauf er sein Werk zu Faden schläget.
Inmittelst einmal auch etwan
Hat er ein Fenster aufgetan –
Ah, Sternenlüfteschwall wie rein
Mit Haufen dringet zu mir ein!

Syne here's King Belshazar* in his banquetin-haa   then
Wi a mengie o weemin an pipers an aa;   crowd
Till a ghaistly haan on the waa did appear
Writin oonchancy wirds that fullt them wi fear.   ill-omened

An last, on the forepairt, see Sarah* stan   front
Bi the door, wi her lug cuppit in her haan,
Harkin oot as her man an the Lord Himsel
Confabit thegither, an she heert God tell   discussed
That Abraham waed faither a bairn, a loon,   boy
An Sarah jist leuch, she cudnae haud on,   laughed; couldn't
For her man an her, they were auld deen folk.   worn-out [help it
But the Lord He heert her, an thus He spoke:
'Fit's that, Sarah? Lachin? Ye'll see   laughing
That fit the Lord wills maun come tae be!'
The auld dame, she ettlet tae deny't;   attempted
'I niver leuch at aa!' she cry't.
Weel, that wisnae far aff tellin a lee,
Bit the Lord, he wiz mercifae an lat it be;
For it wisnae main sleekitness that gart er try   pure disingenuous-
Tae lee; an she wis a Patriarch forby.   made her try to lie [ness

I've com tae think, syn I've been here,
That the winter's the verra croon o the year;   crown
For easy-ozy the days gyang past
Till the en' o the week is here at last:
On Friday at nine a'clock at nicht,
Lief lene in the kindly cannle-licht,   all alone
My Minister maun set tee tae plan
His Sunday sairman as weel's he can.
Thochtfae he'll stan bi the stove a fyle   while
Syne throuw the room his wey he'll wyle   pick his way
Wi restless step, as in his heid
He links God's Wird tae thocht an deed.
In the mids o't, fell distrackit beside,   completely
He's gaen tae the windae an opint it wide
– An oh fit caller air daes blaa   what fresh
Stracht fae the stars tae fresh us aa!

Den Verrenberg ich schimmern seh,
Den Schäferbühel dick mit Schnee!

Zu schreiben endlich er sich setzet,
Ein Blättlein nimmt, die Feder netzet,
Zeichnet sein Alpha und sein O
Über dem Exordio.
Und ich von meinem Postament
Kein Aug ab meinem Herrlein wend;
Seh, wie er, mit Blicken steif ins Licht,
Sinnt, prüfet jedes Worts Gewicht,
Einmal sacht eine Prise greifet,
Vom Docht den roten Butzen streifet;
Auch dann und wann zieht er vor sich
Ein Sprüchlein an vernehmentlich,
So ich mit vorgerecktem Kopf
Begierlich bringe gleich zu Kropf.
Gemachsam kämen wir also
Bis Anfang Applicatio.

Indes der Wächter Elfe schreit.
Mein Herr denkt: es ist Schlafenszeit;
Ruckt seinen Stuhl und nimmt das Licht;
Gut Nacht, Herr Pfarr! – Er hört es nicht.

Im Finstern wär ich denn allein.
Das ist mir eben keine Pein.
Ich hör in der Registratur
Erst eine Weil die Totenuhr,
Lache den Marder heimlich aus
Der scharrt sich müd am Hühnerhaus;
Windweben um das Dächlein stieben;
Ich höre, wie im Wald da drüben –
Man heißet es im Vogeltrost –
Der grimmig Winter sich erbost,
Ein Eichlein spalt't jähling mit Knallen,
Eine Buche, daß die Täler schallen.
– Du meine Güt, da lobt man sich

There's a glint on the Hill o Foundland, see!
An deep snaa lyan on Benachie.

At last he sattles tae write an think;
Taks paper, dooks his pen in ink,
Writes: 'Alpha and Omega He',
Syne: 'Friends, our text this morning we
Take from . . .' and on ma perch up here
I watch ilka move o my maister dear;
I watch him stare intae the cannle-licht,
Ponderin, measurin ilka wird's weicht.   weighing every word
Ae canny sneeshing fae his mull he'll tak,   one surreptitious pinch;
Syne trim the reid-lowin wick richt back,   red burning [snuffbox
An fyles he'll speak a verse til imsel,   sometimes
But I hear't clear aneuch as weel,   enough
Stretch my iron neck oot as far's it'll rax   reach
An intae my crap ilka jewel I pack.
So the twa o's knipes on till the sairman ends,   wrestle on
An the message is clear in: 'So lastly, dear friends . . .'

Alaiven rings oot fae the toonie's clock,
An my maister thinks: Bedtime for all God's folk;
Pits his cheir back in place an taks his licht
An niver hears me fan I bid him Guid Nicht!

Lief lene in the dark I ken nae fear,   left alone
Though ower in the Pairish Office I hear
The deidwatch tickin, an I lach tae mysel   deathwatch beetle
As the tod in the yaird scrats tae nae avail   fox
At the henhoose; an a fluffert, aye, a gale   puff
O weend shaks the reef, an ower in the trees
That the tounsfowk caa the Waed o Birdsease   wood
I hear coorse Winter rage an row,   roll
Ding doon a young aik or a rowan, an wow,   smash; oak
Ye can hear the yark o't the length o the howe,   crash; valley
An fegs, fan ye hear't, I'se warran ye'll bless   upon my word; I'll
The Lord for the stove an its guid-thochtit texts   pious [warrant

So frommen Ofen dankbarlich!
Er wärmelt halt die Nacht so hin,
Es ist ein wahrer Segen drin.
– Jetzt, denk ich, sind wohl hie und dort
Spitzbuben aus auf Raub und Mord;
Denk, was eine schöne Sach es ist,
Brave Schloß und Riegel zu jeder Frist!
Was ich wollt machen herentgegen,
Wenn ich eine Leiter hört anlegen;
Und sonst was so Gedanken sind;
Ein warmes Schweißlein mir entrinnt.
Um zwei, gottlob, und um die drei
Glänzet empor ein Hahnenschrei,
Um fünfe, mit der Morgenglocken,
Mein Herz sich hebet unerschrocken,
Ja voller Freuden auf es springt,
Als der Wächter endlich singt:
Wohlauf, im Namen Jesu Christ!
Der helle Tag erschienen ist!

Ein Stündlein drauf, wenn mir die Sporen
Bereits ein wenig steif gefroren
Rasselt die Lis' im Ofen, brummt,
Bis's Feuer angeht, saust und summt.
Dann von der Küch 'rauf, gar nicht übel,
Die Supp ich wittre, Schmalz und Zwiebel.
Endlich, gewaschen und geklärt,
Mein Herr sich frisch zur Arbeit kehrt.

Am Samstag muß ein Pfarrer fein
Daheim in seiner Klause sein,
Nicht visiteln, herumkutschieren
Seine Faß einbrennen, sonst hantieren.
Meiner hat selten solch Gelust.
Einmal – Ihr sagts nicht weiter just –
Zimmert' er den ganzen Nachmittag
Dem Fritz an einem Meisenschlag,

An the heat it gies oot the lee-lang nicht   live-long
An praise His name and thank Him richt.
– Yet I thinks tae mysel: An noo, nae doot,
There'll be thiefs, ay an murderers oot an aboot;
An I thinks: Ay, Guid be thankit for
Stoot locks an bolts tae haud the door!
But fit wid I dee gin I haird a laidder   what would I do if
Putten tee tae the waa? Fan sich thochts gaither   against
In my heid (as aften aneuch they did),
I swyte a bittie, like ony man wid.   sweat
But bless the Lord, at twa an at three
'Cockalorico!' lichts the dark for me.
Fan the toon's-clock rings five, I tak hairt eence mair,
An at sax, though soondless, I sing yon air:
    'When morning gilds the skies,
     My waking heart arise,
     Let Jesus Christ be praised!'

An oor or so passes; my spurs is turnin
Tae verra ice in the cauldrif mornin;   chilly
Jess clatters at the stove, I can hear her hum
Till the kenlin taks an roars up the lum.   kindling; chimney
Next, up fae the kitchie, the smell o fried finnan   haddock
Gaes roon yer hairt lik a yaird o new flannan,
An the Maister, washen ootwardly an in,
Pits his mind an his pen tae his sairman again.

On Setterdays a minister aye
Maun bide in his study the hale hadden day;   whole day long
Nae pairish visits in the gig,
He daurna brew maut nor delve nor dig.   daren't; malt
Weel, my lad haes seldom sic inclination,
Tho eence he did fa intae temptation
(But tell nae a sowl) – he could be seen   not a soul
Makin a bird's-cage a hale aifterneen

Dort an dem Tisch, und schwatzt' und schmaucht',
Mich alten Tropf kurzweilt' es auch.

Jetzt ist der liebe Sonntag da.
Es läut't zur Kirchen fern und nah.
Man orgelt schon; mir wird dabei,
Als säß ich in der Sakristei.
Es ist kein Mensch im ganzen Haus;
Ein Mücklein hör ich, eine Maus.
Die Sonne sich ins Fenster schleicht,
Zwischen die Kaktusstöck hinstreicht
Zum kleinen Pult von Nußbaumholz,
Eines alten Schreinermeisters Stolz;
Beschaut sich was da liegt umher,
Konkordanz und Kinderlehr,
Oblatenschachtel, Amtssigill,
Im Tintenfaß sich spiegeln will,
Zuteuerst Sand und Grus besicht,
Sich an dem Federmesser sticht
Und gleitet übern Armstuhl frank
Hinüber an den Bücherschrank.
Da stehn in Pergament und Leder
Vornan die frommen Schwabenväter:
Andreä, Bengel, Rieger zween,
Samt *Ötinger* sind da zu sehn.
Wie sie die goldnen Namen liest,
Noch goldener ihr Mund sie küßt,
Wie sie rührt an *Hillers* Harfenspiel –
Horch! klingt es nicht? so fehlt nicht viel.

Inmittelst läuft ein Spinnlein zart
An mir hinauf nach seiner Art,
Und hängt sein Netz, ohn erst zu fragen,
Mir zwischen Schnabel auf und Kragen.
Ich rühr mich nicht aus meiner Ruh,
Schau ihm eine ganze Weile zu,
Darüber ist es wohl geglückt,
Daß ich ein wenig eingenickt. –

For his loonie, an newsin an smoking tee   little son; gossiping
– A richt guid lach for an auld fuil like me.   laugh

An noo the Sabbath day is here;
The kirk-bell summons fowk far an near,
An hark! I can hear the organ, ay,
As clear's if I wiz in the vestry forby.
There's nae a sowl left in the hoose
– A buzzin flee, a scrattin moose –   fly
The saen creeps in throuw the windae yonner;   sun
Throuw atween the cactuses I watch him wanner
Tae the little daskie o walnut waed   walnut desk
(A maisterpiece that an auld jyner made)
– Taks a lookie tae see fitiver there is
Lyin there: Cruden, the Catechis,   Cruden's *Concord-*
The communion breid box, the kirk's ain seal   [*ance*
Refleckit in the inkstan's siller as weel.
Next sand an pounce is cannily surveyed,   ground
An he comes up sharp against the penknife's blade;   [pumice
He hushles joco ower the easy-cheir   slides merrily
Tae the buik-buirds, far buiks o godly lear   bookcase; learning
In perchment an leather stan raa on raa,
The Scots divines at the heid o them aa –
Thomson, Chalmers, Guthrie, a brace
O Browns (a theologick race!)
An readin sic gowden names, the bricht
Saen gars them shine wi the kiss o his licht   makes
An as he touches the Hymnary, belike   just possibly
Ye micht hear a sweet air o John Bacchus Dykes!

A spidery meantime, as spideries dee,
Rins up me, the impident smatchet, an he   cheeky thing
Disnae speir at me, but hangs his web   ask
Atween my collar an my neb!   beak
I niver jow my ginger, jist watch   show no concern
As he wirks awa, the clivver vratch.
An maybe, fylies, it comes tae be
That I drap aff for a meenitie or three . . .

Nun sagt, ob es in Dorf und Stadt
Ein alter Kirchhahn besser hat?

Ein Wunsch im stillen dann und wann
Kommt einen freilich wohl noch an.
Im Sommer stünd ich gern da draus
Bisweilen auf dem Taubenhaus,
Wo dicht dabei der Garten blüht,
Man auch ein Stück vom Flecken sieht.
Dann in der schönen Winterzeit,
Als zum Exempel eben heut:
Ich sag es grad – da haben wir
Gar einen wackern Schlitten hier,
Grün, gelb und schwarz; – er ward verwichen
Erst wieder sauber angestrichen:
Vorn auf dem Bogen brüstet sich
Ein fremder Vogel hoffärtig –
Wenn man mich etwas putzen wollt,
Nicht, daß es drum viel kosten sollt,
Ich stünd so gut dort als wie der
Und machet niemand nicht Unehr!
– Narr! denk ich wieder, du hast dein Teil!
Willst du noch jetzo werden geil?
Mich wundert, ob dir nicht gefiel’,
Daß man, der Welt zum Spott und Ziel,
Deinen warmen Ofen gar zuletzt
Mitsamt dir auf die Läufe setzt’,
Daß auf dem Gsims da um dich säß
Mann, Weib und Kind, der ganze Käs!
Du alter Scherb, schämst du dich nicht,
Auf Eitelkeit zu sein erpicht?
Geh in dich, nimm dein Ende wahr!
Wirst nicht noch einmal hundert Jahr.

Sae tell me, d'y ken, in countrie or toon,
An auld steeplecock wi a better sit-doon?   better provided for

Mind ye, at times it comes tae me
That there's things I think richt lang tae dee   very much long
On simmer days tae stan' ootby   [to do
On the tap o the doocot, far ye can spy   dovecot
The manse's gairden in fullest bloom
An ahint, likewise, a bittie o the toon.   behind
Syne in the winter time o the year
On a day lik iday, saenlighty an clear,   today; sunlit
– I'll come richt oot wi't: doon in the shed   not beat about
There's a grand auld weel-made horse-drawn sled,   [the bush
New-paintit in yalla, green an black
Tae fess its faidit glory back.   bring
An some fremt bird wi his heid casten heich   foreign; held high
Stans at the bow-heid o't unco skeich;   very haughty
But gie me a bittie o a spring-clean, than
Maybe far he swanks I micht stan –   where
I'd nae be misbehaden or oot o place,   inappropriate
An 'twid jist cost a twarthree shillins, or less.
– Noo, noo, I thinks, ye silly auld carl,   chap
Ye're blest! Forget the lust o the wardle!   world
Gin ye fancied yer warm stove lade on tae the runners   if;
O the sled, an yersel' wi't, I widnae wonner!   [loaded
Sic a poppy-show! Or d'ye see yerself   foolish spectacle
Wi the manse-fowk roon ye here, ranged on the
     skelfs,   shelves
The hale clanjamfrey? Ye auld lump o tin,   lot of them
Think shame on yersel for yer vanity, maen.   man
Tak thocht on yer comin hinner-en';   latter end
Ye'll nae see a hunner year again!

Denk es, o Seele!

Ein Tännlein grünet wo,
Wer weiß, im Walde,
Ein Rosenstrauch, wer sagt,
In welchem Garten?
Sie sind erlesen schon,
Denk es, o Seele,
Auf deinem Grab zu wurzeln
Und zu wachsen.

Zwei schwarze Rößlein weiden
Auf der Wiese,
Sie kehren heim zur Stadt
In muntern Sprüngen.
Sie werden schrittweis gehn
Mit deiner Leiche;
Vielleicht, vielleicht noch eh
An ihren Hufen
Das Eisen los wird
Das ich blitzen sehe!

Häusliche Szene

*Schlafzimmer. Präzeptor Ziborius und seine junge Frau.
Das Licht ist gelöscht.*

Schläfst du schon, Rike? – 'Noch nicht.' – Sag! hast du denn
    heut die Kukumern
  Eingemacht? – 'Ja.' – Und wieviel nahmst du mir Essig dazu? –
'Nicht zwei völlige Maß.' – Wie? fast zwei Maß? Und von
    welchem
  Krug? von dem kleinern doch nicht, links vor dem Fenster am
    Hof?
'Freilich.' – Verwünscht! So darf ich die Probe nun noch
    einmal machen,

Oh soul, remember!

In the woods, who knows where,
Stands a green fir-tree;
A rosebush, who can tell,
Blooms in what garden?
Already they have been chosen –
Oh soul, remember! –
To take root on your grave,
For they must grow there.

Out on the meadow two
Black steeds are grazing,
And homewards to the town
They trot so sprightly.
They will be walking when
They draw your coffin;
Who knows but that may be
Even before they shed
That iron on their hooves
That glints so brightly.

A Domestic Scene

*A bedroom. The schoolmaster Herr Ziborius and his young
wife. The light has been turned out.*

Are you asleep yet, Rike? 'No.' Tell me, the cucumbers – did
      you
   Pot them today, and how much vinegar did you put in?
'Two full measures, or less.' What! Nearly two measures? From
      which jug?
   Not from the one on the left! Not from the smaller one,
      there
Outside the window? 'Of course!' Oh God bless us, so now
      the experiment,

Eben indem ich gehofft schon das Ergebnis zu sehn!
Konntest du mich nicht fragen? – 'Du warst in der Schule.' –
  Nicht warten? –
'Lieber, zu lange bereits lagen die Gurken mir da.'
Unlängst sagt ich dir: Nimm von Numero 7 zum Hausbrauch –
'Ach wer behielte denn stets alle die Zahlen im Kopf!' –
Sieben behält sich doch wohl! nichts leichter behalten als
  sieben!
  Groß, mit arabischer Schrift, hält es der Zettel dir vor. –
'Aber du wechselst den Ort nach der Sonne von Fenster
  zu Fenster
  Täglich, die Küche pressiert oft und ich suche mich blind.
Bester, dein Essiggebräu, fast will es mich endlich verdrießen.
  Ruhig, obgleich mit Not, trug ich so manches bis jetzt.
Daß du im Waschhaus dich einrichtetest, wo es an Raum
  fehlt,
  Destillierest und brennst, schien mir das äußerste schon.
Nicht gern sah ich vom Stockbrett erst durch Kolben und
  Krüge
  Meine Reseden verdrängt, Rosen und Sommerlevkoin,
Aber nun stehen ums Haus her rings vor jeglichem Fenster,
  Halb gekleidet in Stroh, gläserne Bäuche gereiht;
Mir auf dem Herd stehn viere zum Hindernis, selber im
  Rauchfang
  Hängt so ein Untier jetzt, wieder ein neuer Versuch!
Lächerlich machen wir uns – nimm mirs nicht übel!' – Was sagst
  du?
  Lächerlich? – 'Hättest du nur heut die Dekanin gehört.
Und in jeglichem Wort ihn selber vernahm ich, den Spötter;
  Boshaft ist er, dazu Schwager zum Pädagogarch.' –
Nun? – 'Einer Festung verglich sie das Haus des Präzeptors,
  ein Bollwerk
  Hieß mein Erker, es sei alles gespickt mit Geschütz!' –

Just as I hoped for results, now it must all be redone.
Wife, why didn't you ask me? 'You were at the school.' Why
    not wait then?
   'Husband, those gherkins had lain long, and enough is
    enough.'
Only lately I told you: use number 7 for domestic
   Purposes – 'Oh, I forget those silly numbers sometimes!'
Seven's not a difficult one to remember, what's easier than
    seven?
   Arabic seven, written large, plain on the label it stands.
'But you keep changing the place as the sun moves, from
    window to window,
   Every day; when I cook, I can't be searching for things.
Listen, my dear: I'm getting quite cross with your vinegar-
    brewing.
   I've endured it till now, peaceably, though it's been hard.
When you began in the washhouse – why, that was the limit
    already! –
   Heating, distilling – when I've no room to work in that place.
Where have my roses all gone, my gillyflowers and my resedas?
   Pushed off the shelf by your pots! Wasn't that bad enough?
    Now
You have surrounded the house with them: window by window
    they stand there,
   Row upon row of those glass bellies half covered in straw;
Four in the hearth to get in my way, and now even in the
    chimney
   One of the monsters (no doubt, some new experiment) hangs!
If you'll forgive me, my dear – we're becoming a laughingstock!'
    What's that?
   Laughingstock? 'I wish you'd heard what the Dean's wife
    said today!
And every word seemed to come from the Dean, that mocker
    and scoffer;
   He's so malicious, and his cousin's Director of Schools.'
Well? 'She said that the schoolmaster's house is a fortress, and
    my bay-
   Window a bastion, the whole place simply larded with guns!'

Schnödes Gerede, der lautere Neid! Ich hoffe mein Stecken-
    Pferd zu behaupten, so gut als ihr Gemahl, der Dekan.
Freuts ihn Kanarienvögel und Einwerfkäfige dutzend-
    Weise zu haben, mich freuts, tüchtigen Essig zu ziehn. –

    Pause. Er scheint nachdenklich. Sie spricht für sich:

'Wahrlich, er dauert mich schon; ihn ängstet ein wenig die
    Drohung
    Mit dem Studienrat, dem er schon lange nicht traut.' –

    Er fährt fort:

Als Präzeptor tat ich von je meine Pflicht; ein geschätzter
    Gradus neuerlich gibt einiges Zeugnis davon.
Was ich auf materiellem Gebiet, in müßigen Stunden,
    Manchem Gewerbe, dem Staat denke zu leisten dereinst,
Ob ich meiner Familie nicht ansehnlichen Vorteil
    Sichere noch mit der Zeit, dessen geschweig ich vorerst:
Aber – *den* will ich sehn, der einem geschundenen Schulmann
    Ein Vergnügen wie das, Essig zu machen, verbeut!
Der von Allotrien spricht, von Lächerlichkeiten – er sei nun
    Oberinspektor, er sei Rektor und Pädagogarch!
Greife nur einer mich an, ich will ihm dienen! Gewappnet
    Findet ihr mich! Dreifach liegt mir das Erz um die Brust!
– Rike, du lachst! . . . du verbirgst es umsonst! ich fühle die
    Stöße . . .
    Nun, was wandelt dich an? Närrst du mich, törichtes
    Weib? –
'Lieber, närrischer, goldener Mann! wer bliebe hier ernsthaft?
    Nein, dies Feuer hätt ich nimmer im Essig gesucht!' –
Gnug mit den Possen! Ich sage dir, mir ist die Sache nicht
    spaßhaft. –
    'Ruhig! Unseren Streit, Alter, vergleichen wir schon.
Gar nicht fällt es mir ein, dir die einzige Freude zu rauben;

That's just vile envious chatter! I say that my hobbyhorse is no
   Less worthwhile than the Dean's; wait till I prove it!
     While he
Passes his time with birdcages and dozens of yellow canaries,
   I brew good vinegar; that happens to be what I like.

   A pause. He seems pensive. She speaks to herself:

'Why, it's a shame, the poor man! He's already alarmed that
     I mentioned
   That official; he's not trusted him now for some time.'

   He continues:

As Praeceptor I never have failed in my duty: as witness
   Lately the mark I achieved, which has been cause for some
     pride.
As to my leisure pursuits, and the long-term material advantage
   They may bring to the State, likewise to many a trade,
And to my family, for whom they promise a prosperous future –
   I make no mention of this, not for the moment at least.
But – to debar a poor honest school drudge of his vinegar-
     making,
   Worn to the bone as he is – what sort of spoilsport is that?
Talks of eccentric pastimes, absurdities – I'd like to meet him,
   Superintendent or not, Rector and Pedagogarch!
You would attack me, sir? Your servant, then, and in full
     armour!
   I shall be ready for you! Threefold, my breastplate of bronze!
. . . Rike, you're laughing at me! You can't hide it: I feel your
     ribs shaking!
   Well, what's got into you then? Making a fool of me, what?
'Darling husband, you poor silly man! How can I help laughing?
   Who would have thought that such heat lived in a vinegar-jar!'
Wife, stop this nonsense! I tell you, for me it's a serious matter.
   'Now, my dear, calm yourself; come, why should we quarrel
     for this?
Why should I dream of depriving you now of your only great
     pleasure?

Zuviel hänget daran, und ich verstehe dich ganz.
Siehst du von deinem Katheder im Schulhaus so durch das
    Fenster
  Über das Höfchen den Schatz deiner Gefäße dir an,
Alle vom Mittagsstrahl der herrlichen Sonne beschienen,
  Die dir den gärenden Wein heimlich zu zeitigen glüht,
Nun, es erquicket dir Herz und Aug in sparsamen Pausen,
  Wie das bunteste Brett meiner Levkoin es nicht tat;
Und ein Pfeifchen Tabak in diesem gemütlichen Anblick
  Nimmt dir des Amtes Verdruß reiner als alles hinweg;
Ja, seitdem du schon selbst mit eigenem Essig die rote
  Tinte dir kochst, die sonst manchen Dreibätzner verschlang,
Ist dir, mein ich, der Wust der Exerzitienhefte
  Minder verhaßt; dich labt still der bekannte Geruch.
Dies, wie mißgönnt' ich es dir? Nur gehst du ein bißchen ins
    Weite.
  Alles – so heißt dein Spruch – habe sein Maß und sein Ziel.' –
Laß mich! Wenn mein Produkt dich einst zur vermöglichen Frau
    macht –
  'Bester, das sagtest du just auch bei der Seidenkultur.' –
Kann ich dafür, daß das Futter mißriet, daß die Tiere
    krepierten? –
  'Seine Gefahr hat auch sicher das neue Geschäft.' –
Namen und Ehre des Manns, die bringst du wohl gar nicht in
    Anschlag? –
  'Ehre genug blieb uns, ehe wir Essig gebraut.' –
Korrespondierendes Mitglied heiß ich dreier Vereine. –
  'Nähme nur *einer* im Jahr etliche Krüge dir ab!' –
Dir fehlt jeder Begriff von rationellem Bestreben. –
  'Seit du ihn hast, fehlt dir abends ein guter Salat.' –
Undank! mein Fabrikat durch sämtliche Sorten ist trefflich. –
  'Numero 7 und 9 kenn ich, und – lobe sie nicht.' –
Heut, wie ich merke, gefällst du dir sehr, mir in Versen zu
    trumpfen. –

It's too important for you; all this I quite understand.
When you are there in the school house and look from
          your desk through the window,
    Over the courtyard, and see your precious jars in a row,
All agleam in the noonday sun as it pours down its splendour,
    Making your wine grow ripe, secretly furthering your plans –
Why, they refresh your heart as you take time off to
          survey them,
    Cheer you as even my best gillyflowers never did me!
And as you light up your pipe and gaze comfortably at these
          treasures,
    They're a distraction, I'm sure, even from your tedious job.
You've even used your own vinegar lately to brew your red
          ink from;
    No need to buy the stuff now, many a sixpence it cost.
That must be some relief, too, in your hateful exercise-marking,
    Soothing schoolmasterly rage with an old favourite smell.
Can I begrudge you all this? – But you are just a little excessive:
    We must do all things, you say, with some restraint and
          good sense.'
Wife, let me be! When my product one day makes you
          famous and wealthy –
    'When you were trying to breed silkworms, you said the
          same thing.'
Was it my fault that something was wrong with the food,
          that the brutes died?
    'Your new venture, I'm sure, will have its own dangers too.'
So: my good name, I suppose, and my honour – you count
          them for nothing?
    'We had honour enough even without vinegar-jars.'
I correspond as a member with three different learned societies!
    'Why doesn't one of them buy some of your vinegar, then?'
You have no notion of rational aims and creative endeavour.
    'You and your notions! A good salad for supper you need.'
What ingratitude! All my varieties have excellent flavours.
    'Well, numbers seven and nine, they're not much good, that
          I know.'
It is your pleasure today, I observe, to cap me with verses.

'Waren es Verse denn nicht, was du gesprochen bisher?' –
Eine Schwäche des Mannes vom Fach, darfst du sie
    mißbrauchen? –
'Unwillkürlich, wie du, red ich elegisches Maß.' –
Mühsam übt ich dirs ein, harmlose Gespräche zu würzen. –
'Freilich im bitteren Ernst nimmt es sich wunderlich aus.' –
Also verbitt ich es jetzt; sprich, wie dir der Schnabel
    gewachsen. –
'Gut; laß sehen, wie sich Prose mit Distichen mischt.' –
Unsinn! Brechen wir ab. Mit Weibern sich streiten ist fruchtlos. –
'Fruchtlos nenn ich, im Schlot Essig bereiten, mein Schatz.' –
Daß noch zum Schlusse mir dein Pentameter tritt auf die Ferse! –
'Dein Hexameter zieht unwiderstehlich ihn nach.' –
Ei, dir scheint es bequem, nur das Wort noch, das letzte zu
    haben:
    Habs! Ich schwöre, von mir hast du das letzte gehört. –
Meinetwegen; so mag ein Hexameter einmal allein stehn.' –

*Pause. Der Mann wird unruhig, es peinigt ihn offenbar,
das Distichon nicht geschlossen zu hören oder es nicht
selber schließen zu dürfen. Nach einiger Zeit kommt ihm
die Frau mit Lachen zu Hülfe und sagt:*

'Alter! ich tat dir zu viel; wirklich, dein Essig passiert;
Wenn er dir künftig noch besser gerät, wohlan, so ist einzig
    Dein das Verdienst, denn du hast, wahrlich, kein zänkisches
    Weib!' –

Er gleichfalls herzlich lachend und sie küssend:

Rike! morgenden Tags räum ich dir die vorderen Fenster
    Sämtlich! und im Kamin prangen die Schinken allein!

'Why not? Have you not been talking in verse all this time?'
It is improper of you to misuse my professional weakness.
   'I quite spontaneously ape your elegiacal speech.'
I took some trouble to teach you this spice for our light-
      hearted discourse.
   'In bitter earnest it sounds very bizarre, I must say.'
Well, I forbid you it now; just talk the way nature has taught
      you.
   'Good; let us see how my prose mixed with your distichs
      will sound.'
Rubbish! Now let us have done! It is fruitless to argue
      with women.
   'I call it fruitless to keep vinegar jars in the hearth.'
Why, devil take your pentameter treading like this on my
      coat-tail!
   'Where your hexameter leads, I have to follow behind.'
Wife, what you like is to have the last word. Well, have it by
      all means!
   I've spoken mine, that I swear; you'll hear no more from
      now on.
'Very well! Let a hexameter stand all forlorn, just for this once.'

    *A pause. Her husband grows restless, it is clearly painful
    to him neither to hear the distich closed nor to be able to
    close it himself. After a while his wife bursts out laughing
    and comes to his rescue:*

   'Husband, I've teased you too much; bless you! Your
      vinegar's good!
And when you brew it still better in future, the credit shall
      all be
Yours; for I'll not have you say you have a quarrelsome wife!'

    He too laughs heartily and kisses her.

Rike! Tomorrow I'll clear every one of those front windows
      for you!
   And your magnificent hams, they'll have the hearth to
      themselves!

Besuch in der Kartause

Epistel an Paul Heyse

Als Junggesell, du weißt ja, lag ich lang einmal
In jenem luftigen Dörflein an der Kindelsteig
Gesundheitshalber müßig auf der Bärenhaut.
Der dicke Förster, stets auf mein Pläsier bedacht,
Wies mir die Gegend kreuz und quer und führte mich
Bei den Kartäusern gleich die ersten Tage ein.
Nun hätt ich dir von Seiner Dignität zunächst,
Dem Prior, manches zu erzählen: wie wir uns
In Scherz und Ernst, trotz meines schwäbischen Ketzertums
Gar bald verstanden; von dem kleinen Gartenhaus
Wo ein bescheidnes Bücherbrett die Lieblinge
Des würdigen Herrn, die edlen alten Schwarten trug,
Aus denen uns bei einem Glase Wein, wie oft!
Pränestes Haine, Tiburs Wasser zugerauscht.
Hievon jedoch ein andermal. Er schläft nun auch
In seiner Ecke dort im Chor. Die Mönche sind,
Ein kleiner Rest der Brüderschaft, in die Welt zerstreut
Im Kreuzgang lärmt der Küfer, aus der Kirche dampft
Das Malz, den Garten aber deckt ein Hopfenwald
Kaum daß das Häuschen in der Mitte frei noch blieb
Von dessen Dach, verwittert und entfärbt, der Storch
Auf *einem* Beine traurig in die Ranken schaut.

So, als ich jüngst, nach vierzehn Jahren, wiederkam,
Fand ich die ganze Herrlichkeit dahin. Sei's drum!
Ein jedes Ding währt seine Zeit. Der alte Herr
Sah alles lang so kommen, und ganz andres noch,
Darüber er sich eben nicht zu Tod gegrämt.
Bei dünnem Weißbier und versalzenem Pökelfleisch
Saß ich im Gasthaus der gewesnen Prälatur,
Im gleichen Sälchen, wo ich jenes erstemal
Mit andern Fremden mich am ausgesuchten Tisch
Des Priors freute klösterlicher Gastfreiheit.

A Visit to the Carthusians

Epistle to Paul Heyse

I once, in my unmarried days, as you'll recall,
Stayed in that breezy village on the Kindelsteig,
Taking an idle rest-cure there for quite some time.
The forester, that good fat man, kept me amused
By showing me the district, and in the first few days
He introduced me to the Carthusian fathers there.
There's much I have to tell about his Reverence
The Prior: how despite my Swabian heresies
We soon made friends, and found much to be serious
And much to laugh about; the little summerhouse,
Where on a modest bookshelf all the good old man's
Favourite authors stood, old worthy pigskin tomes.
How often, as we sipped our wine, they'd speak to us
Of Tivoli's, of Palestrina's groves and streams!
But that tale's for another time. Now he too sleeps
There in his corner of the choir. The other monks,
A remnant of the brotherhood, are all dispersed;
The cloister's now the cooper's workshop, from the church
The smell of malt drifts, the whole garden's thick with hops,
No room in the middle even for that little house
With the discoloured weathered roof, on which a stork
Stares sadly at this jungle, standing on one leg.

And that was all I found of it, revisiting
Its splendours after fourteen years the other day.
Well, past is past, and all things have their time. The old man
Saw it all coming, and foresaw much else as well;
But he was simply not prepared to die of grief.
So I sat now with my pale beer and salted pork
In what were once the Prior's quarters, now an inn,
And in the very room where first, so long ago,
I shared with other strangers the delights of his
Monastic hospitality. They served an eel

Ein großer Aal ward aufgetragen, Laberdan,
Und Artischocken aus dem Treibhaus; 'fleischiger',
So schwur, die Lippen häufig wischend, ein Kaplan,
'Sieht sie Fürst Taxis selber auf der Tafel nicht!'
Des höchsten Preises würdig aber deuchte mir
Ein gelber, weihrauchblumiger Vierunddreißiger,
Den sich das Kloster auf der sonnigsten Halde zog.
Nach dem Kaffee schloß unser wohlgelaunter Wirt
Sein Raritätenkästchen auf, Bildschnitzereien
Enthaltend, alte Münzen, Gemmen und so fort,
Geweihtes und Profanes ohne Unterschied;
Ein heiliger Sebastian in Elfenbein,
Desgleichen Sankt Laurentius mit seinem Rost,
Verschmähten nicht als Nachbarin Andromeda,
Nackt an den Fels geschmiedet, trefflich schön in Buchs.
Nächst alledem zog eine altertümliche
Stutzuhr, die oben auf dem Schranke ging, mich an;
Das Zifferblatt von grauem Zinn, vor welchem sich
Das Pendelchen nur in allzu peinlicher Eile schwang,
Und bei den Ziffern, groß genug, in schwarzer Schrift
Las man das Wort: Una ex illis ultima.
'Derselben eine ist die letzt' – verdeutschte flugs
Der Pater Schaffner, der bei Tisch mich unterhielt
Und gern von seinem Schulsack einen Zipfel wies;
Ein Mann wie Stahl und Eisen; die Gelehrsamkeit
Schien ihn nicht schwer zu drücken und der Küraß stand
Ihm ohne Zweifel besser als die Kutte an.

Dem dacht ich nun so nach für mich, da streift mein Aug
Von ungefähr die Wand entlang und stutzt mit eins:
Denn dort, was seh ich? Wäre das die alte Uhr?
Wahrhaftig ja, sie war es! – Und vergnügt wie sonst,
Laufst nicht, so gilts nicht, schwang ihr Scheibchen sich auf
        und ab.
Betrachtend stand ich eine Weile still vor ihr
Und seufzte wohl dazwischen leichthin einmal auf.
Darüber plötzlich wandte sich ein stummer Gast,
Der einzige, der außer mir im Zimmer war,

Of massive size, salt cod, fresh artichokes straight from
The hothouse, 'fatter and more succulent' (or so,
Wiping his lips repeatedly, a chaplain swore)
'Than any that Prince Thurn and Taxis gets to eat!'
But worthy of the highest praise of all, I thought,
Fragrant as incense, was the golden '34
Grown by the monastery on its own sunniest slope.
When we had drunk our coffee, our good-humoured host
Would open up his box of curiosities,
Full of carved figures, old coins, cameos and the like,
Objects both sacred and profane all jumbled up;
An ivory St Sebastian I recall, likewise
St Laurence roasting on his grill, and neither had
The least objection to being cheek by jowl beside
An exquisitely carved boxwood Andromeda
Chained naked to her rock. What took my fancy most
Was a small antique standing clock, that ticked away
There on the cupboard: to and fro its pendulum
Wagged with disturbing haste before the pewter dial
On which, inscribed beside the figures, black and clear,
We read the words: *Una ex illis ultima*.
'One of these', Father Steward, my companion at
The table, had at once translated for me, 'one
Of these will be your last.' (He liked to show he knew
A thing or two; yet scholarship sat lightly on
This man of steel and iron, who would more willingly,
No doubt, have worn full armour than his monkish garb.)

Thus on the past I mused, when quite by chance my eye,
Glancing along the wall, came to a sudden stop:
For what is this I see? Can that be the old clock?
Indeed it was! And up and down its cheerful disc
(No score unless you're running) wagged as it used to do!
There for a while I stood in front of it and gazed,
And thought my thoughts, and heaved a sigh or two as well.
But now a guest who had not spoken hitherto,
An elderly man, my only fellow-visitor,

Ein älterer Herr, mit freundlichem Gesicht zu mir:
'Wir sollten uns fast kennen, mein ich – hätten wir
Nicht schon vorlängst in diesen Wänden uns gesehn?'
Und alsbald auch erkannt ich ihn: der Doktor wars
Vom Nachbarstädtchen und weiland der Klosterarzt,
Ein Erzschelm damals, wie ich mich noch wohl entsann,
Vor dessen derben Neckerein die Mönche sich
Mehr als vor seinem schlimmsten Tranke fürchteten.
Nun hatt ich hundert Fragen an den Mann, und kam
Beiher auch auf das Ührchen: 'Ei, jawohl, das ist'
Erwidert' er, 'vom seligen Herrn ein Erbstück noch,
Im Testament dem Pater Schaffner zugeteilt
Der es zuletzt dem Brauer, seinem Wirt, vermacht.'
– So starb der Pater hier am Ort? – 'Es litt ihn nicht
Auswärts; ein Jahr, da stellte sich unser Enaksohn
Unkenntlich fast in Rock und Stiefeln, wieder ein.
Hier bleib ich, rief er, bis man mich mit Prügeln jagt!
Für Geld und gute Worte gab man ihm denn auch
Ein Zimmer auf der Sommerseite, Hausmannskost
Und einen Streifen Gartenland. An Beschäftigung
Fehlt' es ihm nicht; er brannte seinen Kartäusergeist
Wie ehedem, die vielbeliebte Panazee,
Die sonst dem Kloster manches Tausend eingebracht.
Am Abend, wo es unten schwarz mit Bauern sitzt,
Behagt' er sich beim Deckelglas, die Dose und
Das blaue Sacktuch neben sich, im Dunst und Schwul
Der Zechgesellschaft, plauderte, las die Zeitung vor,
Sprach Politik und Landwirtschaft – mit *einem* Wort,
Es war ihm wohl, wie in den schönsten Tagen kaum.
Man sagt, er sei bisweilen mit verwegenen
Heiratsgedanken umgegangen – es war damals
So ein lachendes Pumpelchen hier, für den Stalldienst, wie mir
    deucht –
Doch das sind Possen. Eines Morgens rief man mich
In Eile zum Herrn Pater: er sei schwer erkrankt.
Ein Schläglein hatte höflich bei ihm angeklopft
Und ihn in größern Schrecken als Gefahr gesetzt.
Auch fand ich ihn am fünften oder sechsten Tag

Turned to me with a kindly air and said: 'I think
We must have met before somewhere – could it have been
Within these very walls, and quite some time ago?'
And sure enough, I recognized the man at once:
The doctor from the neighbouring town who once had been
Physician to the monastery (and as I
Remembered well, an arch-rogue then, whom the monks feared
More for his ribald jests than for his potent drugs).
So now I had a hundred things to ask this man,
And *en passant* we spoke about the clock. 'Oh yes',
He answered, 'that's an heirloom handed down from his
Late Reverence. The Prior left it to the Steward,
Who in his turn bequeathed it to mine host the brewer.'
'You mean the Steward died here?' 'He had gone out into
The world, but couldn't stand it. In a year, our giant
Returned; we barely knew him in his coat and boots.
'I've come back here to stay!' he cried, 'till you take sticks
To drive me out!' And so, for money and kind words,
They let him have a room on the summer side, plain food,
And a bit of a garden. He had plenty there
To keep him occupied, distilling his chartreuse,
That ever popular elixir, as before;
Many a goodly sum it earned our holy house.
Down here, where such a crowd of peasants used to sit,
He'd spend his evenings with his tankard and his blue
Handkerchief and his snuffbox by him; in the warm fug
Of crowded revellers he'd chatter, read the news
Aloud, and talk of politics and country things:
In short, he was contented as in his best days.
They say that now and then he entertained wild thoughts
Of marriage – at that time, I think, there was a plump
Merry young lass here, working as a stable-maid –
But that's all foolishness. One morning I was called
Urgently to his bedside: he was gravely ill,
They said. Well, a slight stroke had knocked politely on
His door, alarming rather than endangering him.
And five or six days later, sure enough, I found

Schon wieder auf den Strümpfen und getrosten Muts.
Doch fiel mir auf, die kleine Stutzuhr, welche sonst
Dem Bette gegenüber stand und allezeit
Sehr viel bei ihm gegolten, nirgend mehr zu sehn.
Verlegen, als ich darnach frage, fackelt' er:
Sie sei kaputt gegangen, leider, so und so.
Der Fuchs! dacht ich, in seinem Kasten hat er sie
Zu unterst, völlig wohlbehalten, eingesperrt,
Wenn er ihr nicht den Garaus etwa selbst gemacht.
Das unliebsame Sprüchelchen! Mein Pater fand,
Die alte Hexe fange nachgerade an
Zu sticheln, und das war verdrießlich.' – 'Exzellent!
Doch setzten Sie den armen Narren hoffentlich
Nicht noch auf Kohlen durch ein grausames Verhör?'
– 'Je nun, ein wenig stak er allerdings am Spieß,
Was er mir auch im Leben, glaub ich, nicht vergab.'
– So hielt er sich noch eine Zeit? – 'Gesund und rot
Wie eine Rose sah man Seine Reverenz
Vier Jahre noch und drüber, da denn endlich doch
Das leidige Stündlein ganz unangemeldet kam.
Wenn Sie im Tal die Straße gehn dem Flecken zu,
Liegt rechts ein kleiner Kirchhof, wo der Edle ruht.
Ein weißer Stein, mit seinem Klosternamen nur,
Spricht Sie bescheiden um ein Vaterunser an.
Das Ürchen aber – um zum Schlusse kurz zu sein –
War rein verschwunden. Wie das kam, begriff kein Mensch.
Doch frug ihm weiter niemand nach, und längst war es
Vergessen, als von ungefähr die Wirtin einst
In einer abgelegnen Kammer hinterm Schlot
Eine alte Schachtel, wohl verschnürt und zehenfach
Versiegelt, fand, aus der man den gefährlichen
Zeitweisel an das Tageslicht zog mit Eklat.
Die Zuschrift aber lautete: Meinem werten Freund
Bräumeister Ignaz Raußenberger auf Kartaus.'

Also erzählte mir der Schalk mit innigem
Vergnügen, und wer hätte nicht mit ihm gelacht?

Him on his feet again, and in a high good cheer.
But I did notice that the little clock, which had
Always stood opposite his bed, and always been
A thing he greatly valued, was no longer there.
He was embarrassed when I asked him, told some tale
Of how it had got broken, thus and thus, by some
Mischance. Old fox! I thought, he's locked it up quite safe,
Stuffed it into the bottom of his cupboard here,
Or maybe he has smashed the thing with his own hands.
That eery little motto! My good Reverend
Had found the old witch's nagging message more and more
Irksome, till finally he'd had enough of it.'
'Delightful! But, poor innocent, I hope you did
Not question and torment him too unmercifully?'
'Oh well, I grilled him just a bit, perhaps; and he,
I think, never forgave me for it afterwards.'
'So he lived on for some time yet?' 'The Reverend
Continued healthy and as pink as any rose
For four years longer, five perhaps, until at last
The unchancy hour did indeed come, quite unannounced.
Walk down the road towards the village, and you'll find
A little churchyard; that's the good man's resting-place.
A white stone, bearing only his religious name,
Asks modestly for an Our Father for his soul.
As for the clock – well, cutting a long story short –
It had completely disappeared. No one knew how.
But no one now asked questions, and the whole affair
Had been forgotten, when the brewer's wife by chance,
Behind the chimney in an out-of-the-way room,
Found an old parcel, tied up tight and sealed ten times,
From which the ill-omened timekeeper, triumphantly
Unpacked, emerged again into the light of day.
The label read: "To Ignatius Raußenberger, my
Good friend, the master brewer at the Charterhouse".'

This the droll doctor told me, with much obvious glee,
And who indeed would not have laughed to hear his tale?

Erinna an Sappho

Erinna, eine hochgepriesene junge Dichterin des griechischen
Altertums, um 600 v. Chr., Freundin und Schülerin Sapphos
zu Mitylene auf Lesbos. Sie starb als Mädchen mit neunzehn
Jahren. Ihr berühmtestes Werk war ein episches Gedicht, 'Die
Spindel', von dem man jedoch nichts Näheres weiß. Über-
haupt haben sich von ihren Poesien nur einige Bruchstücke
von wenigen Zeilen und drei Epigramme erhalten. Es wurden
ihr zwei Statuen errichtet, und die Anthologie hat mehrere
Epigramme zu ihrem Ruhme von verschiedenen Verfassern.

'Vielfach sind zum Hades die Pfade', heißt ein
Altes Liedchen – 'und einen gehst du selber,
Zweifle nicht!' Wer, süßeste Sappho, zweifelt?
Sagt es nicht jeglicher Tag?
Doch den Lebenden haftet nur leicht im Busen
Solch ein Wort, und dem Meer anwohnend ein Fischer von
        Kind auf
Hört im stumpferen Ohr der Wogen Geräusch nicht mehr.
– Wundersam aber erschrak mir heute das Herz. Vernimm!

Sonniger Morgenglanz im Garten,
Ergossen um der Bäume Wipfel,
Lockte die Langschläferin (denn so schaltest du jüngst Erinna!)
Früh vom schwüligen Lager hinweg.
Stille war mein Gemüt; in den Adern aber
Unstet klopfte das Blut bei der Wangen Blässe.

Als ich am Putztisch jetzo die Flechten lös'te,
Dann mit nardeduftendem Kamm vor der Stirn den Haar-
Schleier teilte, – seltsam betraf mich im Spiegel Blick in Blick.
Augen, sagt ich, ihr Augen, was wollt ihr?
Du, mein Geist, heute noch sicher behaus't da drinne,
Lebendigen Sinnen traulich vermählt,
Wie mit fremdendem Ernst, lächelnd halb, ein Dämon,

Erinna to Sappho

Erinna, a much-acclaimed young poetess of Greek antiquity,
lived around 600 BC, a friend and pupil of Sappho at Mitylene
on the island of Lesbos. She died as a nineteen-year-old girl.
Her most famous work was an epic poem, The Distaff, *of*
which however no details are known. Indeed nothing survives
of her poetry but some fragments a few lines long and three
epigrams. Two statues were raised to her, and the Greek
Anthology contains several epigrams in her honour by differ-
ent authors.

'Many and various are the paths to the land of the dead',
Says an old song – 'and one of them you yourself shall
Walk, do not doubt it!' Who doubts it, dearest Sappho?
Does not each day say the same?
But such a message lies only lightly on living
Hearts, and the fisherman, at home by the sea since
        childhood,
Has a dulled ear that hears the noise of the waves no longer.
– And yet today my soul was wondrously startled. Listen!

Bright morning sun in the garden, gleaming
About the treetops, had enticed me early
Out of my bed, where I love to linger (or so you chide me!)
And out of its sultry warmth. My mind
Was peaceful; but the blood in my veins
Throbbed unsteadily, and my cheeks were pale.

Now, at my dressing-table, as I unbound my hair
And parted it with a spikenard-fragrant comb where it covered
My brow – from the glass something struck me, strangely
        regarding me, a face to my face.
Eyes! You eyes! I said, what are you looking for?
You, my spirit, only today still safe in your house,
Close-wedded there still to my living senses:
With what alien gravity, almost smiling, as a daemon

Nickst du mich an, Tod weissagend!
– Ha, da mit eins durchzuckt' es mich
Wie Wetterschein! wie wenn schwarzgefiedert ein tödlicher
    Pfeil
Streifte die Schläfe hart vorbei,
Daß ich, die Hände gedeckt aufs Antlitz, lange
Staunend blieb, in die nachtschaurige Kluft schwindelnd hinab.

Und das eigene Todesgeschick erwog ich;
Trockenen Augs noch erst,
Bis da ich dein, o Sappho, dachte,
Und der Freundinnen all,
Und anmutiger Musenkunst,
Gleich da quollen die Tränen mir.

Und dort blinkte vom Tisch das schöne Kopfnetz, dein
    Geschenk,
Köstliches Byssosgeweb, von goldnen Bienlein schwärmend.
Dieses, wenn wir demnächst das blumige Fest
Feiern der herrlichen Tochter Demeters,
Möcht ich *ihr* weihn, für meinen Teil und deinen;
Daß sie hold uns bleibe (denn viel vermag sie),
Daß du zu früh dir nicht die braune Locke mögest
Für Erinna vom lieben Haupte trennen.

Now you nod at me, prophesying death!
– Ah, how suddenly it pierced me then,
Like a lightning-flash! as if a deadly arrow, black-feathered,
Were passing close, grazing my temple!
And with my hands I covered my face, staring
Long and astonished, dizzily down into the night's dreadful
    abyss.

And I pondered the destiny of my death;
Still dry-eyed at first, until
I remembered you, dear Sappho,
And all our friends,
And the graceful art of the Muses:
For then my tears fell fast.

And there on the table it glinted, your gift, my beautiful head-
    dress woven
From precious linen, all covered with little golden bees.
We shall soon celebrate the feast of the glorious
Daughter of Demeter, a feast full of flowers:
And this gift I will dedicate to her, for your sake and mine,
That she may still show us favour (for her power is great),
And that you may not too soon be cutting
From your dear head a dark lock for Erinna.

Postscript:
Mörike and Hugo Wolf*

In February 1903 the composer Hugo Wolf, aged forty-three, died in an asylum in Vienna to which he had been confined since October 1898. Like his near-contemporary the philosopher Nietzsche (and like the hero of Thomas Mann's novel *Doktor Faustus*, for whom both he and Nietzsche were partial models), Wolf died of general paralysis of the insane, the final result of an early syphilitic infection. Most of his creative career, like Nietzsche's, had stood under the sign of illness, and shown an astounding alternation between bouts of feverish inspiration and intervals of despairing unproductivity. His main creative period extended only from early 1888 to early 1889, and during it he wrote two of his most important collections of songs: about fifty from Mörike and fifty from Goethe. A third volume of twenty songs from Eichendorff was also completed at this time, and in addition, during the next year or so, Wolf composed most of his settings (about a hundred in all) from nineteenth-century German translations of Spanish and Italian poetry. The years 1892 to 1894 were totally sterile; then he was able to resume work and wrote about thirty more songs and a comic opera, *Der Corregidor*. The composition of a second opera was interrupted by his collapse into insanity in September 1897. As in Nietzsche's case, the illness took the form of *folie de grandeur* (summoning his friends, for instance, he announced that he was taking over from Mahler as Director of the Vienna Opera, where in future only his work would be performed). Wolf had struggled for most of his life with poverty and insufficient recognition, though this had partly been due to his own difficult and domineering nature, his readiness to take offence, his treacherous ingratitude to many of the friends who tried to help him, in fact to a kind of self-aggrandizing pride which his genius excused

* This excursus on Wolf's settings of Mörike's poems has been written in collaboration with Gilbert McKay. We are indebted to the authoritative work by Eric Sams which catalogues the songs (E. Sams, *The Songs of Hugo Wolf*, Faber and Faber, 3rd edn, 1992) and to the expert assistance of Richard Stokes.

but which seems to have anticipated, again like Nietzsche's, his final pathological delusions. He did however live to see Hugo Wolf Societies set up in Vienna, Berlin and Stuttgart, betokening the degree of admiration and good will he had nevertheless inspired.

Having been an enthusiastic and belligerently proselytizing Wagnerite since experiencing a kind of conversion to Wagner at the age of fifteen, he reacted with intolerance to the traditionalist teaching at the Vienna Conservatoire, and was dismissed from that institution when he was seventeen. His musical education was largely autodidactic, based on voracious score-reading and experimentation on the piano. For three years, from January 1884 to April 1887, he was employed as music critic of the *Salonblatt*, a popular Viennese Sunday magazine, in which his fiercely partisan views, anti Brahms and Dvořák, pro Wagner, Liszt and Berlioz, clashed with the predominantly conservative tastes of Vienna and its musical panjandrum Eduard Hanslick, whom Wagner had so detested. The offence his reviews gave to many persons powerful in the musical world was one of the reasons why he found it difficult to get his instrumental works performed. Though a few of these have remained in the general repertoire – the delightful Italian Serenade, one string quartet, very occasionally the opera *Der Corregidor* – it is for his songs (about 240 altogether) that Wolf is still remembered and valued.

The history of the German *Lied* represents a remarkable attempt to create an art-form that would be nothing less than a perfect marriage of poetry and music in which neither element is subsidiary to the other. This was never a one-sidedly musical development: already in the eighteenth century poets were both writing new words to old tunes and composing poems in the expectation that they would be set to music. Nor was it a miniaturist's art: minor composers like Carl Loewe and Robert Franz made their reputations as specialists in the art of *Lieder*-composing, but major figures such as Beethoven, Schubert, Mendelssohn, Schumann, Liszt, and later on Mahler and Richard Strauss, also contributed to the *Lied* tradition and enriched it with works of genius.

In German-speaking countries late in the eighteenth century the presence in many middle-class homes of a clavichord or, increasingly, a fortepiano had led to the cultivation of an intimate, simple mode of song, capable of being sung by an individual alone at the keyboard or in the family circle. The commonest themes were domestic, amatory, patriotic or rural, and the poems, consciously catering for an increasingly confident middle class, were often published in annual anthologies which sometimes also offered a supplement with simple musical settings. In the early nineteenth century the *Lied* spread outside the domestic scene, first to the salon and then to the concert hall, but never entirely lost its intimate character. It always demanded of its audience a sympathetic and informed response to the poems set, and of its performers, both pianist and singer, a high degree of shared understanding and poetic and critical insight into the intentions of both poet and composer. Accordingly, to this day, many great singers – Dietrich Fischer-Dieskau is an outstanding example – have felt that the *Lied* is the greatest test of their artistry, and while gaining international fame as opera singers, have constantly reverted to *Lieder*. The careers of such virtuoso pianists as Gerald Moore who have specialized in the accompaniment of songs also illustrate the vitally important role of the pianist in this genre. From Schubert on, the increasing sophistication of the piano score means that it is no mere accompaniment to the voice but an interpretative medium on a par with it, capable of carrying on the emotional argument of the song when the singer is silent, and able to enrich, complexify, subvert or ironize the utterance of the singer.

This symbiosis of voice and piano reached a culmination with Wolf, above all in his Mörike and Goethe collections. Wolf brought to the *Lied* the new musical techniques he had learnt from Wagner: an enhanced range and complexity of harmony, the subtle and audacious use of dissonance, the creation of additional dimensions by the leitmotif. As Eric Sams remarks: 'Just as Schubert had distilled the essence of classical opera and oratorio (Mozart, Beethoven, Haydn) into the first Romantic *Lieder*, thus creating a new genre, so Wolf in his turn condensed the dramatic intensity of modern (i.e. Wagnerian) music-drama into voice and keyboard, lending fresh life and force to the *Lied* form and enhancing its expressive vocabulary to a pitch never since surpassed.'[*] Corresponding to this new musical element was Wolf's new sophistication and fastidiousness in his treatment of the poetic texts. To a degree unequalled by previous composers of *Lieder*, he gave primacy to the words. At recitals he would insist that each poem should be read out to the audience before each song was performed. Most of his settings are *durchkomponiert*, following the text right through instead of forcing it into a rhythmic or metrical strait-jacket, or constantly repeating words or lines where the poet has not done so. Wolf was able to sense the linguistic register of a poem precisely and to reflect its emotional coloration with perfect fidelity. In his choice of texts for composition, he also shows a wide inclusiveness of taste and

---

* E. Sams, op. cit., p. 2.

a high degree of critical discrimination, and this is confirmed by many perceptive remarks about poetry in his letters to friends.

His collections of songs from Mörike and Goethe were intended specifically as musical homage to two great writers whose work he sought to interpret and reveal, offering a substantial and representative selection of settings from each of them. It was uncommon for a composer to devote a whole volume of about fifty songs to the work of one poet, even if the poet was an international celebrity of the stature of Goethe. It is true that Schubert had planned a collection of twenty-seven Goethe songs in two volumes; he had also written song cycles, *Die schöne Müllerin* and *Die Winterreise*, both based on sequences of poems by Wilhelm Müller; but Wolf's large single-poet anthologies had little precedent. The Goethe volume, moreover, was a particularly bold publication, representing as it did the composer's response to a daunting challenge. Goethe's poetry had been familiar to educated people for more than a century, and had been set to music many times already by Schubert and others; but Wolf's volume was a bid to outdo Schubert, not merely a modest offering of alternative interpretations. It was characteristic that he should place his new settings of some of the most important poems prominently at the beginning and end of his Goethe collection: it began with nine songs from the well-known novel *Wilhelm Meister* (including Mignon's famous 'Kennst du das Land' and 'Nur wer die Sehnsucht kennt') and ended with a group containing the ecstatic meditation *Ganymed* (though Schubert's setting of this is equally beautiful), and above all the young Goethe's defiant dramatic monologue *Prometheus*. In this last composition at least (for which he also wrote an orchestral version of the accompaniment) Wolf arguably far excels Schubert, achieving in *Prometheus* one of the great masterpieces in the repertoire of the *Lied*.

Wolf's *Goethe-Lieder* as a whole represent an astonishingly wide spectrum of the vast work of this most catholic of poets; and even in the lesser case of Eichendorff, who is commonly associated only with relatively conventional, emotionalized landscape poems in the romantic manner, he made a point of including some of the more robust and light-hearted sailor's and student songs which Schumann, for instance, had disregarded. But the most remarkable of the three collections was that of Mörike: it was as substantial and as varied as the Goethe volume and was largely composed before it. Goethe of course did not need to be 'discovered' by Wolf, but the now half-forgotten Swabian poet who had died in 1875 and fallen silent long before then, and who had enjoyed not much more than provincial fame, was a different, more personal matter; and it was with Mörike, too, that the great creative breakthrough had come for Wolf, in February 1888. Before that point he had composed only two Mörike poems, but now he suddenly came to them with a rush, receiving them like a revelation, with an enthusiasm amounting almost to obsession. For weeks on end he carried his pocket-size edition of the poems about with him continually, reading and re-reading them, absorbing them until they seemed to be part of himself. To set them to music became a compulsion: he did so almost somnambulistically, sometimes at the rate of two or three a day. 'On Saturday' (he wrote to a friend) 'I composed *Das verlassene Mägdlein*, already beautifully set by Schumann, without having formed any intention to do so . . . It happened almost against my will. But perhaps it was just because I had surrendered to the spell of the poem that the music turned out so well, and I think my setting can stand comparison with Schumann's . . .'* Between 16 February and 28 November 1888, all fifty-one of the new settings were composed, and the complete volume of fifty-three was published in the following year. Remarkably, again, Wolf stipulated that the title-page should give pride of place to the author of the words: it was to read 'Poems of Eduard Mörike, for voice and piano, set to music by Hugo Wolf', and the frontispiece was to bear a portrait not of himself but of the poet – a gesture which Wolf's contemporary Detlev von Liliencron, in a poem addressed to him, particularly praised.

Between Mörike and Wolf there was clearly that special affinity of genius which German calls *Kongenialität*, almost as if they had been contemporary partners in one of the great collaborations that arise from time to time, such as that between Hofmannsthal and Richard Strauss. Wolf's versatile response to Mörike's own notable versatility is already evidence of this. Limits, of course, were imposed by his genre. Short 'lyrical' or ballad-like poems, of the kind that can normally be turned into *Lieder*, are only one side of Mörike's output: of equal importance are his often quite long narrative or reflective pieces, most of them in classical elegiacs or trimeters. These are obviously debarred, by their length and/or by the technical unsuitability of unrhymed but complex metres, from being set to music as songs. Wolf occasionally made *Lieder* out of short elegiac epigrams: to extremely beautiful effect as in his setting of Goethe's *Anakreons Grab*, but there is only one Mörike example (*An den Schlaf*). The result has been that Mörike's mainly youthful work in what can loosely be called the 'romantic'

---

* For Wolf's discovery of Mörike, see Prawer, *Mörike und seine Leser*, Ernst Klett, Stuttgart, 1960, pp. 35ff.

mode (song-like poems in rhymed verse), which in any case commends itself more readily to most readers, has been given still further prominence by the fame of Wolf's settings. It could not have been otherwise; and we must admire all the more Wolf's choice of a still representative number of Mörike texts and the sensitive diversity of his treatment of them.

The *Lieder* range from the tragic to the comic, from folk-style simplicity to ironic sophistication, from solitary contemplation to humorous sociability, from dramatic action to inward prayer. Within the scope of a relatively brief bilingual selection of Mörike's poems it is not possible to illustrate all these aspects, and we therefore here discuss only a selection within a selection, though this includes some of Wolf's best-known Mörike songs. One of the most beautiful is *Verborgenheit*, which explores the kind of confused emotional state often said to be especially characteristic of Mörike. Here, the conflicting opposites are wonderfully held together by the musical structure, and the positive feeling finally breaks through into an ecstatic climax in the tonic major key just before the reprise of the first stanza. In *In der Frühe*, the anguish of the sleepless night gives way to the reassuring sound of the early morning church bells. In the piano accompaniment a bell-like five-note motif is persistently repeated, mournful at first, then moving into major keys as the divine consolation is felt. Its last three notes seem to echo the simple *mi-fa-sol* melody of the internationally known folk-song about the sleepy monk ('Frère Jacques' or 'Bruder Martin') who is called upon to wake up and ring the bells for matins. This is arguably a conscious musical quotation, one that occurs also in Mahler's first symphony, as Wolf probably knew (the symphony was written a few months before the song); it further reinforces or interprets the poem's religious theme, already established by Mörike in his use of a verse-form reminiscent of the Lutheran hymnal, with corresponding linguistic archaisms (*gehet, herfür, wühlet,* etc.). In *Im Frühling*, the poet's words undergo a remarkable musical elaboration which accommodates all their emotional complexity, his movement outwards into nature and love and back into troubled heart-searching. A less complicated pleasure is expressed in *Er ists!*, another poem about spring (the present edition uses its alternative title *Frühlingsgefühl*). This famous short poem (also composed by Schumann) alludes rather mysteriously (line 7) to the distant sound of harps as a sign that spring has arrived: this is not in fact some kind of mystic, synaesthetic perception, but a reference to the fact that itinerant musicians in early nineteenth-century Swabia, as winter ended, would come out of their town quarters to earn their bread again in the countryside. In Wolf's setting, the suggestion of a harp becomes central: the rapid figurations on the piano are basically arpeggios of chords in bright major keys, and the same structure is repeatedly picked up by the exultant singing voice. Two other moments of comparable happiness, in which the poet for whatever reason seems touched by pre-lapsarian joy and can bless the world as he passes through it, are embodied in *Fußreise* and *Auf einer Wanderung*. It is interesting that the manic-depressive Wolf, an atheist and disciple of Nietzsche, could enter with such ease into these moods of humble contentment. In *Fußreise* a straightforward pervading *andante* motif suffices. In *Auf einer Wanderung* the music again exactly follows the movement of this more complex poem: a dancing 6:8 figure suggests the journey, the arrival in the little town at sunset, the sudden magical voice at the window; then up-and-down-rushing chromatic scales that herald the climax, a central *rallentando* in which the narrator pauses to savour his Faustian moment; then the resumption of the dancing motif in the postlude and a vanishing *diminuendo* as the traveller passes into the distance.

Wolf's special empathy also embraced Mörike's often childlike humour, and he turned into enchantingly appropriate music a number of examples of it, such as *Mausfallensprüchlein* (a child's magic spell for enticing a mouse into a trap) or *Elfenlied*, in which a sleeping elf wakes up in alarm when the night-watchman calls eleven o'clock ('Elfe!'). These have here been omitted as resistant to translation, but *Storchenbotschaft* is retained as a comic variant of a folklore motif; likewise the well-known *Abschied*, in which the poet imagines himself visited by a carping critic who bizarrely urges him to inspect the shadow of his own nose on the wall and admit that it is not a thing of beauty. The poet responds with a polite kick to help him on his way downstairs. The music exactly follows the visitor's behaviour and words, the piano imitating his knock and the more complicated noise of his exit, after which a Viennese waltz motif triumphantly takes over. This poem was normally placed at the end of Mörike's collection of poems, and Wolf's highly comical setting is often sung as a final encore in recitals of the *Mörike-Lieder*.

At the other end of the comic-tragic spectrum is Wolf's extraordinary composition of Mörike's ballad about the abandoned maidservant, *Das verlassene Mägdlein*, a famous and moving lyric of deceptive simplicity; there are estimated to have been about fifty musical settings of it before Wolf, who himself acknowledged the equal beauty of Schumann's version. The girl is lighting the kitchen fire before day-break, and suddenly remembers as she does so that during the night she has been dreaming of her faithless lover. The emptiness and drudgery of her existence is vividly suggested by Wolf's slow repetition of totally bare A minor fifths, and of an insistent dactylic figure modelled on the poem's first line (a crotchet and two quavers, followed by a rising dotted-quaver phrase). This rhythm pervades the entire song; the final stanza echoes the first, and only in the two middle stanzas, as the girl watches the flames rising and her anguish breaks through into consciousness, are subtle harmonic and dynamic complications added to the music, with intensely dramatic effect. The poem has something of the character of a folk-ballad, the figure of the abandoned girl having been a folk-culture motif since long before the young Goethe so notably developed it in his early version of *Faust*. In another folk-style poem in which the speaker is a traditional or conventional figure, the young huntsman compares the imprint of a bird's foot on the pure mountain snow to the handwriting on his sweetheart's letters; Wolf turns this conceit into an exquisite miniature in 5:4 time, exactly crystallizing it in the delicate staccato of the opening piano motif which becomes the central melody. These are two examples of a number of poems in different styles dealing with various aspects of love: tragic loss, tender devotion, mystic adoration as in the formal and rather lush sonnet *An die Geliebte*, worldly-wise sensuality as in *Nimmersatte Liebe*. Wolf's music perfectly matches this diversity. Noteworthy above all are the two enigmatic *Peregrina* songs, in which the tragic colouring of *Das verlassene Mägdlein* returns, but with much greater elaboration. Unlike the ballad, the 'Peregrina' poems reflect a deeply painful personal experience (Mörike's involvement with Maria Meyer), and Wolf complicates the music accordingly with tortured harmonic progressions and pervading chromaticism. A particular figure of descending semitones persistently haunts both songs, binding them together: the voice introduces it in the first ('Der Spiegel . . .'), where the childlike temptress is directly addressed, and the piano then takes it up in the postlude and carries it over into the second song ('Warum, Geliebte . . .') where it is obsessively repeated by the accompaniment as the words narrate the haunting of the poet by the lost beloved whom he cannot forget. This is probably the most developed and dramatic use of a leitmotif device in the *Mörike-Lieder*. In the closing lines the poet-narrator, sitting in a festive gathering of children and friends with the ghost of 'Peregrina' (seen by no one else) beside him, suddenly bursts into helpless tears and leaves with her, 'hand in hand': this ending is realized in music of great simplicity and unexampled pathos. It is very regrettable that Wolf for some reason did not also compose the fifth poem ('Die Liebe, sagt man . . .'), the closing sonnet of the 'Peregrina' cycle.

Personal grief also plays a part in the remarkable poem *An eine*

Äolsharfe. A nexus of associations linked, for Mörike, the wind harps in the *Schloßpark* at Ludwigsburg, the tragic early death (in Ludwigsburg) of his young brother August, and (in the poem's epigraph) a consolatory Latin ode he had picked up from his reading of Horace. In Wolf's setting, as the voice softly muses, the accompaniment subtly suggests the sounds of a wind harp with falling groups of high E major chords in the right hand and persistent rising arpeggio figurations in the left. Wolf had heard a similar effect in Brahms's comparable setting of this poem, though he did not himself hear an Aeolian harp until the summer of 1888, a few months after writing his own version, when he came across one at Schloß Hoch-Osterwitz in Carinthia. A harp-like accompaniment is used again in the mysterious *Gesang Weylas*, the strange brief declamation of the guardian goddess of Mörike's mythical kingdom of Orplid. Wolf, we are told, imagined her sitting on a reef in the moonlight playing a harp; there is nothing about this in Mörike's text, but Wolf's reiterated arpeggio chords add powerfully to the monumental and visionary effect.

There are two further outstanding cases in which Wolf has been inspired by Mörike's contemplative visionary mood. *Um Mitternacht*, perhaps the most profound short evocation in German poetry of the tranquillity of deep night, has been composed in music of equal mastery. Time, weighed in two equal halves, seems to stand still; the silence is such that the mountain streams can be heard murmuring in the distance, and their movement is not antithetical to the night's stillness, but balanced with it in a great harmony of night and day. The voice moves over a continuous accompaniment of quavers rocking ambiguously in 12:8 time, their only change being to modulate subtly to the major key when the streams enter the song. The other great vision of a natural scene or object is *Auf eine Christblume* (the 'two' poems under this title are simply two parts of a single conception). Mörike here contemplates the moon-child, the 'Christmas rose', the wintry hellebore growing by itself in a churchyard, a flower which takes on for him a religious significance enhancing and transcending its natural beauty. It seems both to symbolize the advent of Christ, born at night into the dead world of midwinter, and also to be at home in its own 'magic kingdom' of wandering elves and cold moonlight. Wolf recreates this world in strange, meditative music, in a tonality wandering through successive enharmonic changes, so free of a home key as to be nearly atonal, and reminiscent here and there of the sensuous austerity of *Parsifal*. In the second part, or second poem, the music is delicate to vanishing-point, poised on the very edge of silence and non-existence: it exactly follows Mörike's rarefied vision of an invisible butterfly, doomed as a summer creature never to drink the nectar of this winter flower but still drawn to it out of season, drunk with desire like an unsatisfied ghost, or perhaps like a soul still seeking the grace it has been denied in life.

In general it may be doubted whether Mörike himself would have appreciated Hugo Wolf's settings of his work, *kongenial* or not, if he had lived long enough to hear them. His musical taste had been formed by Mozart and Haydn; he admired Beethoven but felt ill at ease with him, and found even Schubert's setting of Goethe's *Erlkönig* too wild and stormy. Wagner, however, he had heard, and rejected completely.* And yet, without Wagner's inspiration and his musical innovations, it is hard to imagine that Wolf would ever have written the Mörike songs or for that matter anything else; and the publication of Wolf's *Mörike-Lieder* in 1889 was a turning-point in Mörike's posthumous reputation. As they gradually came to be heard by an ever wider public, they introduced his poetry to many who had never even heard of him. It was Wolf, above all, who carried Mörike's name far beyond Germany, and profoundly changed the conventional perception of his personality and art.†

G. W. M., D. L.

---

* For Mörike and Wagner, see Prawer, op. cit., p. 36. A further historical irony (ibid., p. 32) is that, whatever affinities there may have been between Wolf and Nietzsche, they differed in their assessment of Mörike, whose poetry and its much-vaunted musicality the philosopher dismissed as 'sickly-sweet swimsy-wimsy and tinkle-tinkle' (*süßlich weichliches Schwimm-Schwimm und Kling-Kling*).

† For Wolf's influence, see Prawer, op. cit., pp. 36ff.

Notes

Mozart's Journey to Prague

1. *Don Giovanni ... 14 September*: the first performance of *Don Giovanni* took place at the Estates Theatre in Prague on 29 October 1787. Mörike's dates for Mozart's journey, based on earlier biographies, are historically not quite accurate.

2. *wife of General Volkstett*: this name does not in fact occur among Mozart's known acquaintances, though Mörike may have been thinking of Baroness Waldstetten, who was a particular friend and patroness.

3. *Cosa rara ... the Director's intrigues*: the comic opera *Una Cosa Rara* (the 'rare thing' is of course a woman's constancy) was the work of the Spanish composer Vicente Martín y Soler (1754–1806), a protégé of Mozart's envious rival Antonio Salieri (1750–1825), who was Director of the Italian Opera at the Imperial court. According to legend, Salieri deliberately sabotaged the première of *Le Nozze di Figaro* in May 1786 by bribing the Italian singers to perform badly; but *Figaro* was in any case eclipsed in Vienna by the enormous popular success of *Una Cosa Rara*. Mozart nevertheless quotes a few bars of *Una Cosa Rara* in the final scene of *Don Giovanni*, but for which Martín and his opera would now be totally forgotten.

4. *Bondini*: Pasquale Bondini was the director of an Italian opera company in Prague. After his successful production of *Figaro* there in December 1786 he commissioned Mozart to write another opera for him. Mozart wrote *Don Giovanni* for an advance of 100 gold ducats.

5. *King of Prussia*: according to a tradition which lacks supporting evidence, Frederick William II of Prussia offered Mozart the directorship of music at his court, with a salary of 3,000 thalers, an offer which Mozart refused out of misplaced loyalty to his patron the Emperor Joseph II. Mörike antedates this supposed proposal to 1787, before the production of *Don Giovanni*, though historically Mozart's visit to Berlin and Potsdam did not take place until 1789.

6. *Tarare*: when *Don Giovanni* was eventually produced in Vienna in 1788, it was no more of a success than *Figaro* had been: the public preferred Salieri's *Tarare*, given in Vienna under the title *Axur, Re d'Ormus*, with words by Mozart's librettist Da Ponte. In Constanze's fantasy, intended to encourage her husband to seize the opportunity of moving to Prussia, Mozart generously conducts his arch-enemy's mediocre work at the Berlin Opera in 1789.

7. *Schinzberg*: the house and the family remain essentially fictitious, despite attempts to identify them.

8. *display of orange-trees*: the word *Orangerie* usually implies a heated building, of the kind common in baroque or rococo architecture and formal gardens, for the indoor cultivation of oranges and other exotic fruit, but it can also, as here, mean simply a number of orange-trees in tubs temporarily set out in the garden during warm weather. The fruit itself is normally called *Apfelsine* in North German and *Orange* in the south; Mörike in the course of the story uses *Orange* interchangeably with *Pomeranze*, though strictly speaking *Pomeranze* is the smaller and bitterer Seville orange, whereas his first description of the fruit ('magnificent rounded shape . . . succulent coolness') appears to suggest the familiar larger and sweeter variety.

9. *Prince Galitzin's*: Prince Dmitri Mihailovitch Galitzin (1721–93), Russian Ambassador to Vienna and one of Mozart's patrons.

10. *Hagedorn, Götz*: Friedrich von Hagedorn (1708–54) and Johann Nikolaus Götz (1721–81) were representatives of the rococo or 'ana-creontic' style in German poetry.

11. *Susanna's aria*: 'Deh vieni, non tardar' in Act 4.

12. '*Giovinette, che fate all' amore . . . etc.*': Mörike, and the German editions following him, for some reason misquote the text as 'Giovi-nette, che *fatte* all' amore . . .' and attempt to translate it accordingly, though 'che fatte' in fact makes no sense. 'Fare all' amore' is an old-fashioned variant of 'fare l'amore', here meaning no more than verbal dalliance, as 'to make love' once did in English. With this emendation, Zerlina's opening lines could be approximately rendered as: 'You young girls who like kissing and flirting, / take your chance before youth passes by! / If your hearts are on fire and are hurting, / there's a remedy here you should try: / oh, what fun we shall have, you and I! . . .', etc.

13. *Parthenopean*: in ancient myth, Parthenope was one of the Sirens and closely associated with Naples, which was originally called after her.

14. *Ninon de Lenclos's house*: Anne (known as Ninon) de Lenclos (?1620–1705) was famous both for her beauty and for her longevity

and was well acquainted with many of the prominent writers of Louis
XIV's time, though the claim that she presided over a literary salon
which was 'a true centre of refined intellectual culture' is probably
exaggerated.

15. *the Marquise de Sévigné*: Marie de Rabutin-Chantal, Marquise de
Sévigné (1626–96), is now remembered chiefly for her letters to her
married daughter living in the provinces, which over a period of
twenty-five years contain many vivid and witty evocations of Paris
society under Louis XIV.

16. *Chapelle*: Claude-Emmanuel L'Huillier (1628–86), known as
Chapelle, a minor writer of the classical period.

17. *Phoebus*: one of the names of Apollo, the god of (among other
things) music.

18. *Chiron*: a wise centaur, half-brother of Zeus, skilled in various arts
which he learnt from Apollo and taught to Achilles and other heroes.
His role (in the picture) as tutor to Apollo is possibly due to a confusion
by Mörike.

19. *he who on his shoulder . . . Apollo*: the alcaic lines from Horace
(*Odes* III 4) are

> . . . numquam umeris positurus arcum,
> qui rore puro Castaliae lavit
> crines solutos, qui Lyciae tenet
> dumeta natalemque silvam,
> Delius et Patareus Apollo.

Mörike quotes them in a translation which in the German text he
attributes to Karl Wilhelm Ramler (1725–98), though in fact it is his
own. I have retranslated the passage directly from the Latin. Horace
refers to Apollo's bow (his deadly weapon, not the bow for a violin as
the Count supposes) and to places associated with him: the island of
Delos as his reputed birthplace, the coastal city of Patara in Lycia (Asia
Minor) and the sacred stream of Castalia near his oracle at Delphi.

20. *Da Ponte and the clever Schikaneder*: the Abbé Lorenzo da Ponte
(1749–1838), writer for the Italian Opera at the Imperial Court, earned
a measure of immortality as the author of the libretti for *Le Nozze di
Figaro*, *Don Giovanni* and *Così fan tutte*, as did Emanuel Schikaneder
(1751–1812), a popular Viennese theatre director, who wrote the
libretto of *Die Zauberflöte*.

21. *Signor Bonbonnière*: 'Bonbonnière' was the nickname given by
Mozart and his friends to Salieri, who was a compulsive eater of
confectionery.

22. *modicum of truth*: Mörike at this point adds a footnote stating that he had in mind a specific lifelike drawing of Mozart in profile which he found on the title page of a score. Although he does not further identify this portrait, it is possible that he is referring to the drawing by Doris Stock (1789), well known as an engraving.

23. *Prince Esterhazy ... Haydn*: Nicolas Joseph, Prince Esterhazy (1714–90) was an important patron of the arts and sciences, resident at Eisenstadt in what is now Burgenland, where he founded an academy of music. Joseph Haydn (1732–1809), the most eminent composer of the Viennese classical school after Mozart and Beethoven, was his Director of Music for over forty years. Mozart dedicated six of his greatest string quartets to Haydn.

24. *The Dušeks*: the Bohemian pianist and composer Jan Ladislav Dušek (1760–1812) and his wife, the singer Josefa Dušek (1754–1824), were friends of the Mozarts.

25. *Florentine master ... Ambras collection*: the sculptor and goldsmith Benvenuto Cellini (1500–1571), whose remarkable autobiography Goethe translated, was commissioned by Cardinal Ippolito d'Este to model a gold salt-cellar, and this remains one of his most famous pieces. Schloß Ambras or Amras near Innsbruck was the seat of the Counts of Tyrol and housed a magnificent collection of weapons and works of art, most of which, including the salt-cellar, were later transferred to museums in Vienna.

26. *Leporello ... Sillery*: the Count, addressing his footman by the name of Don Giovanni's servant, calls for a vintage champagne from the village of Sillery near Reims. This dry amber-coloured wine had been famous since the seventeenth century and remained in fashion long after Mozart's time, being for instance consumed in large quantities by the Prince Regent. Today the name has been absorbed into the Moët empire and forgotten.

27. *Di rider finirai pria dell' aurora*: 'You will have stopped laughing before dawn.'

28. *many a false prophet will arise*: this has been read as an allusion by Mörike to Wagner and Liszt, whose music he disliked.

29. *Chevalier Gluck*: the successful operatic composer Christoph Willibald Gluck (1714–87), known especially for his *Orfeo ed Euridice*, settled in Vienna and was ennobled by the Emperor as Ritter von Gluck. Historically he was still alive at the time of Mozart's supposed allusion to him.

Selected Poems

'On a Winter Morning before Sunrise' (1825): See note on 'Urach Revisited', below.

'Peregrina I–V': The third poem ('A madness . . .') is known to have been written in the summer of 1824, at the time of the Maria Meyer affair, and the other four not later than May or June 1828, but possibly at some time in the preceding four years. A version of II, I, III and V (grouped in that order and not including IV) was among quite a number of Mörike's early poems to be scattered here and there in *Maler Nolten* and published in it in 1832; all five then appeared, revised and rearranged, as a cycle under the title 'Peregrina' and with the note 'From *Maler Nolten*', in the 1838 and subsequent collections. It is not certain, though probable, that all five of the poems refer directly or indirectly to Maria Meyer.

'Two Voices in the Night' (1825): This piece of dialogue, which could equally well be a monologue, is extracted from 'The Last King of Orplid', a fantastic verse intermezzo in dramatic form which Mörike inserted into *Maler Nolten* as a magic-lantern show. In this original version (written in 1825) the two speakers or singers are King Ulmon and the elfin princess Thereile. The lines were later published in the 1838 collection under the title 'At night' ('Nachts'), and eventually in the final 1867 edition with the present title.

'At Midnight' (1827): The phrase 'stieg . . . ans Land' seems to suggest that the night has 'come ashore' from the sea, and thus that the imagined landscape is that of a mountain range on the sea coast, though Mörike had never actually seen any such place. The mysterious central image of an equally balanced pair of golden scales is given special emphasis by its occurrence in both stanzas: 'Waage', 'in gleichen Schalen';' Joch' (= crossbar), 'gleichgeschwungen'. In his 1838 collection Mörike placed this poem at the end of the book.

'In the Early Morning' (1828): I have not attempted to imitate Mörike's slightly archaic language which gives this poem something of the character of a Lutheran hymn. See also the discussion of Hugo Wolf's remarkable setting (Postscript, p. 200).

'A Journey on Foot' (1828): It has been interestingly suggested that the words 'im leichten Wanderschweiße' of the penultimate line are linked to the earlier references to Adam (lines 10, 15) and thus subtly allude to the curse imposed after the Fall (Genesis 3, 19: '. . . in the sweat of thy face shalt thou eat bread'). In his present self-accepting mood, the poet seems to feel the curse only vestigially.

'Intimation of Spring' (1829): First published without a title in *Maler Nolten* (1832). From the 1838 and later collections it has become known as 'Er ists!', i.e. 'he (the Spring) is here!', but in 1844 Mörike prepared a manuscript copy of his poems for presentation to the King of Prussia (the so-called 'Königshandschrift'), in which he gave this poem the more translatable title 'Frühlingsgefühl', a variant which I have here adopted.

'In the Spring'(1828): An exactly similar physical intimacy with nature is experienced by the young Goethe's Werther in his novel of 1774 (letter of 10 May).

'Urach Revisited' (1827): In 1818 the fourteen-year-old Mörike entered the Theological Seminary at Urach, where he studied for four years. He revisited Urach in 1825. Here he evokes his nostalgic memories, interweaving them with reflections on the mystery of nature and its changing relationship with the human soul. This poem, reminiscent in some ways of Wordsworth's famous meditation on Tintern Abbey, ranks with 'On a Winter Morning before Sunrise' as a major expression of the poet's youthful sensibility. It is commonly interpreted as the record of a frustrated attempt to recapture past experience and emotion, though like 'On a Winter Morning . . .' it ends with a sense of renewal.

'Love Insatiable'(1828): This curious combination of old-fashioned proverbial worldly wisdom with bold erotic realism shocked some nineteenth-century critics who failed to distinguish naive sensuality from salaciousness and condemned the young Mörike's reference to love-bites as immoral, savage and disgusting.

'The Forsaken Girl'/'The Forsaken Lassie' (1829): The subtle folk-ballad-like simplicity of this lyric makes it as untranslatable as Gretchen's 'Meine Ruh ist hin'. We offer two alternative attempts. Gilbert McKay's gives it a Scots colouring (less pronounced than in 'The Auld Steeplecock'). In the fourth stanza, 'tears' and 'nears' should be read disyllabically.

'The Song of Weyla' (?1831): Mörike's most elaborated, though still brief, description of his mythical land of 'Orplid' is given in Book I of his novel *Maler Nolten*. Speaking as one of the characters, the actor Larkens, he recalls his youthful friendship with Bauer and their collaborative invention of the Orplid story: 'When I was still at school, I had a friend whose artistic aims and way of thinking went hand in hand with mine. In our free time, following our natural bent, we soon constructed a poetic world which even now I cannot recall without emotion . . . For our literary purposes we invented a territory situated outside the known world, in complete seclusion, an island of which the supposed inhabitants had been a strong, heroic people, divided into various tribes and regions and with differences of character, but having a more or less uniform religion. The island was called Orplid, and we thought of it as being somewhere in the Pacific Ocean between New Zealand and South America. Orplid was more particularly the name of the city in the most important kingdom: it was supposed to have divine founders, and was under the special protection of the goddess Weyla, after whom the island's main river was also called. In fragmentary fashion, and selecting the most important periods, we would tell each other the history of these peoples. There was no lack of remarkable wars and adventures. Our theology had some points in common with Greek polytheism, but retained its own character on the whole; we also did not exclude the subordinate world of elves, fairies and goblins.

'Orplid, once the treasure of the immortals, was doomed in the end to perish by their wrath, as gradually its ancient simplicity gave way to a corrupting refinement of thought and morals. A terrible fate snatched all living humanity away, even their dwellings sank out of sight; only Weyla's favourite child, the castle and city of Orplid itself, was permitted to remain, extinct and desolate though it was, as a sad and splendid monument of bygone grandeur. The gods turned their faces from the scene for ever, and the noble goddess who ruled it now scarcely vouchsafed it a glance, and then only for the sake of a single mortal who by higher decree was destined long to outlive the general destruction . . .'

'Seclusion' was written in 1832.

'To an Aeolian Harp' (1837): The alcaic strophe of the epigraph is from a consolatory ode (II, 9) addressed by Horace to his friend Valgius Rufus, a contemporary poet whose favourite Greek slave-boy Mystes had recently died (or so at least Mörike reads it, though some Horace commentators suggest that Mystes deserted Valgius for another lover, or perhaps never even existed). Aeolian or wind harps were instruments known to Mörike; in Ludwigsburg, for instance, which he revisited from time to time, he 'heard them murmuring as usual' (letter to Luise Rau, 14 May 1831) at the Emichsburg, a baroque artificial ruin in the park of the royal palace. Ludwigsburg was where the poet's beloved younger brother August had died in 1824 and was buried; Mörike's grief for him is expressed, thirteen years after the event, in this complex of associations.

'News from the Storks' (1837): In German nursery lore it was necessary to explain not only the arrival of a new baby (a stork has brought it) but also its mother's temporary indisposition (she can't walk because the stork has been pecking her leg).

'A Huntsman's Song'(1837): The 'huntsman' was a traditional folklore figure who from Goethe's 'Jägers Abendlied' ('A huntsman's evening song', 1775) onwards frequently appears in German romantic poetry.

'A Prayer': The two quatrains of this poem did not originally belong together: the second was written in 1832 and appeared, without a title, in *Maler Nolten*, whereas the first was not written until 1845 or 1846. In the 1848 and 1856 collections the two appeared together as a poem in two parts, with the present title; the numbering was then dropped in 1867. The final result is nevertheless a perfect and touching expression of the ideal of 'holdes Bescheiden', a phrase hardly translatable but implying unembittered acceptance of a state of limited contentment 'midway between' too much woe and too much joy. The 'prayer' is ostensibly Christian, but embodies the ancient wisdom of the 'golden mean' (*aurea mediocritas*) with which Mörike was familiar from his study of Horace (*Odes* II, 10).

'Johann Kepler' (1837): Mörike's fellow-countryman Kepler, a contemporary of Tycho Brahe and Galileo, was born in Württemberg in 1571 and died in 1630; he became court astronomer to the Emperor Rudolf II in Prague and was for a time employed by Wallenstein. He was a brilliant pioneer of mathematical and astronomical theories, famous above all for his discovery of the laws of planetary motion, to which he was led by his special study of the orbit of Mars.

'To Sleep' (1838): This Latin elegiac epigram, which Mörike has translated into trimeters, is attributed to Heinrich Meibom, a seventeenth-century German academic; Mörike found the lines quoted in a work on Hogarth's engravings by the humorist and satirist Georg Christoff Lichtenberg (1742–99), who was one of his favourite authors.

'At Daybreak': A first version, with the title 'A conversation before daybreak' ('Gespräch vor Tage', 1837), was later much improved, and the revised text of the 1867 edition is a perfect example of the classical epigram in two elegiac distichs.

'The Tale of the Safe and Sound Man' was written in 1837–8.

'The Woodland Pest' (1841). 'Classical six-footed line': in Latin verse the trimeter was reckoned as a line of six iambic feet (senarius) rather than three double-iambic metra as in Greek verse. 'A poet': Friedrich Gottlieb Klopstock (1724–1803) had a certain historical importance in German literature as a pioneer of classical verse forms. Mörike alludes with a trace of irony to the dedicatees and titles of some of his well-known odes ('Fanny', 'Cidly', *The Lake of Zürich* and *The Early Graves*, which is parodistically quoted in line 51).

'To the Nightingale' (1841): Mörike's use of strophic forms is rare and usually parodistic, as here.

'To a Christmas Rose' (1841): 'I' and 'II' were first printed in a periodical as separate poems; from 1848 onwards Mörike numbered them as two parts of a single poem under one title.

'The Beautiful Beech-Tree' was written in 1842.

'Divine Remembrance' was written in 1845.

'A Walk in the Country' was written in 1845.

'The Falls of the Rhine' (1846): The falls here described are at Schaffhausen, on the German–Swiss border.

'Inscription on a Clock with the Three Hour-Goddesses' (1846): The 'Hours' (Latin *Horae*) were goddesses personifying the seasons or other fixed natural periods, and thus associated with the passage of time generally.

'On a Lamp' (1846): Since the verb *scheinen* can mean either 'seem' or 'shine', it has been suggested that the last line of this epigram could mean either that what is beautiful seems blessed in itself, or that it shines blessedly within itself. This ambiguity has stirred up a continuing but perhaps unnecessary academic controversy. The poem is often quoted as a celebration of the autonomy and self-sufficiency of beauty, but such a conception is not really characteristic of Mörike, especially not in his later period. The lamp by its nature is associated not with aesthetic isolation, but with human companionableness: it hangs in a room used for entertainment, and is decorated with a circle of dancing children. The same could be said of 'Inscription on a Clock . . .' (above), in which the dance of the goddesses of time symbolizes the orderly divisions of human life and social activity.

'The Auld Steeplecock' (1840, 1852): The regional and rather archaic folk-German of this *Knittelvers* poem has been translated by Gilbert McKay into the Buchan Scots still spoken in the Aberdeenshire and Banffshire area, which is perhaps a nearer equivalent than southern English to its down-to-earth style and subject-matter. 'An Deil kens . . .': since Dutch-tiled stoves are unknown in Scotland, these four lines are a discreet interpolation. 'Hatto the Bishop': according to legend, Archbishop Hatto of Mainz was eaten alive in his castle on the Rhine (still called the Mouse Tower) by a plague of rats and mice, as punishment for his cruel oppression of the starving people. 'Belshazar': Daniel 5. 'Sarah': Genesis 18, 9–15.

'Oh soul, remember!': The manuscript of an earlier text of this poem, with the title 'Grabgedanken' ('Thoughts of Mortality'), is dated September 1851. Mörike then used it, slightly revised and dropping the title, as his epilogue to *Mozart's Journey to Prague*. He also included it among his collected poems, adopting the new sixth line ('Denk es, o Seele!' as the title by which the poem has since become commonly known.

'A Domestic Scene' (1852): An example of the comic use of the elegiac metre.

'A Visit to the Carthusians' (1861): The 'Kindelsteig' and its village and monastery are fictitious, as Mörike indicates in a letter of 11 August 1863 to the Stuttgart bookseller Julius Krais, remarking 'we therefore cannot here properly gratify the self-indulgent craving for actuality [*realistische Verwöhnung*] of certain readers'.

'Erinna to Sappho' (1863): Mörike's epigraphic historical note is inaccurate, since Sappho was born in the late seventh century BC, whereas Erinna is thought to have lived in the fourth. She did, however, write a 300-line epic poem called *The Distaff* and died at the age of nineteen. 'Struck me': 'betraf mich', here scarcely translatable, suggests both 'encountered me' and 'amazed me' as well as 'concerned me (referred to me)'. 'Daughter of Demeter': Persephone (Proserpina), the goddess of the dead in the underworld. 'Cutting . . . a dark lock': as a ritual token of mourning.

Title Index of Poems